I'm Gonna Make You Love Me

Tracey Richardson

BELLA
BOOKS
2018

Bella Books, Inc.
P.O. Box 10543
Tallahassee, FL 32302

Printed in the United States of America on acid-free paper.

First Bella Books Edition 2018

Editor: Medora MacDougall
Cover Designer: Sandy Knowles

ISBN: 978-1-59493-614-2

Other Bella Books by Tracey Richardson

Blind Bet
By Mutual Consent
The Campaign
The Candidate
Delay of Game
Heartsick
Last Salute
No Rules of Engagement
Side Order of Love
The Song in My Heart
The Wedding Party

Acknowledgments

My foremost thanks is for the readers—to those of you who've stuck with me novel after novel, as well as to those who are taking a chance on their first Tracey Richardson novel. Without all of you, I wouldn't be doing this. Also my thanks to the reviewers out there who tirelessly promote lesbian fiction—you folks have my respect and admiration. My editor, Medora MacDougall, is simply the best, and I'm delighted to have been able to work with her for several novels now. Erin Hodgson, thank you for taking a peek at my manuscript while it was still a work in progress and making some great suggestions. Bella Books is like a family to me, and I am grateful for their top-notch work and dedication. To my wife, Sandra, thank you for putting up with me being in my own head so much of the time! I can't even describe how lucky I am to be able to call myself a full-time fiction writer.

About the Author

Tracey Richardson lives in the Georgian Bay area of Ontario, Canada, with her partner and their dogs, and grew up near Windsor, Ontario. She retired from a long-time newspaper journalism career a few years ago and devotes her time to writing, reading, playing (and watching) hockey and walking her dogs. Life is good!

Author's Note

Ah, Motown music. The songs of my youth, heard while growing up a stone's throw from Detroit, Michigan—the birthplace and heartbeat of Motown. I can so clearly remember as a kid listening on my little transistor radio to CKLW, The Big 8, a radio station shared jointly between Detroit and Windsor. It played all the best music back in the 1970s, including tons of Motown music. Motown music struck a chord in my young, music-loving soul. As my character in this novel, Claire Melbourne, says of the music, even when the songs are about getting your heart handed to you, they make you want to get up and dance. I had my own little record player back then and a nice little collection of forty-fives (they're still in the closet at my childhood home!). The coolest thing about the Motown label back then? It featured a map of Detroit, which included a highway that ran right through my small town near the city of Windsor, Ontario. It made me feel like Motown was *my* music, like I too was on the map. This novel is a tribute to what I think of as some of the finest music to have emerged from the 1960s and '70s.

CHAPTER ONE

Nowhere To Run To

It'd been one of those days from hell that demanded a massive drink or five—anything, Claire Melbourne prayed, to obliterate the sting of having to fire someone *and* losing a scoop that turned out to be the city's biggest story in months. It should have been their story, it *was* their story, right in the palm of their hands—an exclusive, a scoop, about the deputy mayor on the take. Her newspaper had been gifted the chance to break the story, and now it was too late. Rival print and broadcast news outlets had grabbed the ball and run with it, leaving her paper to follow like a dog looking for scraps. *Goddammit*, she thought with fresh outrage. It was the kind of story that made careers, won awards, brought in new subscribers and advertisers. They blew it. Or rather, their clueless intern blew it. Hence, the firing.

The drink could wait. Claire palmed the keys to her mom's— no, *her*—1965 convertible Mustang the color of a shiny red apple. Speed. The top down. An empty road unspooling ahead of her like a black ribbon. Music cranked to compete with the wind. It wouldn't be enough to make her forget today, but it would be a start. Driving the old girl always gave her overloaded mind a badly needed distraction. And a cool antique car like the 'Stang with its V-8 engine was exactly the permission she needed to be a little reckless, a little daring, and a whole lot immature.

Five minutes later the city grew smaller in the rearview mirror. The late spring sun was glorious, warming Claire's face while the wind tossed her collar-length, honey-blond hair in about six different directions. She tugged on her Oakley sunglasses and punched the stereo on—the only modern thing in the car because, hell, you *needed* a good sound system in a car like this. And on a shitty day like today, rock music, maybe even metal that she could scream to, would definitely help. But same as always, she felt the familiar tug—guilt too—and hit the pre-set button to the only oldies station in the city. It was, she was sorry to admit, sacrilegious in this car to listen to music any more contemporary than the seventies.

Claire tightened her grip on the nubby steering wheel, its solidness making her feel connected to the road and to the machine traversing it. The steering was loose, though, not like modern cars; you had to pay attention, keep your hands on the wheel and your eyes on the road and *feel* everything. No checking texts or fiddling with the radio or you'd be on the shoulder before you knew it. She never understood why her mother withdrew a big chunk of her retirement savings to buy this thing nineteen years ago. Never truly appreciated it until her mother was gone and it ended up hers, along with a simple three-bedroom ranch-style home in disrepair and a bone-dry savings account. She'd almost sold the car after the funeral, but after taking it out a couple of times, she discovered it was more liberating, more relaxing, way more playful than she had expected—something her mom would have enjoyed teasing her about. This car, her mom had told her on more than one occasion, could teach a person to appreciate life. While Claire never entirely believed her, the car stayed, and she'd not regretted it.

She tapped the wheel distractedly. Ellie Kirkland was the girl's—correction, the intern's—name. Thick, wavy dark hair and big brown eyes that were too sensitive, too expressive, too vulnerable to belong to a reporter. Claire had thought so right from the get-go, but her best friend Jackson Hurley, who also happened to be Claire's best reporter, convinced her to give Ellie a try for the twelve-month internship. Claire hadn't wanted to. Ellie, she told Jacks, looked like she didn't have the chops to be a reporter. Looked too trusting or something.

"What, because she's pretty?" he'd countered.

"Maybe." Pretty was for television, not print. Pretty didn't like to get down and dirty, where the real news took place. "You know pretty doesn't always get taken seriously, Jacks. This isn't a goddamned fashion magazine. It's a newspaper. A *daily* newspaper."

"What, are you saying I'm not pretty?" He batted his long blond eyelashes at her, his hand on his hip. Indeed, Jackson was far too pretty for a guy. "Fine," he snorted. "But don't be like that."

"Like what?"

"Like some chauvinistic man in a three-piece suit with slicked back hair and a wife at home who won't give him a blow job."

Claire was used to Jackson's crude talk, but she rolled her eyes out of duty. He'd hit a bulls-eye with the chauvinism comment, though, and so she relented and brought Ellie aboard, because women in any business sometimes needed a hand up, especially from other women. But oh, god, how she wished now she hadn't. What a fucking mistake! The blunder was ultimately Claire's responsibility as city editor of the newspaper, and she was fully expecting to be called up on the carpet for it. The only silver lining, if there was one, was that she'd saved this Ellie girl a lot of future heartache by firing her, because whatever she was, she was not a reporter.

Motown music—*what else!*—poured cheerfully from the speakers. The damned station was fixated on the stuff, and yes, this was Windsor with the real Motown only a stone's throw across the Detroit River, so *of course* Motown was her mom's favorite and *of course* Claire grew up on a steady diet of it. She'd tolerated it for her mom's sake, but when it came to sixties and seventies music, if pressed, she preferred the pre-disco Bee Gees, Jefferson Airplane, the Doors, Hendrix, Elton John, America, and of course Janis. Always Janis. Claire hadn't been born until 1976, so her taste in music was more Prince, Madonna, Bryan Adams, The Pretenders. The stuff you could really party to. Party to like it was 1999. Every generation had its signature music. Her mom's was Motown. Someone like Ellie, Christ, it was probably Lady Gaga or Katy Perry, or worse, Justin Bieber. *Ugh*!

She glanced at the rising needle on the speedometer. The gauge was laid out horizontally on the dash with a big orange needle crawling up the miles per hour: thirty, thirty-five, forty, forty-five. Everything was simple in this car. A shifter on the floor between the seats, the round gas gauge with another orange needle, a headlight knob that you pulled out to turn on the lights, a cigarette lighter, windows you had to manually roll up or down. She had just finished college when her mom bought the car, and with typical know-it-all, new-to-adulthood arrogance, Claire had asked her why she hadn't gone for a hot little foreign job. A BMW or a Porsche—something cool like that. Her mom wouldn't bite, though. Just smiled and announced she was in love with this car and had wanted one since the day Ford began making them.

"Ain't No Mountain High Enough." Not the Diana Ross version but the Marvin Gaye-Tammi Terrell one, and Claire couldn't stop her mouth from twisting into a smile because dammit, her mother was right. Motown music, even when the songs were about getting your heart handed to you, made you want to get up and dance. Which was exactly what her mom did whenever she played the old records or the songs came on the radio. She'd grab Claire by the hand and twirl her around in their little linoleum and Formica kitchen and dance like it was some kind of contest she wanted desperately to win. They'd spin and mimic the sleek Motown choreography, as if they were a couple of Supremes, before collapsing into a heap of giggles. For all the rough moments they'd endured together, there was always a Motown song waiting to be played.

It struck Claire that something about this Ellie kid reminded her of her mother. Ah, yes, of course. It was that annoying, perpetually sunny outlook. The *nice* factor. It was what had turned her off Ellie in the first place, made her want to teach her that life wasn't ice cream and sunshine and bright red convertibles (like this one) flying down an open highway. The newspaper business was about ferreting out controversial stories, working up contacts, sitting through boring old board meetings, or poring through two hundred pages of meeting minutes to find one decent storyline. It was about talking to murder victims' families, watching EMTs scrape up the injured or dead from the pavement. It was about reporting on poor kids whose only good meal of the day was being cut by the school board, about city politicians or bureaucrats taking kickbacks over paving jobs and garbage pickup. The news business didn't happen on the sunny side of the street, which was exactly where her mom, and this Ellie, preferred to dwell. It wasn't reality, all that Pollyanna bullshit. And it didn't get anybody anywhere. Just meant you sailed through life without a clue as to what was really going on around you. *Christ.*

So many times Claire wished her mother had been a fighter, that she'd possessed even the tiniest nasty streak. Like when Claire's dad left her for that floozy who worked at the diner out in the industrial park. Yeah, that would have been a good time for Claire's mom to let out her inner bitch. Also, the times when he was late with child support payments or withheld them altogether because floozy Cheryl *needed* a new car. Nice didn't keep your husband at home. Nice didn't pay the mortgage. And nice sure as hell didn't qualify you for a job in journalism. *But what the hell, eh Mom? Throw on the old Motown tunes and act like none of this shit is happening to you. Yeah, that's the way to do it, right, Ma? That'll make it all better. Not!*

"I'm Gonna Make You Love Me" was next on the hit parade, by Diana Ross and the Temptations. She knew the damned words by heart, had almost started singing them when instead she ground her teeth in frustration at how perfect this little spit in her eye was. The song was her mother's favorite. She used to sing it to Claire when Claire was a kid, sing it while dancing her around the kitchen floor. Against Claire's will, the memory began to soften her mood. Because whatever her shortcomings, her mom—

"Shit! Shit!" Claire jerked the wheel in the direction away from the furry black animal that had darted out beside her right front tire. There was a screech of rubber on pavement before the car launched into a fishtailing skid and onto the gravel shoulder, missing the animal as far as Claire could tell. She fought the wheel to hold it steady, prayed the tires did their job. They did. When the car mercifully came to a halt, Claire hopped out, pissed. Pissed that the car could have been damaged or, worse, that she could have been injured. These old cars didn't come with airbags and side impact panels. Didn't even come with shoulder strap seatbelts.

She cast around for the animal that she'd like to kick into the next county, and there it was, a medium-sized, curly-haired, black dog, one of those whatcha-ma-doodle things. Labradoodle? It sat shivering in the ditch like it was the middle of winter instead of the end of May.

Goddammit. It was looking at her with big wet brown eyes that would surely be weeping if the thing were human, but she refused to let the pathetic sight defuse her anger. "Come here, you little bastard," she yelled, but the dog only hunkered deeper into the mud and tall grass. "Don't make me come and get you."

That was exactly what it did, and Claire cursed as she hopped the ditch and grabbed the thing by the collar. Not that she'd ever be mistaken for being a dog lover, but she couldn't bring herself to leave it there to get hit by the next car that came along. Plus it had a collar and tag, with a pink leash dangling from it—*pink, for fuck sakes!*—which meant it was somebody's pet—somebody who did a shitty job of watching their pet, mind you. Piper, the bone-shaped metal tag said, with a phone number and address on the back. With one hand she hung on to the quivering dog and with the other pulled her cell phone from a cargo pocket in her pants. The line was busy. Of course it was, because it was one of those fucking days.

"Are you a girl or a boy, Piper?"

The dog stared at her like she was a complete idiot.

"Fine." She peeked underneath, saw it was a girl. "What the hell are you doing all the way over here, anyway?" The address was at least three kilometers away. "Fine mess you've gotten yourself into, girl. All muddy and covered in burrs now. I'm sure your owner will be thrilled."

The dog looked like it wanted to cry again, and Claire looked skyward in frustration because the poor thing and its plight were actually softening her sour mood. *Jesus, now I'm turning soft over a dog?* She dialed the number again. Still busy. *Great.* And it was going to rain soon, judging by the black clouds scudding along the western horizon.

Well, rain or not, it wasn't her fault the dog had run away. And besides, she was hungry for dinner. And thirsty for the stiff drink she hadn't yet fixed. Claire turned and hopped back in the car, but before she could shut the door, she pictured her mother frowning at her. And shaking an accusatory finger. *You can't leave that poor dog out there, Claire Catherine. Now do the right thing, for goodness sake, and see that that dog gets home safely. It's the least you can do since you almost hit it with* my *car.* Claire dragged herself back out of the car. *Aw fuck.* If she didn't do exactly what she suspected her mother was telepathically ordering her to do, she could expect something catastrophic to happen. Like her coffeemaker exploding and sending coffee spewing everywhere, like it did the time she'd boxed up her mom's Harlequin romance novels—all three hundred of them—intending to donate them to the thrift store. Even now, the boxes of books sat in her unfinished basement because she was afraid to test her mother again.

She sighed at the curly-furred mutt, which only looked at her quizzically. "All right, Miss Piper, goddammit. Ever ride in a 1965 Mustang before?"

Ellie Kirkland paced the small living room, her heart beating like she was running a marathon. She glanced out the window and frowned at the sprinkle of rain that had begun falling.

"That's it," she announced to Marissa, her cousin and roommate. "I'm going out again to look for Piper." She'd spent the last two hours driving around and had only stopped back at their rented townhouse for a pee break and to see if Piper had returned on her own.

"It'll be dark soon, and since Piper's black, we'll never spot her." Marissa was always the calm, sensible one. Which was probably why she'd graduated at the top of her nursing class. "We'll keep calling animal control. Hopefully somebody's picked her up by now. Or she'll make her way back. It hasn't been that long. Let's give it a little more time."

"But it's starting to rain, Riss. I can't leave her out there. She'll be scared, and..." *And I'll die if anything happens to her!*

She was near tears again, unable to forgive herself. She'd been walking Piper when a cat ran across their path and that was it, the chase was on. The leash ripped away from her hands before she knew it, and Piper was gone. *If I hadn't been using my other hand to hold that damned coffee cup, it would have been fine. That's it. No more mocha lattes on dog walks, even if the cute barista around the corner is serving them naked next time.*

"She's a smart dog, Ellie. And she won't melt from the rain, trust me."

"There's cars out there. And other animals. The poor thing isn't used to fending for herself. She's—"

The doorbell rang. *Oh shit.* What if it was bad news? What if it was somebody who'd run over Piper and now they'd come to tell her? Or the cops, coming to deliver the bad news? She'd never forgive herself, and the thought of Piper's poor little limp body made her feel instantly sick to her stomach. The dog had been her graduation present a year ago from her parents. They'd actually gotten a clue and figured out somewhere along the line how much she liked dogs. Piper was more like Ellie's baby, to the point where Marissa had thrown her a "puppy shower" last August. At Halloween and Christmas, Easter too, Ellie liked to dress Piper in cute, frilly, themed costumes, to endless teasing from her Facebook and Instagram friends. She couldn't lose this dog. And if she did, she'd never hear the end of it from her parents…that she was too immature to look after a dog, that she could never see anything through, that it was so typical of her inability to handle responsibility. Piper's disappearance was the icing on the cake that was made purely out of shit today.

"Don't," she called out weakly to Marissa, as in, don't answer the door. But it was too late. Marissa was letting someone in, talking in a low voice, and Ellie's imagination ran wild again with visions of Piper dead or injured, her heart cracking with each dreadful thought. And then came the unmistakable flurry of the click-clacking of dog nails on the tile floor. *Piper?* "Oh my god, is that you, girl?"

The dog, damp from the light rain and smelling of grass and mud, bounded into the living room, practically bowling Ellie over. She dropped to her knees and let Piper lick her face before furiously hugging her. She was wet, a little muddy, but Ellie didn't care. "You've come back! Oh, thank god. You bad, bad cat chaser, you." She stroked Piper's curly head and gave her the blackest stare she could summon, which really wasn't much. "No more chasing cats for you. I'm getting you a harness. And a muzzle. And maybe a ball and chain to slow you down. But a bath is the first thing you're getting."

Piper's ears drooped at the word *bath*.

"A-hem." It was Marissa, inclining her head toward someone in the foyer that Ellie couldn't see. The hero who'd brought Piper home.

"Oh, god," Ellie said, jumping to her feet and dashing for the foyer, anxious to thank whomever it was. "I can't thank you enough for returning my d—"

Holy shit! It was her boss, Claire Melbourne, right here in the flesh. Well, ex-boss as of noon today. Like a sudden dropped cell phone call, she lost the link between Claire and Piper and could only replay in her mind the moment this woman had fired her. She'd not been very nice about it either. Her face all red and tight so that you could see every muscle in her jaw and neck. She was super pissed, and rightly so, Ellie supposed. She'd fucked up big time. And she was very sorry about it, but Ms. Melbourne—Claire, everyone else called her—wasn't handing out any second chances. Wasn't entertaining excuses either. Just told her in a don't-fuck-with-me voice that her time at the newspaper had come to an abrupt end and to please pack her things immediately and hand in her key card and ID card. It wasn't entirely a real job, only a twelve-month internship that paid little more than minimum wage, but still. To Ellie it was a job, and one she'd gotten all on her own. She cried all the way home, then took Piper out to walk off her sadness and frustration. Which was how Piper had gotten away on her.

She fought to regain her voice, fearing it sounded embarrassingly trembly and high-pitched. "Ms. Melbourne, w-what are you doing here? Did I…are you…" *Here to fire me again?* No, that couldn't be it. People didn't get fired twice.

"Oh!" her ex-boss exclaimed, looking, for the first time Ellie could ever recall, completely rattled as she ran a hand through her hair. "It's you."

Marissa's eyes swung from one to the other, like she couldn't quite figure out what the hell was happening. *Well, neither can I,* Ellie thought.

"Your dog," Claire Melbourne said. "It…she…"

"Piper! Oh god, she got away on me this afternoon when I was walking her. She chased a cat and…well, I'm so grateful you found her, you have no idea." Civility won the day because Ellie would do anything for the person who'd rescued Piper. Even if that person was Cruella De Vil in cute cargo pants and a tailored blouse and leather ankle boots that looked like they were made for walking. Walking all over people. And which were now covered in mud, thanks to Piper's little escapade. Ellie gulped. If Claire Melbourne demanded new boots out of this ordeal, Ellie was in big trouble. She could never afford it.

Claire Melbourne pointed her chin at Ellie. "Well, I was driving and she ran out and I almost hit her."

Ellie's hand flew to her mouth. "Oh you didn't, did you? I mean, she's okay, right?" Piper was already playing with one of her stuffed toys, squeaking the shit out of it, and looked absolutely fine, but you never knew.

"Yes, she's okay, and no, I didn't hit her. Her tag had your address on it."

"Well," Marissa interjected. "We're so glad you did. It was very kind of you. Would you like to come in for coffee? Or a drink?"

Ellie wanted to die. What the hell was Marissa doing inviting the boss-from-hell in for a drink? Oh, wait. Marissa couldn't possibly know this was the same Claire Melbourne who was her boss. Nor had she yet told Marissa her news about being fired. It wasn't that Marissa would be judgmental, or go blabbing it to Ellie's oh-so-judgy, overachieving, perfectionist parents, Dr. and Dr. Kirkland. Ellie had been so caught up in Piper's disappearance that there hadn't been time to tell Marissa.

Claire's eyes widened in alarm, probably matching the fear in Ellie's, as an uncomfortable moment of silence passed.

"Actually," Claire said, rescuing them both, "I have somewhere to be. I just wanted to return, er, Piper, home."

"Right," Ellie said, leaping to the door because she couldn't open it fast enough to get this woman the hell out of here. "And thank you again. Thank you so much! You...you're a life saver."

"Well, it...it was no trouble." A smile weaker than water, and then Claire Melbourne was striding purposefully to her Mustang. Her Mustang of the ancient and very cool variety. Okay, it was a pretty sweet car but it did *not* match the driver's personality.

"Wow," Marissa said. "Look at that car! Sexy, wouldn't you say?"

Ellie rolled her eyes. Yes, the car was lovely, but the fact that it was owned by Claire Melbourne was all she could see.

"What?" Marissa continued. "I think it's sexy. Its owner is not bad either. If you like the domineering type." She laughed at her own joke. "Ms., what was her name? Melbourne? Did you see the way she—"

"I don't want to talk about her. Or her damned car." Ellie stalked to the kitchen, pawed through the Keurig pod collection, dug out a cappuccino, and popped it into the machine.

Marissa, hot on her heels, wouldn't drop it. "Look, I thought she...Oh wait. Melbourne. Isn't that your boss's name? Ellie, was that your *boss*?"

Tears pricked at the back of Ellie's eyes. "Yes."

"Why didn't you say? You know I like a woman who knows how to take charge. Geez, I'd have been visiting your office on a daily basis. I mean, I know she's older, but, like, hello, cougar!"

"Look, she's not…" Ellie couldn't quite manage to get out the words that Claire wasn't her boss anymore. "She's not *that*…I don't know. And jeez, Riss, I don't look at her that way. It's, like, icky to think of your boss as sexy. She's…Ms. Melbourne. Claire." Ellie had always had a hard time calling authority figures by their first name. It felt weird. Probably because she didn't truly feel like a grownup yet, even though most of her high school friends were set in careers now, a few were married, a handful even had a kid or two.

"All right, agreed on the boss thing, but holy Jesus, El. I've never seen eyes that shade of blue before. They're like sexy wolf eyes. Like…like…chips of pale blue ice I'd love to melt. Ooh, and that mouth, it's begging to be kissed, don't you think?"

Ellie slammed her eyes shut. She did *not* want to think of the woman who'd fired her that way. "Can we please stop talking about her?" She knew her cousin was simply having a little fun, plus she was still sowing her wild lesbian oats (which she seemed to have an unending supply of) and never seemed to grow tired of talking about women. But if Ellie didn't succeed in changing the subject, Marissa would be at it all evening.

Piper bounded into the kitchen, trailing a blue towel in her mouth.

"Where did you get that from, Piper?"

She growled, clamped down harder on the towel, and wouldn't let go when Ellie tried to extract it from her teeth.

"I think the hot Ms. Melbourne used it to dry Piper off and left it near the door." Marissa handed Ellie her mug of cappuccino and put a coffee pod in the machine for herself.

"Crap," Ellie said, plucking a dog treat from the pottery canister on the counter and trading it for the towel in Piper's mouth.

"What's wrong? Just bring it back to sexy boss lady when you go to work on Monday."

"I can't…exactly."

"Why not?"

This was the part where Ellie—again—got to feel like the perpetual loser she was. Nothing had ever come easy to her, at least not in the career department. Unlike Marissa, who'd sailed through nursing school a couple of years ago and was regarded as something of a young ER hotshot at Windsor Regional Hospital's downtown location. Nor was Ellie anything like her twin sister Erin, who was finishing her fourth year of medical school and happily following in the footsteps of their parents, both of whom had family medicine practices bursting with full rosters and both of whom had known since they'd played doctor with their Barbie dolls exactly what they wanted to do when they grew up. Doctors Emily and Elaine Kirkland were the perfect physicians, the perfect lesbian couple with the perfect little family. Erin was their little chip off the old block, their little mini me. But not Ellie. Ellie still couldn't seem to figure out what the hell to do with the rest of her life, and at twenty-six, there was little family patience for what they considered her inertia, her inherent lack of ambition. Worse was they thought of her as not as smart as the rest of them, with their dinner table talk of gene mutations and stem cell therapy and Freud versus Jung that was pointedly meant to exclude her.

Marissa wasn't like them. She had infinite patience for Ellie and her indecisiveness, which was why Ellie roomed with her instead of living at home, where her mothers sucked the life out of her with their judgment-laced questions and their barbed advice. She'd never get out from under their aura of overachieving ambitiousness, and it was almost enough to make her want to give up even trying.

She struck a casual pose. "You know, I'm not so sure the whole journalism experiment is working out."

"What? I thought you loved it?"

"I did. I'm…sort of…not very good at it."

"But you did well enough in it at school. And you've been at the newspaper for eight months now."

It was now or never. "Claire Melbourne fired me today."

Marissa's hand flew to her mouth. She sat down on the stool at the breakfast bar, stunned into silence. Which Ellie knew wouldn't last long. It didn't. "Is she nuts? Why would she fire *you*? You're so happy and friendly and helpful, like the cute puppy everyone loves."

"Gee, thanks. I think."

"No, really! You're, like, the person least likely to get fired from anything in the whole world."

"You're being nice, and I appreciate it, but being a cheerful puppy dog doesn't cut it in the news business. I sucked at it, Riss. I blew a big scoop."

"What do you mean you blew a big scoop? And why was an intern entrusted with a big scoop anyway? Didn't you have a mentor reporter or editor? Someone to help you out? Take the reins?"

"I happened to answer the phone yesterday from an anonymous caller letting us know he had some kind of incriminating tape of the deputy mayor and somebody doing some sort of shady business deal. I scribbled it on a piece of paper. And then I had to run out to interview somebody about therapy dogs. I was going to be late, so I didn't have time to pass on the message. And then, by the time I got back, everybody was gone for the day. And, well…"

"You also lost the piece of paper?"

The memory of her screw-up brought tears to Ellie's eyes. "I didn't mean to, Riss. But it turned out to be a really big deal." Her absentmindedness was another thing her mothers liked to harp on. It's not like she could help it. She simply got… distracted easily.

"Come here." Marissa pulled her in for a hug. "You'll find something else. I know you will. Trust me, it's not the end of the world."

Ellie wasn't in a mood to believe her. "First I dropped out of pharmacy school, now I'll never be a journalist."

"Stop it. Pharmacy wasn't for you and you know it. And yesterday was one mistake. You can try for a job at a radio station or another newspaper. Television is where you really belong anyway, with your looks."

Marissa was an excellent cheerleader, and Ellie was eternally grateful to have someone in her corner, backing her up no matter what or how often she screwed up. "I don't know. To be honest, I don't think I have the heart—or the heartlessness, I should say—to be a news reporter anyway. I need to figure something else out."

Back to square one. Yet again.

"Riss, please don't tell my moms about this. They don't need to know until I decide what I'm doing next, okay?" She could practically hear them, accusing her of changing careers as often as she changed socks. And Erin, who had her own charmed life to live, wasn't around to be a buffer.

"I wouldn't dream of it. Now come on, let's go out for dinner and a drink. My treat."

"You picked up dinner last time."

"So what. I'm not keeping track."

"Tell you what. I'll buy dinner if you do me a favor and take that blanket back to boss-from-hell next week."

Marissa broke into a devilish grin. "I would have given anything to do that before you told me about her firing you. Now I'd want to slap her silly, so no. I'm afraid you'll have to do it, sport."

Crap.

CHAPTER TWO

Every Little Bit Hurts

Claire continued to feel the sting of last week's lost scoop, but at least Jackson Hurley had dug up a good story today about an off-duty city cop who'd been caught smuggling cases of booze across the border from Michigan and reselling it at a rate that was cheaper than the local government stores charged. Modern-day bootlegging, and while it didn't quite make up for last week's screw-up, it was something. Claire planned to milk it for all it was worth by splashing it across the top of tomorrow's front page.

She stood and stretched, her back cramping from sitting too long. Jacks was across the newsroom tapping away on his keyboard. It was a large, open-concept room with rows of desks for more than a dozen reporters and a central hub for editors, which was where Claire spent most of her day. She had a small glassed-in office as well if she needed privacy to chat with a staffer or someone else, but she preferred being in the middle of the constant thrum of phones ringing, the chattering police scanner, reporters and editors keyboarding away or interviewing people over the phone. It was also the best way to keep tabs on emerging stories.

She glanced at the wall clock. Time to remind her best reporter that deadline was approaching. It wasn't truly, but she wanted to read through the story before it went to a copy editor, then got "webbed up" and out onto their social media sites. After that it was onto the electronic layout department this evening, then the printing presses overnight for tomorrow morning's early print edition. Claire already had a headline and layout design in mind for the bootlegging cop story.

She tapped lightly on Jackson's shoulder and earned a smile in return.

"You owe me one, my friend," he whispered. "And I plan to collect, so you know. Saturday night. Me and you. The Red Zone. Drinks on you, of course."

"Ha. Like you need an excuse to get your crazy on at the Zone. Or for me to buy you a drink."

The Red Zone was Windsor's only LGBTQ dance club, and Jacks was a regular patron, or used to be, back when he was single. Claire's presence there was rare, except for when her friend managed to drag her along. Their friendship reached back to high school, a couple of queer outcasts who'd teamed up out of necessity, only to realize they actually enjoyed hanging out together. They were still best friends, and everyone in the newsroom knew it. That Claire was Jackson's boss failed to raise eyebrows, because she was harder on him than anyone else. Which he thrived on. He was more than adept at handling Claire and her tough expectations, plus he was a damned good reporter.

"After last week," he said on a theatrical sigh, "we both deserve to get our crazy on."

"I'll say. Speaking of work, are you almost—"

"Well, look who's come to visit." Jacks leaped out of his chair. "Hey, girl!"

Aw shit. It was Ellie Kirkland. What the hell was she doing here? She'd removed her personal belongings minutes after Claire had fired her, so that couldn't be the reason she was back.

But Jacks, who was overly demonstrative with his emotions, began hugging her like a lifelong friend who'd returned from an extended absence. What the hell was with that?

"It's so great to see you, kid." Claire was sure Jackson was laying it on thick for her benefit. He was pissed that she'd fired Ellie, had made no secret of the fact that he thought it was a rash and unnecessary decision. Not to mention harsh. He'd been sulking about it ever since. "Did you come back to visit us, sweetie?"

Claire began to back away. Discreetly, or so she thought.

"Actually, I came to return this to Ms. Melbourne." She held up the blue towel, the one Claire had used to protect her car's backseat from a wet and muddy Piper.

Two sets of eyes halted Claire's not-so-smooth retreat. "Oh, I, ah, that wasn't necessary, really. You could have thrown it out or kept it." *God, anything but bring it back here.*

Ellie shook her head, slow to smile, but when she did, it was like a full-on blast of sunshine. Right. The kid was the perpetually cheery type, a sunny side of the street dweller. And she was damned good at it, a natural, even though it must be killing her to have to—again—be in such close proximity to the person who'd fired her. She had balls. Or a shitload of denial going on.

"Returning it's the least I could do after you saved my dog." Dimples, deep and irresistible, oozed charm in Claire's direction, throwing her off. And Claire didn't like to be off balance, on the defense, like this. Maybe she'd seriously underestimated the kid, but only if a killer instinct lay beneath the charming little games. Which she highly doubted and had never witnessed.

Jackson's eyebrows nearly shot off his head. "You saved her dog, Claire? How did I miss that?"

"I did not save her dog. It was nothing, really."

Ellie's smile dissolved and those huge brown eyes of hers began to mist over. Oh Christ, was she going to cry now? Was it another of her little tricks to make Claire feel sorry for her? Or guilty for firing her?

"It's not nothing to me, Ms. Melbourne. Piper's like my baby, and if you hadn't returned her, I don't know what I would have done."

Jackson patted Ellie's hand and dropped his voice to a stage whisper. "That's our Claire. She's a lot nicer than she wants anyone to believe."

Claire coughed. It was a conspiracy to embarrass the crap out of her. And she didn't like it. She snatched the proffered towel from Ellie's hands. "Well, thanks for dropping this by." She caught Jackson's eyes. "I need your story in the next ten minutes, all right?"

She walked away, feeling the unmistakable laser beams of Jacks's eyes on her back. She'd hear it from him later. And she did, in the form of about a dozen texts after he ignored her for the rest of his shift and fled out the door promptly at five. Claire was logging out of her computer and about to head home when the first text came in.

Did you have to be so mean to the poor girl? Again???

I'm not being mean to her. She came to deliver something to me. I took it. I was polite. Okay?!?

Considering you FIRED her last week, you could have been nicer. Like asked her how she's doing!

Jacks, don't start. I'm not in the mood.

Fine. At least tell me how the hell you became a doggie superhero.

Did not.

Did too. I thought Ellie was going to hug you.

Wasn't a big deal. I found the dog by the road and returned it. End of story.

I doubt that. Your deed might have actually made up for being such a big meanie to her in the first place.

Claire sighed. Jackson and his drama. She texted back that she was driving and had to put her phone away. A lie, but she wasn't in the mood for further discussion about Ellie Kirkland.

* * *

I must be crazy, Ellie thought. *No, scratch that. I'm a glutton for punishment.*

She pulled into the driveway of her childhood home, interlocking brick leading to a rather palatial five-bedroom, Tudor-style home in Windsor's posh south end. Her moms had been inviting her for dinner all week; she finally accepted when they were no longer buying her excuses. Returning the towel to Cruella De Vil yesterday had left her with a small measure of residual courage. She'd need as much of it as she could get, because she had to tell her parents sometime about her current sad state of affairs. And her pathetic plans for the future. Which actually meant zero plans at this point.

"Let's get this over with," she mumbled to herself and took a deep breath before exiting her crappy old Honda Civic with the scratched paint and the missing hubcap. Her mothers had offered to buy her a new car many times, but to Ellie it was a point of pride and independence to turn them down. She would do things her way, even if those things were substandard and woeful. Not to mention that a new car was one less thing they could hold over her head like the blade of a guillotine.

"Darling," Emily said, greeting her with a kiss to both cheeks. Emily was Ellie's birth mother, while Elaine's brother had been the sperm donor, which technically made Elaine her aunt if you went by blood, but to Ellie they were both her moms. Emily was Mom, Elaine was Mama.

"Hi, Mom." She held up a bottle of wine.

"Oh, you shouldn't have, dear."

Yes, she should have. It was considered bad manners in her family if you showed up empty-handed, though the wine had cost the kind of small fortune she didn't have.

Elaine was the cook in the family and a good one. Of the four of them, Ellie was the least functional in the kitchen, which the others often teased her about. She followed her nose to the kitchen. Or rather, she followed the pungent scent of basil, garlic, and tomato sauce; it smelled divine.

"Sweetheart," Elaine said, leaving the stove and wrapping Ellie in a bear hug.

"Hi, Mama."

Her mothers had always been warm and affectionate, doling out an endless supply of both during her childhood and adolescence and even now. Tears had always been met with gentle murmurings and rocking, sickness with homemade chicken soup, birthdays with parties like the neighborhood had never seen before. Life would be perfect if only that same love and acceptance had extended to Ellie's adult choices. There were no more kid gloves, no coddling, where Ellie's future was concerned. It was her mothers' version of tough love.

They made small talk until dinner was served. No sense in ruining anybody's appetite, Ellie decided. The casserole was a concoction of Elaine's, something she called "Italian Surprise." It had all kinds of mouth-watering stuff in it: Italian sausage, the garlic and basil she'd smelled earlier, shell pasta, spicy tomato sauce. And lots and lots of gooey cheese. Simply smelling it added a couple of pounds to her hips, but what the hell. It was worth it.

"Your sister's coming home for the month of July and part of August," Emily announced, beaming with pride. She always beamed with pride whenever Erin was the subject of conversation. Which was often.

"Oh, good. We can hang out, talk about obstructive jaundice and acute subdural hematomas." Ellie tried, really tried, to keep the sarcasm from her voice, but Emily's frown told her she hadn't been very successful.

In that lecturing doctor voice of hers, Elaine said, "Considering you're twins, I can't believe how different you are." Which really meant, how the hell did you turn out to be such a dud?

Ellie sighed an apology for her cranky comment. "I'm glad she's coming home. I look forward to spending some time with her." They weren't as close as they used to be, mainly because of geographical reasons, but right now, Ellie could sure use another friend in her corner.

"How are things at the newspaper?" Emily asked innocently. On any other day, Ellie would have welcomed the change of subject and prattled on and on about her latest assignment.

"Actually, that's what I want to talk to you both about." She pushed her empty plate aside. This was it. Time to—yet again—disappoint her mothers. Because that's what she did. Why break with tradition now? "I'm not working at the paper anymore."

"What?" The two women said in unison.

"I said I'm not wor—"

"We heard you, dear." Elaine gave that long, beleaguered sigh that said the world had once again delivered a massive weight onto her shoulders. "What do you mean you're no longer working at the newspaper? What happened?"

"I…" Ellie wavered between honesty and a fabulous lie that would lay the blame somewhere else. But she wasn't a liar, which was partly why she always seemed to be getting into trouble. When she was a kid and played hockey, she'd practically sprint to the penalty box in guilt, earned or not, whenever the ref blew the whistle and raised his arm to signal an infraction. "I sort of made a mistake, a big mistake, and got fired last week."

Emily leaned closer, her expression neutral, but not her eyes. Her eyes were probing, concerned. And of course, full of displeasure and disappointment. "What kind of mistake? What did you do?"

She told them matter-of-factly what happened. She'd long since wrung out her emotions with a few good crying jags. The gossamer of despair that remained was mostly from feeling lost, directionless, back on the gerbil wheel of here-we-go-again.

"Well," said Elaine, "that's rather harsh, to be fired for one mistake. Who is this heartless, intractable boss who would do such a thing?"

"It doesn't matter, it's done." It would be easy to hate Claire Melbourne, to pin the blame on her. And Ellie had wanted to do exactly that, but as the days passed, she began to consider that Claire Melbourne might have actually done her a favor. In a perverse, humiliating way, mind you, but deep down, she knew she wasn't cut out to be a journalist. She loved meeting people, hearing their stories, and writing was super fun. But she didn't possess a hard-nosed edge, nor live for the dogged pursuit of truth and justice and all that journalistic dogma crap. She wasn't meant to save the world…another reason why she didn't quite fit in with the rest of the Kirklands. The Kirklands wanted to save everybody and look good doing it.

Silence ensued, during which Ellie straightened her back and mentally prepared for the onslaught. She didn't have to wait long.

"What are you going to do?" Emily asked in a slightly panicked voice. Ah yes, the million-dollar question.

"Get a job, obviously." If she could at least reassure her mothers that she wouldn't need financial help from them, it would be a start. "I've already put my application in at a bakery/café downtown." The Café Au Chocolat. It was as upscale as Starbucks, but independently owned by an acquaintance of Marissa's. The place had the best coffee and the best homemade scones and lemon bars in the city.

"But that's not…" Elaine paused in a thin attempt to calm down. Her face was noticeably pinched and red—the look of disapproval Ellie knew well. "You have a university degree, Ellie. I should think Starbucks is—"

"Beneath me? Mama, I hate to tell you, but all the restaurants, coffee shops, and department stores are full of workers who have university degrees. My degree isn't worth much in the real world, you know." She'd never told them about her dog-walking gig. It was only one client and it didn't pay well, but that's not why she did it. She did it because she loved dogs, but her moms would never understand. Money, prestige, titles, and letters after your name, those were the measuring sticks in the Kirkland household.

"Well, your education was *supposed* to qualify you to work at the newspaper." There was a bite to Elaine's words, and it hurt.

Ellie closed her eyes briefly and tried to count how many times she'd been through this same scenario. Her first failure was her desire back in high school to be an interior designer. That simply wasn't good enough for the daughter of two physicians. Then it was off to get a pharmacology degree, which lasted three semesters (she dropped out before she could be kicked out of the program). Journalism, via a communications/

journalism degree at the University of Windsor, was supposed to lead to her dream job, except her dream job had turned into a nightmare.

"I'm not going to be a journalist," she said matter-of-factly. "I don't have what it takes. And I probably knew that before I even finished my program, but I didn't want to again drop out of something. I wanted to actually finish what I started, for once."

"And you did, dear." Emily's smile was pathetic, pitiful. "Do you have an idea of what you'll try next?"

"No." The word *try* wasn't lost on her, as in, what flavor of ice cream would you like to try next? No one in her family had confidence in her. And who could blame them?

Emily and Elaine exchanged a look, and it was enough to almost send Ellie spiraling into what she knew would be a cascade of tears if she didn't make a quick exit. "You know what? I really have to go now. I'm sorry. Thank you for dinner. It was lovely."

"Ellie, wait." Elaine stood and pulled her into another hug. "Honey, please don't leave like that."

"It's fine. I'm fine. I promise." It wasn't. *She* wasn't. But it was temporary. If there was one thing Ellie was good at, it was at bouncing back.

Emily kissed her on the cheek at the door. "We love you. You'll think of something."

Yes. They did love her in their own way, she supposed. And as much as her family often annoyed her—no, pissed her off—they were still family. And one day maybe they'd find a way to be proud of her. Maybe. But not today.

CHAPTER THREE

The Way You Do The Things You Do

If she was going to have to sit through a couple of hours of dance music and watch Jacks make a fool of himself, Claire figured the least she could do was get a little drunk. Which probably wouldn't take more than three drinks, given that she wasn't a huge drinker. A glass of wine after work, another with dinner was more than enough to take the edge off. She'd not been drunk in years—she hated feeling like crap the next day—but the prospect of submitting herself to the salvos of alcohol held particular appeal tonight. She'd never admit it to Jacks, but this foreign feeling that kept pulling her spirits down, making her feel like shit, was guilt. And it was Ellie Kirkland returning her towel to her that had set her on this little trip down Guilt Lane. The kid was undeniably sweet. And most alarming of all, she didn't seem to harbor any ill will toward Claire. Not even a whiff of it. Was she not human, for Christ sakes?

Jacks stuck his nose close to her drink and inhaled. "Ooh, a mojito. You're either celebrating something or trying to forget something."

He knew her too damned well, but with eighteen years of working together, not to mention their time in high school and college, it was a given. "I thought I'd be…" she waggled her eyebrows, "…a little adventurous tonight."

"I like Adventure Claire. Much more fun than Crabby Claire. Or Ogre Claire."

"I am not an ogre."

"All right, normally you're not, but with Ellie Kirkland, you—"

Claire rounded on him. "Can we please, for one teeny, tiny day, stop talking about Ellie Kirkland? What is she, your long lost kid sister or something? I've never seen you so protective before. I swear she's related to you. Or she's got something on you that even *I* don't know about."

Jacks took a delicate sip of his Salty Dog. His live-in boyfriend, Julian, was away on a business trip and it was obvious by the way he nursed his drink that Jacks was planning to behave himself tonight. "Come on. Us queers have to look out for another, that's all it is. You should understand that."

Ellie Kirkland was queer? How had she missed that?

"Plus she's a good kid, Claire Bear."

"All right, fine, so she's a good kid. You've made your point. About three thousand freaking times." Was he going to make her pay for this for the next twelve months? "Even you can admit she's not driven enough for this job. She's not ruthless enough. She doesn't *want* it bad enough."

Jacks heaved a weary sigh. "I know, you're probably right."

"Probably?" Claire and Jacks had been through hell and back together. Not quite war, but they'd shared the same foxhole covering many unpleasant events. There was the massive passenger jet crash early in their careers, more gory murder trials and sex assault trials than they cared to count, and a horrendous nursing home fire nine years ago that left six people dead. They'd also survived their first city editor at the newspaper—a homophobic, habitual pot smoker who enjoyed making their lives miserable. The joke was on him when he was finally fired for getting the newspaper sued—not once but twice.

Jacks relented. "All right, all right. I know this job isn't for everybody. I just hate to see—" His mouth fell open, his eyes suddenly glued to something near the door, and the massive grin splitting his handsome face made Claire instantly relax. Until she followed his gaze.

Oh no, it couldn't be. Except it was. Ellie Kirkland and the woman she lived with—what was her name again?—were coming through the door, nodding their heads at people, stopping to hug a few others. Of course they would know everybody in the place, unlike Claire and Jacks who were among only a handful of people in their forties and who stuck out like old farts at a kiddie parade. Ellie and her friend, meanwhile, looked totally at home.

"Well, well." Jacks nudged her playfully. "We can't seem to get rid of our little Ellie Jelly lately. Must be karma." He stared at Claire. "Your karma. And I have to confess, I'm kind of loving it."

"You would." Jacks was a practical joker, with a sense of humor that could cut deep and hard. Ellie was the gum on her shoe and Jacks was making sure she stepped in it. Over and over again. She took a long sip of her drink because it was going to be a long night. "Did you know about this?"

"About what?"

"Playing dumb isn't your style."

"Fine. No, I didn't know she would be here. How would I know a thing like that? I haven't been to this place in three months. Ellie! Over here!"

Oh god, he was waving her and her girlfriend over to their table. At least, she assumed the woman was Ellie's girlfriend.

The two inched their way through the crowd. "Hi!" Ellie yelled over Lady Gaga. Claire nodded. She could do polite, but she wasn't going to do super friendly, because she couldn't stomach the possibility of Ellie and her girlfriend hanging out with them for an extended amount of time. Was there a way to say "get lost" nicely?

"This is Marissa," Ellie said by way of introduction. "My cousin and roommate." She looked at Claire with raised eyebrows. "You met her when you returned Piper?"

"Of course." Claire shook Marissa's hand. So they weren't a couple. Which meant Jacks might be wrong about Ellie being gay. Not that it mattered, of course. "Nice to meet you again."

"Likewise." The frost was radiating off Marissa. Not that Claire could blame her. Ellie had probably spared no detail in explaining how rude she had been in firing her. She greeted Jacks with a much warmer demeanor.

"Oh!" Jacks threw up his hands, leapt from his chair, and twirled. "I LOVE Jennifer Hudson! Who's with me?"

"I am!" Marissa followed him to the dance floor.

Great, Claire thought. He was leaving her alone with Ellie. *Now what?*

Ellie studied the glass of wine in her hand like it was the Rosetta Stone. Claire did the same with her mojito. Fine. She could be a big girl. She was, after all, the supervising editor of thirteen reporters, two photographers, and three copy editors. She could be civil to Ellie. What she wouldn't do was apologize.

"Ellie, look, I think…"

Dammit. Even in the dim lighting and the laser strobe lights bouncing around the place like tennis balls, Ellie's eyes were huge and full of…Not need, exactly, but vulnerability. Innocence. Exactly like her damned dog's. Claire's heart did a little backflip.

She tried again, defeated by Ellie's guileless eyes. "I feel like we should talk about what happened at the paper." Because they hadn't. At all. The day she'd fired her, Claire had cut off Ellie's explanation for failing to pass along the important message that lost the paper what would have been its biggest scoop of the year. She'd fired her, right there on the spot.

"Sorry, what?"

Jennifer Hudson had segued into a seventies' disco tune and Jacks was pulling out all the stops on the dance floor, doing his best John Travolta impersonation. All he needed was the white suit and the dark, slicked-back hair.

Claire raised her voice. "At the newspaper. I may not have properly explained why I needed to…"

Jacks and Marissa were waving them over, and Ellie jumped to her feet. Her smile was like a blast of sunshine. "Come on,

Ms. Melbourne. Who can resist an actual disco song from the seventies?"

Huh. She actually knows what disco is? But she followed Ellie to the dance floor anyway because, well, she could be cool. Okay, not cool, perhaps, but she could be human. She could dance, even if it was usually in the confines of her own four walls.

"You should probably call me Claire."

Ellie smiled as Donna Summer's voice floated over them like glitter from above, singing about McArthur's Park melting. Ellie loved music from that era. She never understood why, and it made her the butt of much teasing when she was growing up. She swore she'd been born a couple of decades too late. "Sure," she answered absently, not really caring what she did or didn't call Claire Melbourne. She'd not been thrilled to see her former boss here, but she really liked Jackson Hurley, and if she had to put up with Claire, be nice to her for an hour or so, she could handle it.

Ellie threw her hands in the air and lost herself in the music, moving to the beat, picturing in her head tight miniskirts and sequined tops, platform shoes, big hair, eye shadow that went on forever. She'd seen that old *Saturday Night Fever* movie about a million times, wishing she'd actually been alive when iconic places like Studio 54 were in their heyday.

One of her all-time favorite songs came next, the Temptations and Diana Ross's "I'm Gonna Make You Love Me." *Crap.* It was a slow song and she'd just bumped up against Ms. Melbourne. Er, Claire. She cast around for an escape route, a rescuer, something to get her out of having to dance with the boss from hell. Ex-boss from hell. But no, they were all jammed in like sardines, and Jacks and Marissa were dancing together. *Whatever you do, don't panic!*

Claire backed away into somebody's hip, looking slightly horrified (which made Ellie feel perversely good) and managed to find a space between bodies through which to squeeze. *Thank god.* Dancing a slow song with the woman who'd fired her? *Please!* Ellie would rather dance with a straight man drooling all over her than dance with Claire Melbourne. She'd rather dance with anyone else, if it came to that. Which was slightly unfortunate, because on the surface, Claire seemed like a good catch. She was a lesbian, according to the rumor mill, and a single one at that. She had great cheekbones, a very kissable mouth (Marissa was right), but mostly it was those eyes of hers— they were movie star quality. Ellie had never before noticed how good looking Claire was, mainly because she'd always been so intimidated by her. One icy look from those blue eyes used to send her scurrying back to her desk and behind her computer screen, her heart in her throat.

She sauntered to the bar for another glass of wine to dull the burn of Claire's dance floor rejection. Not that she'd wanted to dance with Claire, but still. When she chose to go clubbing here, which was barely every six weeks or so, there was never a shortage of women who wanted to dance with her. She wasn't typically the kind of person that people ran away from. Claire probably wasn't either, and yet Ellie had wanted to escape from her too, if she were honest. Fine. So they both disliked one another.

"Hey." Marissa bumped shoulders with her and ordered a gin smash. "Some cute girls here tonight, don't you think?" She was perpetually single, perpetually looking, and having a world of fun with it.

"I guess." Ellie wasn't in the market for a girlfriend. Not really. If one stumbled into her lap, someone who was a good catch, she wouldn't say no to a date, but otherwise she was happily single. Mostly, she didn't want the encumbrance of a relationship until she figured out what to do with her life. Something like settling her ship on smooth waters before adding all the ups and downs, the turbulence and thrills, of a committed relationship.

They both sipped their drinks, in no hurry to return to the table where Jacks and Claire sat.

"You know what I've decided?" Marissa said. "That for a first-class bitch, your boss is still hot. I don't think I've ever seen her here before, have you?"

Definitely not. Ellie would have remembered. "I don't want to think of her as hot."

Marissa clinked glasses with her. "All right, then let's think of her as a bitch."

"I don't think I want to do that either."

"What? Why not?"

Marissa was like that. Black and white. Someone was either a bitch or they were a saint. Nice or a jerk. Maybe it was from working in the ER, dealing with all kinds of people, mostly at their worst, that forced her to make snap judgments. "I think, I don't know, that maybe she's not as bad as she seems," Ellie offered. Well, sometimes she was. Ellie once saw her tear a strip off some lawyer who'd come into the newsroom, full of bluster and bullshit and threats, wanting the name of his client, who was up on robbery charges, to be kept out of the paper. But this was also the Claire Melbourne who'd returned Piper to her. And the Claire Melbourne who, at Christmas, Ellie saw slip a one-hundred-dollar bill into the Salvation Army kettle outside the news office.

"Huh. She was bad enough to fire you. That makes her a bitch in my books."

"Maybe." Ellie sipped her wine, glanced across the bobbing heads to the table where Claire and Jacks sat. Claire was smiling at something Jacks was saying. She looked relaxed. Normal. Like she might even be having fun. "Maybe not."

Marissa wasn't listening anymore. She'd turned to chat with a long-legged brunette who'd sidled up to her, and the take-me-home game was on. It was a good time to leave, before Jacks noticed she was alone and waved her over again. She finished off her wine in one long swallow, signaled to Marissa that she was catching a cab home, and walked out the door without a glance back.

Claire Melbourne was one complicated lady. Ellie was not unhappy to think that she would probably never see her again.

CHAPTER FOUR

Come See About Me

A bad storm early that morning had wiped out power and knocked down trees along the lakeshore, and Claire and her team spent the day chasing down the story. The photos of the damage were good—a tree right through the middle of someone's living room, a child's bicycle perched on the roof of a neighboring shed—and eyewitnesses had given good interviews. No injuries, which was great, but plenty of damage to give the reader enough visual shock and awe. With only an apple for lunch and the hour approaching six in the evening, Claire was in no mood to cook supper.

The deli sandwiches at the Café Au Chocolat, around the corner and down the street from the newspaper office, were to die for, and Claire had had the forethought a few hours ago to phone and ask them to hold back a roast beef sandwich for her. She'd make it there with only minutes to spare before the place closed.

She rushed in. And stopped dead in her tracks. There was Ellie Kirkland behind the counter, wiping things down, preparing to close up. She wore a bright yellow apron over a short-sleeved white blouse and beige Capri pants. The unhurried, fluid movements of her arm reminded Claire of the dance club last week, of Ellie dancing as though she were the only person in the room, letting the music dictate her movements, her body a river flowing with the currents. Maybe it was because of her age that she could act so carefree, or maybe it was simply the way she was, but something about her devil-may-care attitude intimidated Claire a little.

She remembered what it was like to be twenty-five, twenty-six. When you think you have a million tomorrows, that you can still have any life you want, that there's plenty of time for a second, a third, a fourth chance. You think you can start over any damned time you want. And then before you know it, you realize your life is going by, that there's precious little time left to dither and daydream.

Oh hell, who was she kidding. She'd never been the type to roll with the punches, to let life take her wherever it might. Having the rug pulled out from under her, when her father abandoned her and her mother, put an end to any of that airy-fairy bullshit. Claire Melbourne would never jump without a parachute, would never embark on something without a plan. She liked—needed—predictability. She'd planned out her career path like she was mapping out victory strategies for the Allies in World War Two.

"Oh!" Ellie said, turning. Her surprise morphed into a smile that put Claire back on her heels. "Hi."

"I...Hi. You work here now?"

"I do. Since two days ago."

Shit. From an apprentice journalist to a counter person at a café. *I did that to her*, Claire thought. Took away her future, made her have to wear an apron the color of a banana. *No, wait.* Claire did a mental shake of her head. Ellie did it to herself by not being diligent enough, not focusing on priorities. She was not a journalist and if Claire hadn't fired her, someone else would have someday. There. That felt better.

But damn if Ellie didn't continue to be friendly, solicitous. Like she would to any customer, Claire supposed, when really, she had every right to be rude to her, to tell her to take her sandwich and stuff it where the sun doesn't shine.

"I have your sandwich for you, Ms. Melbourne. And I've added an extra pickle on the side."

"Thank you, Ellie. But please, um, call me Claire." *I'm not your boss anymore*, Claire prattled on in her head. *And if you call me Ms. Melbourne one more time I swear I'm going to lose it, because it reminds me of…everything that happened.*

"Okay, sure thing. How would you like to pay for that?"

"Um, I'll use my debit card, please."

Ellie rang the purchase through, handed Claire the paper bag, then followed her out the door, which she locked behind her.

"Oh, I'm sorry if I held you up in there."

"You didn't." She gazed forlornly toward the empty bus stop down the street. "But I think I missed the six o'clock bus."

Oh no. Claire's fault again. How was it that she kept messing with this girl's life? Ellie had even left the dance club early the other night. Probably on account of Claire. Claire's mouth started working, spewing things—nice things—before she could get control over it. "My car is not far. Um, why don't you let me drive you home?"

"It's okay, I can walk."

Claire knew that Ellie and Marissa lived a good piece away. It would take probably forty minutes for her to walk home. Not something she likely wanted to do after being on her feet all day at the café. "No really, I insist. It's the least I can do." The least she could do to make up for a lot of things.

"All right. Thank you."

They walked in silence to the parking lot behind the news building. Claire didn't always drive the Mustang to work—she was too worried about door dings and mischief—but it was a spectacular day. Sunny, warm. The kind of day made for a convertible.

"Wow. I love this car." Ellie ran her hand along the ridge of the passenger door, the shiny chrome handle. "Are you sure about this?"

"Well, it was good enough for your dog. It's more than good enough for you." Claire winked before she had time to think, then coughed away her horror. The last thing she wanted was for Ellie to think she had an ulterior motive in offering her a ride. *Jesus!*

She started the ignition, pressed the button to retract the roof, and nudged the car into traffic heading south on Ouellette Avenue.

"Wow," Ellie said again, the breeze tossing her dark hair across her face. "I keep saying it, but this is awesome. I hope Piper behaved in here when you drove her home."

"She did. I think. But she was in the backseat, so..." Not that this backseat had ever seen any action. Not as long as her mother owned it, nor as long as she'd owned it either. And why the hell was she thinking about the backseat and its lack of action while Ellie was sitting beside her, looking like she was made for this thing—her head thrown back, a smile that had settled permanently on her lips, her long legs stretched out in front of her, hair that looked so post-sex it wasn't funny. She even looked as though she'd settled in for a long trip, not a fifteen-minute drive.

"How's the radio in this thing?"

"Good. The original was pretty horrible. I updated it a couple of years ago."

"You can't have a car like this and not have a good stereo system. May I?"

"Go for it." *Find your Justin Bieber or Taylor Swift.* But to her surprise, Ellie didn't change it from the oldies station. In fact, she cranked the volume on "The Way You Do The Things You Do."

"Oh, I love Motown music!"

"Oh no, not you too."

Ellie bopped her shoulders to the beat. "Cool. You love Motown too?"

"Let's say I've come to grudgingly appreciate it later in life."

"It totally suits this car, don't you think?"

No, but strangely enough, it suits you, Claire thought. Ellie looked as happy as a cat sunning itself on a comfy windowsill. Just like her mother when she listened to the same music. It energized her while at the same time it calmed her—a yin and yang effect that seemed to both draw on and replenish the well of her very life force. How could one or two simple songs do that?

Claire eased the car to a stop at the side of the road, an idea occurring to her. "How would you like to drive the rest of the way?"

Ellie hesitated, but only for a moment.

The steering wheel was as big as the moon and as hard as a rock. It was loose too, like you had to turn it almost all the way around to turn a corner. The pedals were much bigger than she was used to, almost the size of her entire foot, and the gear shifter wasn't as smooth and tight as her Honda's. But it was no problem for her as she transitioned the car in and out of traffic smoothly. It was zippy and it responded to her, and the way the wind sprayed her hair in a million directions and the way the setting sun warmed her cheeks made her wish the car, or one like it, was hers. Because she felt free, on top of the world in this thing. Felt like anything and everything was hers to conquer. No wonder Claire liked the car. It suited her: the power and the head-turning part of it, anyway.

Claire. Ellie sucked in a breath because she was enjoying the way Claire was looking at her, like she couldn't quite believe Ellie could handle the Mustang so expertly, driving it like it was an extension of herself. Claire even settled deeper into her seat with each passing kilometer, a silent contract with Ellie that she trusted her.

It was a triumph for sure. A small one, but important nonetheless because it demonstrated to Claire that Ellie wasn't some stupid, immature woman who couldn't do anything right. She could drive this car and drive it well. There was no need to prove anything to her anymore. Except she wanted to.

The realization made her jerk the wheel a little. *God.* What would Marissa say about that little self-realization? Well, Ellie knew exactly what Marissa would say. That Ellie was nuts, that she had a mommy complex, ergo, she needs to impress older women because she can't seem to impress her mothers. Well, Marissa was wrong because she didn't feel the need to impress anybody. Those days were gone. It was time now to figure out what she really wanted to do with her life. And no, it wasn't working in a café, not for the long term, but she needed to feed herself. And pay her share of the rent. And pay for the new alternator her car needed.

Ellie pulled into the parking slot normally reserved for her car, which was in the shop. "Thank you for this. Um. Claire." Okay, that felt weird. "I really appreciate it. And driving it was, like, way cool, so thank you for that too. In fact, if you ever need a car sitter or a driver, I'd be more than happy to volunteer. I can even come up with a pet name for your car, give it a little polishing too." She was babbling, nervous suddenly. Because they were at her house and Marissa wasn't home and she wasn't sure if she should invite Claire in for a drink or a cup of coffee or something as a way to thank her for the ride. "I...would you like to come in for a cup of coffee or tea? Or something stronger?"

Claire was exiting the passenger door and stumbled a little. For someone who liked to hold her cards close to her chest, she had the most readable face sometimes, and right now it registered surprise, bewilderment. Ellie bit back a smile. Seeing Claire off balance like this gave her an unmistakable thrill.

"Thank you, but it's been a long day. And I have a lovely roast beef sandwich waiting for me."

"That you do. Well, thank you again."

"You're welcome, Ellie."

Wow. The iceberg otherwise known as Claire Melbourne was melting a little.

Ellie unlocked the front door and was nearly bowled over. Piper bounded out, and she felt more like a ninety-pound bowling ball than one that was half that weight as she almost leveled Ellie. *Oh no.* "Piper, wait! Come back here!"

Piper was a black streak as she shot straight into Claire's open door and into the backseat. Where she sat with what Ellie swore was a giant grin on her face. Claire, on the other hand, wasn't grinning. Claire was frowning. And swearing a little.

"Oh god, I'm so sorry." Ellie scurried to the car and tried her best to verbally coax Piper out. Which, of course, wasn't working one bit.

Claire tried to coax Piper out too, but Piper was holding her ground.

"I'll get some dog biscuits from the house. She loves the chicken and rosemary ones I made for her." Homemade chicken and rosemary dog biscuits. Jesus, Claire was going to think she was a freak.

By the time she returned outside, Piper had moved to the driver's seat and was panting happily, while Claire leaned against the closed door, stroking Piper's head and talking to her. Actually talking nicely to her and not swearing. Or threatening her. *Wow.*

"I think my dog likes you."

"I think she likes my car."

"Well, she has good taste. And you did spoil her by driving her home in it."

I could be spoiled by that car too, Ellie thought, then grew horrified because Claire looked like she was reading her mind. And she looked like she was amused rather than annoyed, which, in a way, was even more horrifying.

"Okay, Miss Piper," Claire said, returning her attention to the dog. "Will you come out of there if I promise to take you for a ride another time?"

Wow, was she serious? Ellie hoped so. Especially if she got to go with Piper and drive the car again.

"Piper would love that."

"She would?" The diminishing sunlight planted different shades in Claire's eyes, the light blue of them tinted with gold around the edges. The effect was startling. And it was doing something funny to Ellie's stomach. Sprouting little butterflies in it. What the hell was that all about?

Ellie held a biscuit out to Piper, who finally relented and hopped down from the seat. "Wouldn't you like a car ride, girl?" Piper gently took the biscuit from Ellie's fingers and chewed happily. "I'd say that's a yes."

"All right. Well. I guess I'd better make good on that promise sometime, eh?"

Was she serious? Ellie was going to have to think on this for a while because the offer seemed so un-Claire-like, but then, Claire wasn't the type to say stuff she didn't mean. She swallowed her nervousness. "I think we'd both like that."

CHAPTER FIVE

Too Busy Thinking About My Baby

Claire sipped her wine and forced her attention back to the woman sitting across from her. She was on a rare date. As in, she could barely remember the last time she'd been on one. Oh, wait. How on earth could she forget? It was around Valentine's Day over a year ago. And it'd been an unmitigated disaster. A waiter spilled red wine all over her date's lap, and that was only the beginning. Two hours later, as she and her date were kissing in her car, Claire suddenly felt her stomach clench in pain. The shellfish she'd had for dinner was about to make a horrible reappearance. And it did, all over the front seat. Embarrassment had kept Claire from ever calling the woman again.

"Something on your mind, Claire?"

Sandy was her name. She was a banker, specializing in loans for small businesses. Nice enough, but a little on the dull side. A lot on the dull side, actually. A little plain looking too, and then Claire felt bad for focusing on something as superficial as the woman's looks. But if she was only going to go on a date once a year, couldn't it at least be with somebody really hot?

"Sorry, not really, no." It was her chance to change the subject, except she couldn't think of anything to say. They had so little in common that it struck her that she had no business agreeing to the date in the first place. Sandy was a friend of Jacks's boyfriend, Julian, and Claire had only agreed to it because Jacks had practically begged her and, in Jacks-like fashion, wouldn't let it drop. He'd owe her one now.

Sandy returned to her favorite subject, her work. This time she was going on and on in a monotone voice about helping to secure financing for a small company that made and sold essential oils. Essential oils to help you sleep, essential oils to help you digest food, essential oils for every possible affliction under the sun. Bowel movements too, probably. *Ugh.* Claire's mind wandered again, this time to her spontaneous, and insane, offer the other day to take Ellie's dog for a ride in her Mustang again. Ellie too, of course, because she sure as hell wasn't taking the dog on her own. With her luck, the thing would jump out of the car in the middle of the highway or something. She'd almost killed the dog once already.

What was it about Ellie Kirkland that made her do spontaneous, ridiculous things? Like dance at that club. Like let her drive her Mustang. And then there was that damned dog, Piper, who was actually starting to grow on her. Claire was becoming a stranger to herself, ever since she'd fired Ellie. Ever since Ellie kept reappearing in her life, to be more precise. Just last night, she'd had a dream about Ellie. Ellie diving into a swimming pool, all lithe and athletic, popping out of the water and beckoning Claire with the most beguiling smile she'd ever seen. She fought wanting to join Ellie in the pool, yet her feet inched closer and closer to the edge. And then she woke up, ready to cuss out her mother, because she swore it was her mother pulling all these otherworldly strings that kept Ellie reappearing in her life. And in her dreams. It was punishment. Punishment for firing her, clearly.

"Sorry, what?" she said to Sandy.

"I said, what kind of music do you like?"

"Oh, you know, rock music, contemporary stuff. What about you? You don't happen to like Motown music, do you?"

"Oh no, I can't stand Motown music. It all sounds the same to me."

Claire smiled. "Good." Oh, wait, not good. It should be good, because it wasn't Claire's favorite music either. Yet there was Ellie in her mind's eye, dancing at The Red Zone to the Temptations—twirling, grinning blissfully, looking lost in a world of happiness. She had to admit, there was something about the music that not only made you want to dance, but sent you back to a time that was simple and uncomplicated—when all that mattered was getting the person you liked to like you back. It was the blind innocence of youth, of fragile but hopeful hearts, compacted into a three-minute song. Maybe that was why the music had been so popular in its day and why its charm persisted today. Who didn't want to *like* somebody and be liked back by that person?

Claire only knew of the sixties what she'd read and seen on documentaries, plus what her mom told her. She understood that it was a time of great social upheaval. Young people demanding a slice of the power and respect so closely guarded by their parents' generation, women growing restless, wanting a different life, black folks raging at generations of injustice. The Vietnam War dividing the United States, making the Western world reexamine its priorities. Rock music of the era no longer apologized, no longer tried to make nice with songs about holding hands and blue suede shoes. It was Janis screaming about a piece of her heart, the Doors lighting fires, the Stones painting things black. And then there was soul music dancing itself into the mainstream, making people remember what it was like to have a good time, to forget their troubles for a minute, an hour, an evening.

Yeah, Claire got that. But okay, so Sandy didn't. No big deal. She looked into the woman's eyes. They were brown, but a thin, watery brown and not at all like Ellie's. Not even close. Ellie's eyes were a dreamy, swirling dark brown that reminded Claire of decadent things like hot fudge sundaes. They were like solid earth too, a warm hug that made you feel safe, grounded. Jesus Lord, it was so not fair. Those eyes did not belong on someone sixteen years younger (Claire had looked up Ellie's age yesterday in the personnel files) and certainly not on someone completely inappropriate and unavailable. *What a waste.*

Claire blinked herself back to the present as the server deposited their bill. They argued politely over it, Claire finally claiming it while Sandy paid the tip.

"Thank you for dinner," Sandy said outside the restaurant. "Will I see you again?"

Good question, Claire thought. Instead, she said, "Perhaps. I'm afraid I've got an early day tomorrow and need to get home."

After dropping Sandy off and avoiding an awkward goodnight kiss, Claire realized she'd also gotten away without exchanging phone numbers.

* * *

Maggie was the sweetest Labrador retriever Ellie had ever met, but man, she was strong when she wanted to be. More like a husky when she pulled like this, and Ellie fought to bring her back from the rose bushes on someone's lawn she was intent on sniffing. Three houses down, Maggie was at it again, sniffing a hydrangea bush before trying to chew on a leaf. The heavy wood front door opened and Ellie braced for the scolding that was sure to come.

Her mouth fell open in surprise. "Claire!"

"Ellie? What are you doing at my house?"

Oh great, she's going to think I'm stalking her now. "Um." For help she glanced at Maggie, who sat on her butt and wagged her tail furiously. "I'm walking Maggie, actually. Mrs. Gartner's dog. You know, the lady who lives in that white stucco house down the street?"

Claire shielded her eyes against the sun to look in the direction of Mrs. Gartner's house. "You know Helen Gartner?"

"I do. Well, only for a few weeks now. I walk her dog three times a week. She seems very nice. Mrs. Gartner, I mean." *Why am I so freaking nervous?* "Maggie too, of course."

"So you do this for a job? As well as work at the café?"

Ellie shrugged. "The dog walking doesn't feel like work. But I, um, could use the money."

Claire frowned, narrowed her eyes in that way that used to make Ellie tremble in fear, back when Claire was still her boss. Claire was a master at it. Still. "Hi, Maggie." She sauntered down the steps to pet the dog. When her gaze returned to Ellie, she still looked displeased. Ellie seemed to have that effect on her. A lot. "I, ah, thought maybe you were here to collect."

"Collect?"

Claire's face relaxed into a modest smile, and Ellie wondered if the scary act was just that, an act. When her face softened the way it did now, she was beautiful—blessed with flawless skin and high cheekbones that automatically drew attention to those incredible eyes of hers. She was tall, a couple inches taller than Ellie, and she was not especially thin, did not look like she swam fifty laps a day or jogged regularly. Claire Melbourne looked exactly the way a mature woman should look, it occurred to Ellie—a few extra pounds but in a healthy way. She wore her clothes well, regally almost, and carried herself with the confidence and the bearing of someone who knew exactly where she was going and what she would do when she got there. Jacks had let it slip that both he and Claire were forty-two, which Ellie would never have otherwise believed. Late thirties, maybe, but not forties.

"Yes, collect. On the ride. In the Mustang. You know, for you and Piper."

Ah, yes. So Claire had been wondering, probably dreading, if Ellie would show up and demand that promised ride in the car. She smiled, determined to enjoy this. "Well, now that you mention it, a ride would be nice sometime soon. Especially since it's officially the first day of summer today."

At the mention of summer, Maggie lay down on the sidewalk and began panting. It was hot for June.

"I guess that means the dog would like some water?"

"If it's not too much trouble."

"And you? Would you like a glass of water too?"

Ellie nodded and grinned, satisfaction streaking through her at the faint pink blush working its way up Claire's neck. When Claire returned, she placed a bowl of water on the ground for Maggie, who eagerly lapped it up, and handed a glass to Ellie.

"Would you like to sit while you drink that?" She motioned to one of two Adirondack chairs on her front porch. They were bright red, matching her painted door, which was very stylistically brave for Claire. Though there was the red Mustang too, of course, but Claire usually dressed in dark greys, dark blues, dark greens, black. The only bright color Ellie had ever seen on her was her eyes and occasionally some lipstick, but that was usually a pale shade of pink or red.

"I like your bright colors here," Ellie said, tying Maggie's leash to one of the porch posts before claiming an Adirondack chair. "The red is really nice." So were the blue of her eyes too, but she'd die before she'd admit that. "You should do more of it."

"Shh, don't tell anyone."

They sat in awkward silence before Ellie felt compelled to break it. "I'm not, like, stalking you, in case you're wondering."

"Hmm. It is a little weird that we keep running into each other." Claire looked skyward for some inexplicable reason. "And the funny thing is, I think we're going to keep running into each other like this if I...we...don't talk about what happened." She sighed heavily and rearranged her expression into something less frown-y.

"Okay."

"The thing is, Ellie..." She looked skyward again. What was it with that? "I may have been a little hasty when I flat-out fired you. The mistake you made, I didn't let you explain and I—"

"No, it was a huge mistake. I get that. And there really wasn't an excuse for forgetting to pass along that phone message. I was distracted and I...Well, I guess it doesn't matter now."

Claire sipped her water and seemed to be pondering something important. She actually respected that about Claire, that she thought before she spoke. Well, usually. It was something Ellie knew she herself could improve upon because her go-to was to start talking without thinking first.

"Ellie, would you like a second chance? Would you like to come back to the newspaper?"

Wow. She hadn't seen that coming. The tough, unforgiving, uncompromising Claire Melbourne was offering her a second chance? And admitting she was wrong in firing her? Ellie had never witnessed the woman backtrack on anything before.

"Actually, I don't. But thank you."

Claire's eyebrows rose in puzzlement, but she didn't speak, instead she waited for Ellie to fill the space and explain. Which was Ellie's nature to do.

"I mean, that's really nice of you to offer. It means a lot to me." And it did. It meant she wasn't irredeemable, that she had hope, potential. It also cemented the discovery that Claire wasn't as big a meanie as she had once thought. "However, I... can't accept your offer, Claire." She stood up and went to untie Maggie's leash from the post.

Claire stood too. "Are you sure?"

"I am, thank you. And thanks for the water. You ready to go, Mags?"

The dog wagged its tail happily. Ellie waved goodbye to Claire, pretty sure Claire was right about their running into one another again. For whatever reason, they were interacting more now than when Ellie worked at the paper. And it was weird. Super weird, seeing Claire outside of work like this. But it was also kind of...well, not so terrible.

She looked back one last time and saw Claire lean against the porch post, shaking her head. There was an odd half smile on her face.

CHAPTER SIX

My Mistake (Was To Love You)

"You sure you still feel like eating lunch?" Claire asked Jacks on the way out the door. He'd been come back from covering a bad motorcycle crash, and Claire knew from experience what gory scenes did to your appetite. After covering one of her early crashes, in which four teenagers had been instantly killed, Claire could barely eat for a week. Every time she thought of food, never mind smelled it, she almost threw up.

"As long as there's not ketchup involved, I'll be fine."

Claire rolled her eyes. Her friend would never suffer from PTSD, that was for sure. Nor would he ever starve.

She steered him down the sidewalk in the opposite direction from the Café au Chocolat, where Ellie worked, because with her luck, Ellie would be there, looking cute and perky and friendly and not at all bitter about being fired. How could she not be disappointed about losing her dream job? About seeing her journalism aspirations go up in smoke? The worst part was that Claire couldn't shake her these days, even in her own neighborhood. If only her mother would lay off from this little haunting, throwing Ellie in her path over and over again. What more could she do? She'd offered Ellie her job back, had sort of apologized. *I'm out of ideas, Mom. There's nothing else I can do to atone for firing her.*

"What's with the look?" Jacks said as they snagged a table for two at The Cellar Deli, a basement restaurant around the corner that made to-die-for soups and wraps.

"What look?"

"A minute ago, you looked like you were having a conversation in your head. You have invisible friends now or something?"

"Nope. My *visible* friends are more than I can handle, thanks." Damn Jacks and his astute sense of observation. No, forget that. It was what made him such a good reporter. And if she didn't confess, he'd get it out of her eventually. She sighed loudly. "It's Ellie Kirkland."

Jacks's entire face broke into a grin. "Don't tell me you finally figured out what a great kid she is."

"Fine. She's a good kid."

"And?"

The waitress set her beef barley soup in front of her. Claire ate a few spoonfuls to stall, but Jacks was staring her down. Pointedly. Not many people said no to Jacks when he singularly focused his attention on them. Plus his patience was almost criminally infinite.

"All right, look. You were right. I shouldn't have fired her so quickly."

Jacks motioned in the air with his finger as though writing in a notebook. "Sorry, need to write this down. 'June 24th, Claire Melbourne admitted she was wrong.'"

Claire rolled her eyes, knowing full well Jacks was right. Admitting she was wrong didn't come easy. And probably not often enough. "I should have given her another chance. Not because I think she's got a future as a reporter, but because she deserved more consideration. She was more than halfway through her internship and I probably...All right, I should have let her finish it."

"Yes, you should have. But there's a simple solution to that, my friend. Call her up and ask her to come back."

Claire winced as she felt the unmistakable tingling of a blush stamping her cheeks. "I sort of already offered."

"Oh, goodie." Jacks clapped his hands together. "So when is she coming back?"

"She's not."

He threw his veggie wrap down on his plate in disgust. "Were you mean to her again?"

"No, I was not mean to her!" Why did everyone think she was mean? Just because she had high standards that included things like deadlines and attention to details and—horror of horrors—getting facts right. *Jeez!* "I was extremely nice, I'll have you know. And she turned me down."

"Why? I thought she loved it at the paper?"

"Apparently not. I don't know, she didn't say why." Claire had spent hours trying to puzzle out why Ellie didn't want to come back. It could be that Ellie didn't like her, didn't want to work for her again. And while that idea hurt, it didn't feel accurate, because Ellie had never given off those kind of vibes. She'd have every right to hate Claire, but Claire guessed that she rarely, and probably never, made enemies of people. She was too kind for that, too forgiving.

Jacks went back to devouring his wrap, staring off into space while he chewed. Claire didn't trust that look. So she asked, "What are you thinking?"

"What makes you think I'm thinking about anything?"

"Because you're never not thinking. Scheming, more like."

"I'm only thinking that it bothers you that she said no to you. Which you're not used to, right? I mean, you go out of your way to admit you were wrong about something, and the person rejects you anyway."

"If you think I'm personally insulted that Ellie doesn't want her internship back, you're wrong." Claire went back to her soup. Well, she wasn't exactly being honest. She indeed was insulted that Ellie had turned her down, until she remembered that it really was no skin off her nose if the kid didn't want to return. The important thing was she'd offered, that she tried to make amends for firing her. Her mother had to at least give her credit for that.

"So. Julian's back from his business trip to Hong Kong?" Julian Smithson was a corporate lawyer who traveled in some pretty rich circles from what Claire could tell. He and Jacks had only been together a year, but Julian seemed to spoil him, and that made Claire happy. Jacks hadn't had it very easy in the love department up until now. In fact, being with the same guy for over a year was probably a new record for him.

"Yes, my darling returned safe and sound to me. Though exhausted. I always tell him he works too hard, but does he listen? Oh, and you're coming to our backyard pool party slash barbecue next weekend, right?"

Claire pretended to check her calendar. Her weekends were almost always blank. "Yes, I'll be there."

"Good. And bring your bathing suit. We opened the pool yesterday."

"My bathing suit? Seriously? What is this, fifth grade?"

"Just do it. With any luck, you'll catch the eye of some gorgeous gal."

"Yeah, right."

"Oops, wait. I should warn you that Julian invited Sandy to the barbecue." Jacks had the good sense to look sorry. Claire had told him all about their dull date the other night. A glass of water had more chemistry going on in it than she'd had with Sandy, was how she'd worded it.

"Great. And you want me to bring my bathing suit?" Sandy would probably be all over her if she wore a bathing suit. The thought made her involuntarily shiver.

"Good point."

* * *

The door jingled to announce a new customer. Ellie had finished cleaning and reassembling the espresso machine while her boss, Pam, worked on a couple of cold turkey sandwiches for the young couple seated in the corner. Ellie gave a start when she saw it was her twin sister, Erin. The same Erin who wasn't due back in town yet.

"Hey, sis!" Erin sprinted to her and pulled her into a full-body hug.

"Ah, the star of the Family Kirkland returns. And early by about six days."

Erin had long ago stopped trying to disabuse Ellie of the notion she was the family favorite. "Come on. You know you missed me and couldn't wait for my return."

"Hmmm. If you say so." But Ellie was grinning. Her sister's accomplishments hadn't truly diminished her love for her. Any tension between them had more to do with their mothers than them. Besides, having an identical twin was something you were stuck with forever, and it would totally suck to be stuck with somebody you didn't like.

"So." Erin looked around, a deep furrow etched in her forehead. "I came to ask a favor."

"Of me?" It was almost always the other way around.

"Yes, of you. Can I stay with you and Riss for a little while?"

"Sure, but why not stay at home? Your room is its usual shrine, pining for your return."

Erin rolled her eyes, then leaned in to whisper, "Your boss is looking at us. Can we talk about this when you get home?"

"All right." Ellie couldn't afford to lose this job too. "See you at home in a few. You know where the spare key is hidden, right?"

"Sure do, though I wish you guys were more imaginative than taping it underneath your mailbox."

Ellie watched her sister leave with the usual brew of envy and admiration and wondered for the millionth time how the two of them could be so different. How Erin had sucked up all the DNA for smarts and drive, how she'd been born with a halo over her head, while Ellie had been the afterthought, the hapless twin along for the ride in their mother's womb.

At home later the two devoured a pepperoni pizza. It was one of the weird things about being identical twins—they liked the same food. The same books and movies too.

"Should we save some for Riss?" Erin asked without enthusiasm.

"Nah!" Marissa could fend for herself when she finished her shift.

Erin grabbed the last piece and began shoving it in her mouth. What, had she not eaten in a month or something? Oh, wait. Erin always ate with a bottomless stomach when something was bothering her. "So, are you going tell me or what?"

"I'll opt for the *what* because I have no idea what you're talking about."

Oh, so they were going to play a guessing game, were they? "You always eat like a Labrador retriever when something's wrong. Plus you don't want to stay at our moms'. So, what gives?"

"Look, Nancy Drew, it doesn't mean anything's wrong, okay?"

"Don't tell me you're not graduating from med school?" That would be a family disaster of epic proportions. Erin had just completed her fourth and final year and was to begin some kind of residency later in August. Toronto was her destination, though Ellie wasn't clear on what kind of residency. Last she heard, it was a toss-up between emergency medicine and radiology. Which were nothing alike, of course.

Erin passed her a look of annoyance. "Absolutely not! Are you kidding me? Of course I finished, and with flying colors."

"Then what?"

"Who said anything's wrong? I'd like to crash here, that's all. Enjoy a few days before the E's start smothering me with—well, you know how they are."

Did she ever. The attention their mothers showered on Erin was the exact opposite of the attention they gave Ellie. She wouldn't mind, for once, to be the one smothered by all that positive attention and overbearing pride. To be made to feel like she could do no wrong. She'd even sacrifice her independence and move back home if that were the case, and yet here was Erin, wanting to escape it.

Erin carried their plates to the sink, then refilled Ellie's glass from the bottle of merlot on the table. Erin was drinking sparkling water, and when Ellie quizzed her about it, she said she'd gotten out of the habit of alcohol because med school had been so demanding and needed all of her energy and wits. Drinking red wine now would give her a headache and leave her feeling like crap tomorrow. "Speaking of flunking out, what's this about you getting fired from the newspaper?"

Of course, her moms had ratted her out. They were as quick to share her failures as they were to share her sister's achievements.

"There's nothing to say. I bombed out. Again."

"Aw, Ellie." Erin clutched her hand across the table and held it firmly. She had every right to make Ellie feel small, to lord her success and her charmed life over her. But she never did. Ellie remembered when they were kids, and it was report card day. Erin had straight A's (as usual), while Ellie struggled to maintain B's and C's. Their mothers gave them each five dollars for every A and two dollars for every B. Ellie would watch Erin collect her pile of money, her face blank for their moms, but in private with Ellie, guilt would twist her mouth into a grimace. From her little owl purse she'd carefully extract half of her windfall and give it to Ellie.

"You know you're going to be okay, right?"

Ellie shrugged. She didn't know that at all. But if Erin thought so, maybe there was a chance.

"Hey." Erin squinted at the wall calendar beside the table. "What's this barbecue you've written down for Saturday?"

"A former co-worker from the paper is having a backyard barbecue and invited me. I'm not sure I'm going."

"Oh, come on. You must be on good terms with everyone there if you've been invited."

"Not necessarily," Ellie mumbled.

"What was that?"

"Nothing."

"Good, then take me as your date."

"What?" Crap. This was exactly what she did not need: the smarter, cuter, more successful version of herself tagging along at the party. She'd had enough of that when she was younger, thank you very much.

"We'll be the dynamic duo. We'll kick any asses that need kicking. It'll be like the old days when we used to go to parties together."

"You mean when everybody flocked to you and ignored me? Or do you mean the times you went off alone to parties and pretended to be me?" Erin sometimes did that, because if everyone thought she was the flawed twin, she could get away with taking a few drinks, sharing the occasional joint, because perfect, overachieving Erin didn't do those things.

Erin's face predictably colored. "You still aren't going to let me forget that stuff?"

"Nope. And I *will* get you back one day."

Erin grinned. "Whatever. I promise to be on my best behavior. Besides, what else is there to do in boring old Windsor anyway?"

CHAPTER SEVEN

Something About You

Jacks's eyes were locked on Claire, watching her watch Ellie. Claire knew it and yet she couldn't keep her eyes from following the young woman across the lawn. Christ, Ellie was like a magnet for her eyes. What the hell was wrong with her? She had never looked at Ellie when she was working at the paper, never gave her a second thought except when she annoyed the hell out of her. Like the time she was sent to interview the family of a victim who'd died in a house fire and came back with nothing.

"What do you mean you have no story?" Claire said to her, her exasperation getting the best of her. "I thought you were supposed to talk to the woman's sister?"

Ellie pulled on her fingers nervously, avoiding eye contact. "I did, but what she told me was, like, too personal."

Claire's blood pounded in her ears. "Excuse me? Too personal? That's a journalist's job, Ellie, to get those personal things, to put them in the story so readers can learn about the victim. We're not looking for the simple press release from the cops or the fire department. We want to know who the victim was, what she was like. We want a sense of the kind of person whose life was cut short. Personal is exactly what we want."

It took Ellie a few moments and a couple of false starts before she could look Claire in the eyes. "It was too sad. And it was stuff strangers don't need to read about. Plus it had nothing to do with the fire anyway."

"What is this personal stuff you're guarding with your life?"

"Her sister told me how she was seeing a psychiatrist, how she was depressed, how she'd never gotten over the death of her baby a couple of years ago."

"But that's exactly what the reader needs to know. What if the fire was set intentionally? What if it was a suicide? What if she was flaked out on pills or booze while the fire was raging away? Let me see your notes."

Ellie blinked, her resolve crumbling. Most people's did when Claire got her ire up. "I didn't take any notes. Didn't record anything either. The conversation wasn't relevant. So I just... listened."

Claire turned on her heel then, knowing if she said one more thing, she'd end up screaming at Ellie right there in the middle of the newsroom. Or firing her. Which of course she did a couple of months later. The kid had no business being a journalist, and Claire still believed that. She conceded she could have been gentler with Ellie when it was time to let her go, and for that she was sorry. But if Jacks or Ellie herself or anybody else said one more thing about the firing, she'd unearth this little gem as a reminder she'd done Ellie, and future readers everywhere, a favor by firing her. Even if it was a little on the harsh side.

"You do realize, my dear Claire," Jacks said to her now, a barbecue brush dangling from his hand, "she's no longer off-limits to you."

Claire's brain was on a treadmill going nowhere because she couldn't get it to catch up to what her friend was saying. "What the hell are you talking about?"

"Ellie, of course, and don't pretend you haven't been watching her in that little red bathing suit of hers. I'd be watching her too if I were straight. Or if I were a lesbian. Actually I'd like to be a lesbian for a day."

Jacks was always saying weird things like that. "And what would you do if you were?"

"Teach you all how to dance." He nudged her to show he was kidding. "Her twin sister Erin is equally cute, which I'm sure you noticed. And she's gay, too, in case you're wondering."

Claire hadn't been wondering, but she had noticed how much they looked alike. "Aren't you the fountain of knowledge."

"Always."

"Must be strange growing up with an identical twin." She wondered if Ellie and Erin had ever fought over the same girls in high school.

"Ellie tells me she finished her last year of medical school and that she starts a residency program later in the summer."

Huh. An overachiever, unlike Ellie, it seemed. And Jacks was right, the twin was equally good-looking, though she seemed to carry herself with an almost brazen confidence Ellie didn't quite possess. Who wouldn't be self-assured if they were so good-looking and a newly minted doctor too? Erin practically glowed from all the gifts that had been bestowed upon her, and Claire felt a twinge of pity for Ellie, growing up in the shadow of someone who had probably always been more popular, more successful. Might explain a few things about Ellie, come to think of it.

"Anyway," Jacks said, setting down his barbecue brush. "Why don't I take you over there and introduce you to her twin?" His tone was totally meant to provoke. "Then you'll have a reason to look at Ellie."

"For Christ sake, I was not looking at her."

"Were too. And like I said, she's not off-limits anymore, you know."

"What the hell do you mean, not off-limits?"

"To date! You're not her boss anymore."

"Wait, where is *this* coming from? Have you lost your mind? Did you fry it when you lit the barbecue?"

"Ha ha, very funny. It's the whole opposites-attract-thing with you two. I can see it with my own eyes. And you *are* attracted to her."

"Your own eyes are blind, thank you very much. And in case you haven't noticed, she's sixteen years younger. And I'm not attracted to her, so there."

"Age schmage. She's almost twenty-seven years old, which makes her a long way from jailbait. And you're absolutely attracted to her. Who wouldn't be? She's a real cutie. And very nice."

"Jacks, you're being an ass."

"No, sister, you're being a stubborn mule." He picked up the barbecue brush again and pointed it at her. "Claire, you need to do something drastic to break out of the boring old life you've settled into. It's unhealthy. It's…it's pathetic."

Boring old life? Settled? *Pathetic?* Just because she didn't go out on dates all the time or go dancing at the club every week did not mean she was boring. Her face was so hot as she contemplated his insult and how to respond to it that combusting on the spot was a real possibility. "You're overstepping, mister. And I don't appreciate you getting all judgy on me."

Jacks set his jaw, but his eyes softened and so did his voice. "Fine. I'm sorry. I want you to have some fun, that's all. And Ellie—or somebody like her—would be good for you, okay? She's the opposite of uptight. She's kind and she's funny. It doesn't matter that she's younger, that's a stupid excuse anyway."

It wasn't a stupid excuse to Claire. Ellie was from a different generation. She was someone who'd never used a dial phone or a typewriter and might not, for all Claire knew, even know what the hell those things were. She definitely wasn't walking the earth pre-Internet, pre-cell phones, pre-MTV, pre-Netflix. To Claire, there'd been a whole world before all this technology, a clear dividing line between the two. Like, hell yeah, she knew how to read an actual printed map. Knew how to not only take photos with an emulsion camera but how to develop film too (or used to). You wanted to talk to your schoolmate, you bicycled to her house or you telephoned her house or you caught up with her in the schoolyard at recess. You didn't text or email or Facebook or Instagram or Snapchat her or whatever the fuck it was today. *Okay, calm down*, she told herself. People are people. It didn't have to be a big deal, especially since she had no intention of ever dating Ellie or anyone from her generation.

"I can assure you," Claire said from between clenched teeth, "I know how to have fun without dating a twenty-six-year-old."

"Almost twenty-seven."

Claire rolled her eyes, about to tell Jacks to fuck off, when she spied Sandy on the massive deck at the back of the house. Sandy the boring banker who was, mercifully, her own age.

"Where are you going?" Jacks called after her.

"To talk with Sandy."

Jacks jogged to catch up with her and caught her arm. "I thought you didn't like her?"

"I don't, especially."

"Then why…?"

"Bye, Jacks."

"Who's *that* hot cougar?"

Ellie discreetly followed her sister's pointed finger, which landed squarely on Claire Melbourne. "Um, which one?"

"Honey blond, collar-length hair, dimples when she smiles and crystal blue eyes to die for. Jesus, you could make jewels out of those eyes."

"Oh. Her."

Erin stared at Ellie, all wide-eyed and accusatory. "Don't tell me you didn't notice her. Come on, you know most of these people here. Who is she?"

"Why, are you on the market? I thought you were dating Shelly what's-her-name from your class. The one who wants to be a psychiatrist."

"No. We broke up months ago. Those psych people are all a little nuts."

"Ah, so you *are* on the market!"

Maintaining eye contact suddenly became too onerous for Erin. That was interesting. Erin was fearlessly confident, and with that ballsy attitude, she had lived her life as an open book and kept no secrets. Until, quite possibly, now. "I'm thinking of *you*, silly. Come on, introduce me."

"No, wait. There's something about her you should know." Okay, this was the part where Erin, in her blind loyalty, would hate Claire as soon as she learned the backstory.

Erin held up her hand. "Only thing to know is if she likes women."

"She definitely does. That's what Jacks says, anyway." Ellie had never given much thought to Claire's romantic life before, but now that Erin had planted the seed, she wondered what kind of woman turned Claire's head. Wondered if Claire had ever been in love, unrequited or otherwise. Had she ever lived with a woman before? Or was she a player with two or three women at a time she strung along? Ellie didn't get that vibe from her, but you never knew. She looked like the kind of person who, if she ever focused all that laser-like attention and confidence and power on some poor soul, they wouldn't have a chance of saying no to her.

"Single?"

Ellie took a deep breath. She wanted Claire to be single for a reason she couldn't explain. Now that she looked at her—really looked at her—those long, strong legs, that ass that filled out her shorts, the stocky shoulders, breasts that—Ellie felt heat rush to face. *Stop looking at her breasts, dammit!* Claire Melbourne was gorgeous in a totally grown woman way, and now that she saw her through Erin's eyes, there'd be no going back to thinking of her as that scary boss lady who was untouchable, a mystery. Not that Claire was nearly as scary anymore. Not since they'd had a couple of not-unpleasant run-ins. And not since she'd found little ways—a few words, a look—that seemed to throw Claire off balance. Now *that* was fun.

"I…I'm not sure if she's single. Look, let's forget—"

"Ooh, wait, I think that woman she's talking to is hitting on her. See how she keeps touching her arm or her shoulder when she says something to her? And how she inclines her head toward her when she speaks? You should take notes, El."

"Or I could learn from a pro like you, right?"

"Exactly. Watch and learn." Erin never had any problem getting women to fall all over her. She was rarely ever without a girlfriend. And contrary to what Erin believed, it wasn't that Ellie didn't know how to attract a woman. It was that she'd never found anyone who truly made her want to become attached. She wasn't the butterfly flitting from flower to flower, sampling all the nectar, the way Erin was. The same Erin who was being super evasive about her love life these days.

"Come on," Erin said, tugging her along. "I want to meet her."

Claire's head swung toward them as they approached, her eyes registering something between amusement and horror. The woman she was with—shorter, a little on the plain side—stopped talking and turned her attention to Ellie and Erin's approach.

"Hello," Claire said carefully, coolly.

"Hi…er, Claire. Um. I'd like you to meet my sister, Erin." *My twin sister who suddenly seems to think you're the most fascinating person at this party.* God, Erin and her little games. What was she up to, anyway?

"So pleased to meet you," Erin said, shaking Claire's hand, then leaning close and whispering something to her. Claire laughed. Of course she did. When Erin turned on the charm, no one was immune. Except the woman beside Claire, whose frown was growing deeper by the second. Any deeper and it might end up permanently engraved on her face.

"Oh," Claire said, finding her manners. "This is Sandy. She's, um, a friend of Jackson's partner, Julian."

The frown deepened another notch.

"Hi," Ellie and Erin said in unison.

Sandy nodded at them, dismissing them as she turned to Claire and began talking quietly. Big mistake, because Erin thrived on challenges, especially if another woman was at the center of it.

"Did you bring your bathing suit, Claire? The water's warm." Erin touched her wrist. "And it'd be even warmer if you were in it. What do you say? Would you like to join me for a swim? Ah, you too, Sandy. And Ellie, of course."

Claire's eyes grew so wide, Ellie worried she might pop a blood vessel. It took another moment before her mouth closed enough to allow her to speak. "I...uh...actually, no. I didn't bring my swimsuit. But...wait." There was a definite glint of mischief in her eyes when she turned to Sandy. "Why don't you go for it, Sandy? You were just complaining about how hot it is. A swim would cool you right down. Isn't that right, Erin?"

"I...ah..." Sandy looked as stunned as Erin did, but finally Erin's manners won out and she gamely hooked an arm through Sandy's.

"Come on. Go get changed and I'll meet you at the pool." She shot Ellie a discreet eye roll. Ellie's herculean effort to keep from laughing was nearly giving her an aneurysm.

"Well done," Ellie murmured to Claire once Erin and Sandy were out of earshot.

"Was I that obvious?"

"Yes. Well, to me anyway, but hopefully not to Sandy. Is she your girlfriend?" Okay, that felt weird asking such a personal question, but Claire immediately shook her head and said no. "You'd like her to be?" God, what was getting into her, asking all these personal questions? Yet she wanted to know the answers. Desperately.

"No. But she'd like to be."

"Ah, I get it. So you were looking to be rescued, is that it?"

"More like looking for Sandy to be rescued. I'm not exactly the damsel-in-distress type. Although your sister is certainly charming."

Ellie felt her mood shift. "That she is." Erin had been a whirling dervish of bonhomie since they'd arrived at Jackson's, flitting from group to group, telling jokes, paying compliments, reciting anecdotal stories from medical school that alternately made people laugh or fall into empathy with her. Ellie wasn't exactly an introvert, but her sister took extrovert to a whole new level. Ubervert, if there was such a thing.

Ellie's eyes traveled to the pool, where Erin was splashing around, a semicircle of people captivated by her. What else was new?

"Come on." Claire nodded at Ellie's empty glass. "Let's go get a top-up."

Now who was doing the rescuing? Ellie thought.

Fresh mojitos in hand, Claire steered Ellie to a quiet corner of the patio under a pergola of flowering wisteria. She was miraculously managing to avoid looking at Ellie's mesh cotton swimsuit cover-up, though a few times she caught her eyes beginning their downward, blissful, shameless journey. *Eyes up, Claire, eyes up.* Because she did *not* want Ellie to think she was checking out her cleavage or her boobs or the tight, twenty-six-year-old abs that the cover-up didn't exactly, well, cover up. There was at least a four-pack under there. *Just stop it, Claire.*

"So what's it like being a twin?" *Wow, that's a new level of lameness for a question from a journalist*; Claire mentally kicked herself.

"Peachy." Ellie downed nearly half her drink in two gulps. "Man, these are good."

"I think they're a crime in at least four provinces and thirty-two states. Though not in Cuba."

"Then we should definitely go there. Know any good travel agents? My schedule's pretty light these days." Ellie laughed at her own joke, and instead of it being annoying, it was charming. Cute. Claire found herself wanting to make Ellie laugh again.

"Next time I'll get you a Cuban cigar to go with your mojito." Next time? Maybe Claire was the one who was on her way to getting drunk.

"Ooh, yes, a cigar would really make me feel adventurous. And kinda butch." Ellie laughed again, and it sent a warm ripple up and down Claire's spine. "In fact, I think I'm going to have to get another one of these. You?"

"I'm good, thanks." Claire would have bet money it was Ellie's excuse to ditch her as she watched her march off. To her surprise, she returned a minute later, another mojito in her hand.

"You might want to be careful with those," Claire warned. "When you can't taste the alcohol in a drink, you quickly become its bitch."

"Ha, you're kind of funny, Claire Melbourne. I like that about you."

She likes that about me? Whoa! Were they *liking* one another now?

"So…about being a twin." Time to wrestle this conversation back to safer territory.

Ellie shrugged like it was a run-of-the-mill topic, which it probably was for her. But Claire really did want to know what it was like. "Sometimes it's kinda cool. Like knowing what the other one thinks before she says it. And liking or not liking the same stuff. If Erin goes to a movie and hates it, I won't bother going to check it out. That kind of thing. But other times it kinda sucks too, to be honest."

"Like when your twin gets all the attention?" Claire flicked a glance at Erin and her audience in the pool.

Ellie's gaze followed, her mouth turning down. "Something like that."

Claire had hit on something that felt a lot monumental and a little insurmountable, judging not only by the look on Ellie's face, but by the sudden thickness in the air between them. She'd overstepped.

Ellie caught her eyes and said, "My turn."

Claire raised her eyebrows but didn't object. Where was all this gumption from Ellie when she'd had a chance to prove her worth in the newsroom? The kind that would have saved her job?

"So…um." Ellie took another swallow of her drink and seemed to decide something. "How come you don't you show your humorous side more often?"

"Excuse me?" Was that a backhanded insult?

"I mean…you're actually quite funny when you let yourself be. Like, when you're not all…you know…" An adorable blush bloomed on Ellie's cheeks. "All boss-like."

Clearly the alcohol was loosening Ellie's lips, though none of her observations were things Jacks hadn't already told Claire a million times. *Don't be such a grouch, Claire Bear. Smile like you mean it. Have some fun for once in your life.* Or her favorite, *It's okay for people to see you're actually a very nice person.*

All right. So Ellie wanted to see more of her sense of humor. She tightened the muscles in her face, narrowed her eyes. It was the kind of look that made the poor little newspaper carriers run for dear life. Reluctant interview subjects too. "I see what's going on here. You think I'm a mean boss. Is that what you're saying?"

Oh shit, now I've gone and done it. Ellie finished off what was her third mojito for the afternoon and tried to ignore the rubbery feeling in her legs. Because she did *not* need to embarrass herself further in front of Claire. "Um…I don't think I said that." *Oh, god.* "Did I?"

"Is that why you rejected my offer to come back to the paper?" A visible swallow made Claire's throat bob a little. "Because I'm a mean boss?" The line between serious and funny had become so blurred, so confusing, that it wasn't…funny.

"No, I…I can handle mean bosses. I mean…" Dammit, she was making this worse. Classic Claire, giving her no latitude, her eyes blue laser beams that were both cold and hot at the same time. How did she do that?

"Don't you mean *I'm* mean?"

Mortification and horror gathered in a tight knot in Ellie's stomach, making her nauseous suddenly. She was sure she could think her way out of this if only her brain would cooperate. Those damned drinks! "No, um. Crap, that's not what I meant. I…I…"

And then Claire's hand was on her arm. Surprisingly warm, surprisingly…not tender but something like it. Forgiving? Reassuring? "I'm messing with you, Ellie. Forgive me." Claire's grin reached all the way to her eyes, and coupled with her soft hand on Ellie's arm, the dual effect left her light-headed. Made her want to giggle too. Claire wasn't a big meanie, not at all.

Apparently, it was an act she could conjure at will. "Oh!" Ellie stumbled a little, laughed.

Claire's arm wrapped around her waist, amazingly strong and steady. "I've got you, Ellie."

"I'm fine. Really." Ellie righted herself under her own power. "Sorry, but you…"

"Threw you off? Had you going?"

"Yup. Definitely had me going. And threw me off." It was liquid courage, but Ellie intended to get the last word. "And for that you owe me."

"I do?"

"Absolutely. How about that ride in your Mustang? Piper too."

"Oh, right. I did promise that, didn't I?" Claire said it more to herself than to Ellie.

"You did. What are you doing tomorrow afternoon?"

CHAPTER EIGHT

Heaven Must Have Sent You

Out of reflex, Claire checked her hair in the rearview mirror. Oh hell. What did it matter? Ellie certainly wasn't going to care how she looked, yet she couldn't resist finger combing it back into place as she slowed to the curb in front of Ellie's house. She was still a little in awe and disbelief that Ellie had shown the gumption to press her into making good on her promise for another ride in the Mustang. And as much as she'd initially wanted to avoid her at Jacks's barbecue, she was glad she hadn't. She'd learned things about Ellie she hadn't known—that she had a twin who took up all the oxygen in the room, that she was funny in a totally charming way, and most surprising of all, that she was much more self-possessed than Claire had ever given her credit for. Ellie seemed miraculously no longer afraid to challenge her, which was a complete one-eighty from the young woman at the newspaper who would barely look her in the eye or would scurry away at the least provocation. *This* confident Ellie was someone Claire could picture herself getting to know better. Well, if the opportunity arose, which it probably wouldn't. And that was fine too. Even with the thaw between them, becoming friends was extremely unlikely. *As in, don't even go there, Claire.*

"Good afternoon!" Ellie bounded out the front door before Claire had even brought the car to a full stop, looking every bit like a woman who was far younger than Claire. Her smile was radiant and carefree, and her body moved with a graceful agility that Claire could only dream about now. No bad knees yet, obviously. And was there such a thing as a bad hair day for Ellie Kirkland? *She probably wakes up looking like that. Shit, stop thinking about her waking up!*

Piper, sporting a red collar and matching leash exactly the same shade as the Mustang, pranced with attitude behind her master. The dog, Claire had to admit, was kind of cute. As far as dogs went, anyway.

"Well, look at you two," Claire said, and damn if she couldn't keep from smiling. "All ready for a ride?"

"Absolutely. We'll be your trusty co-pilots. And your furry one has had a bath, so she won't mess up your car. She even matches the car, did you notice?"

"I did. Please don't tell me it was on purpose."

"Nope, but it is kind of karma cute."

"Karma cute?" Claire shook her head, but her smile had yet to dim. How was it possible that a simple, silly phrase from Ellie could make her feel happy? Had it come from anyone else, she would have rolled her eyes and dismissed the phrase as goofy. But Ellie made it sound fun, perfectly appropriate.

Claire got out and pushed the bucket seat forward for Piper, who leapt into the back like it was her second home. "I see she remembers the car."

"Who wouldn't?" Ellie's eyes stroked the car lovingly, raking over its sparkling chrome and the shiny candy apple-red paint. The woman was clearly in love and didn't bother trying to hide it.

Claire gave the Mustang a grateful pat before she returned to the driver's seat. Who knew this thing was such a chick magnet? Not that Ellie was some chick she wanted to pick up, nor was Claire some icky perv preying on young women. The thought alone made her shiver involuntarily. "You're not in a big rush to get back, are you?"

"No, why?" Ellie climbed into the passenger seat and snapped the lap belt around her.

"Nothing. Except…have you had lunch yet?"

"As a matter of fact I haven't."

"Good. I have a surprise for you, then. And for Piper."

Ellie quirked an eyebrow at her. A perfectly shaped, gorgeous eyebrow that, well, drew Claire's gaze to those incredible dark eyes that seemed to contain all of the world's great mysteries. She'd not been very successful recently in trying to forget those eyes.

Just drive, Claire, so you'll have something to look at besides her. To make matters worse, all she could hear in her head was Jacks telling her that Ellie was no longer off limits, that she could date her if she wanted to. Like, seriously? Not a chance in hell. And not because Ellie wasn't attractive and nice and, sure, fun to be around. It came down to two simple reasons. One, Ellie was more than a decade and a half younger; and two, there was no way Ellie would ever be interested in dating someone so old and, well, opinionated and set in her ways as Claire. Even if she hadn't been the mean boss who fired her, Ellie would so not be into someone like her. They were opposites. In fact, they were about as dissimilar as two people could be. So there. Now that that was settled, maybe she could enjoy the afternoon with Ellie. And Piper, who didn't seem the least bit fazed by having the wind whipping around her, her nose jutting into the air trying to identify every scent that flew past.

"I think your dog likes riding in my car."

"Good. That makes two of us."

"Actually, you two kinda look like you were made for this car."

"We do?"

Ellie was giving her that look again. A look, Claire swore, that was part flirtatious, part mischief, part innocent. Like, how did she manage to express all that in one look? A look that would be trouble if not for the simple fact there was absolutely nothing going on between them. Not even a flicker. They were acquaintances. Friendly acquaintances, former colleagues, and, okay, someone Claire felt she needed to redeem herself with. Ellie was a nice kid who hadn't deserved to be fired the way she had.

"Say, Claire, what made you get this car anyway?"

"Why? Does it surprise you that I own it?"

"A little. I would have pegged you for having a super sleek, super fast sports car. Something contemporary."

"Well, you'd be right. But it was my mom's and I inherited it from her. Couldn't bring myself to sell it."

"I'm sorry. How long has she been gone?"

"Almost ten years."

"Were you close?"

"Yes and no."

Ellie didn't say anything, but her expression was one of patient encouragement.

"She pretty much raised me on her own. So yeah, we were close, but not very much alike."

"What was she like?"

Claire concentrated on the road while she thought about her mom. There were still times when her anger at her mother reared up because they'd had a much harder life than they needed to. If only she'd held Claire's father's feet to the fire, things could have been easier for them, financially at least. But as she stole a glance at Ellie—at those kind, inquisitive eyes and gentle smile—Claire's heart softened. Ellie was a lot like her mom—the type to give people the benefit of the doubt, honest to a fault, always looking for the silver lining—and it was almost impossible to stay angry with someone who refused to let life beat them down.

"She was a lot of fun, actually. She loved to dance, especially to that old Motown music. And she loved going for rides in this car. Said it made her feel like she was living her adolescence all over again."

"So…if you're not much like her, are you saying you're *not* fun?" A little smirk was the exclamation mark. Was Ellie teasing her?

"Hmm. Guess I walked into that one, huh?"

"You did. And for the record, I think you *are* fun."

"Trying to flatter me, are you?"

"Nope. I can see it in your eyes. There's a whole world of fun inside you that's dying to break free. And I think this car definitely helps bring it out. I'm glad you have a car like this, Claire."

Claire laughed. "Okay. What else besides the car would help with my makeover?"

"Hmmm…more dancing at the Red Zone, definitely. Especially to Motown music. And another mojito at Jackson's party yesterday would have helped too."

"You wanted to see me make a fool of myself, is that it? Would that have been *fun*?" Claire couldn't remember the last time she'd had too much to drink in public. Probably well before she'd been promoted at work. It wasn't her style, and now she worried Ellie's needling might not be so innocent or altruistic after all.

Ellie's eyes grew deadly serious. "Actually, no, I don't want to see you make a fool of yourself. I don't wish anything bad for you at all, Claire. Ever."

Claire's heart skipped a beat. The fact that Ellie seemed to hold no grudge about being fired was somewhat miraculous. Astonishing, really, because if the tables were turned, Claire knew she'd never be as gracious. Or as forgiving. "You should hate me, you know," she said quietly.

Ellie shrugged and looked away. The city was behind them now. Fields and fields of corn, about knee high, sped past in a blur of green. Much of the bounty would go into animal feed, some into cans or bags for human consumption too. The sandy soil in the area, along with the heat and humidity of summer, made for excellent growing conditions for cash crops. Strawberries, asparagus, peas, and tomatoes were also plentiful. Grapevines too. The area's wineries had really taken off in recent years.

After a moment, Ellie finally said over the wind and the car engine, "I get why you fired me, I really do, so don't worry about it."

Claire wasn't worried. Not really. But the more she got to know Ellie, the more she wished she'd been patient, perhaps even nurturing with her, instead of so, so…exacting, so blunt, so inflexibly demanding. She'd done a disservice by letting Ellie sink or swim on her own at the paper instead of doing more to mentor her, of trying to bring her along, though Claire remained convinced that journalism wasn't truly Ellie's destiny. Still. She could have handled things differently. Except sunshine and rainbows and motherly hugs were not the way she conducted herself. She didn't even know how to do those things, truth be told.

"Journalism isn't for me," Ellie confessed, as though reading Claire's mind. "I know that now, so you were right. I didn't belong there."

"But you're good with people, I understand that better now. And you're smart. And inquisitive. You could try again, you know."

"Nope. I do like talking with people and getting to know people, but I don't want to put their story out there for everybody to see. I don't want to have to tell their secrets. I don't want to be the conduit to people judging other people."

"But the business isn't always like that. We do good things too. We make a difference in people's lives. Maybe not every day, but a lot of the time. And I'm talking real change. Like that judge who constantly blamed sexual assault victims, do you remember him? The only reason last year he was finally fired is because we wouldn't let it go. Or how about that suicide helpline for teenagers that was about to go under? Our stories generated a big community fundraiser that means it will continue for at least another year, maybe two. I could name a hundred examples like these."

"I know. And I do want to make a difference, but not on that kind of scale. I want it to be more one on one, you know? Small-scale differences. It took me until now to realize it."

In Claire's world, things were very much black and white. There was a wrong that needed to be righted, a crime or wrongdoing needing to be exposed, a better path brought to light. People like Ellie, like Claire's own mother, didn't think on a grand scale like that. Alberta Melbourne worked for over thirty years as a personal services worker at a nursing home, doing other people's laundry, cleaning up vomit and shit, helping clients bathe and dress. For the longest time it embarrassed Claire, until she slowly began to realize—was still realizing—that it took many hands, and many types of people, to make the world go around. And that small changes, small differences, were much more effective and monumental if a person's world was small. To the nursing home residents and their loved ones, it mattered if they could move about, if they had clean clothes to wear and decent food to eat, if they were treated with dignity and respect. She'd been stunned by the dozens of clients and colleagues who showed up at her mother's funeral to pay their respects.

"I get it, I do," Claire said quietly. "Somebody once said that you can't solve the big problems until you've solved the little ones first. And that making a difference, doing good, doesn't have to be in some splashy, obvious way all the time. I'm sort of working on that." She smiled to cover the discomfort of never having confessed her feelings about the subject to anyone before. "Ellie?" She captured the younger woman's eyes with her own and held them for instant, then smiled. "Thank you for not holding a grudge."

Ellie was quite sure by now that she wasn't imagining the interest in Claire's eyes. She was definitely scoping her out—well, she had a couple of times today anyway, and it made Ellie tingly all over. When she was working for Claire, there'd never been a hint of attraction or interest. Not even of the mild variety. Claire was the kind of boss who was cool, unflappable, always in control, tough more often than not, and whose intense gaze and perpetually furrowed brow created a wall between herself and those not in her intimate circle. Professionally aloof was a good description. But *this* Claire's defenses melted more and more each time Ellie interacted with her and it was…interesting. Okay, more than interesting, it was fascinating, alluring in an almost forbidden way. Claire was human, fallible, imperfect. She also wasn't as emotionless as she liked to pretend. Her guard wasn't exactly down with Ellie, but at least there were cracks now where light peeked through, and oh, what a light it was. It was like seeing a flash of something in the sky that might be a meteor, and all you want to do is see it again.

"You're not going to tell me where you're taking us?"

"Nope. But we're getting close."

They'd driven east out of the city, down country roads and through a small town. The land was flat, open. Dotting the roadsides were small mom-and-pop produce stands advertising freshly picked asparagus and strawberries.

"If it's okay with you, I thought we'd stop at one of these on the way back," Claire said, pointing to a fresh produce stand. "I love to cook with fresh veggies. You can do so much with fresh asparagus, everything from omelets to fettuccine alfredo. And when you grill the asparagus? Mmmm. Nothing like it."

Ellie's mouth watered at Claire's description. And then she wanted to pinch herself. Claire Melbourne was driving her around in her cooler than cool Mustang and talking about food. And talking to her like they were almost friends. Ellie didn't know this woman. At all. Or at least, this wasn't the same woman who could tear a strip off a junior reporter in twelve words or less. "Okay, that sounds good. But on the way back from where?"

Claire laughed. "Ha, almost got me!"

She had a nice laugh. A nice smile too. Like, a *really* nice smile that showed off perfect teeth and sent little earthquakes up and down Ellie's core. She didn't want to think about what the sensation meant, because that would be too…weird.

Claire geared the Mustang down and hit the turn signal for the drive-in restaurant. It was like something from the 1950s where carhops came out to take your order and deliver your food. A giant ice cream cone sign out front announced it as The Dairy Freez.

"Cool!" Ellie said. She'd never seen anything like it except in that old *American Graffiti* movie she'd watched on late-night TV back in her teens. "This is the neatest thing I've seen in, like, forever." It was more than cool, it was thrilling, it was fucking amazing and totally perfect in this vintage car, but Ellie commanded herself to chill. She didn't want to do anything that would make Claire regret bringing her here. She could imagine nothing more off-putting to Claire than being around someone who acted like an excitable child.

Claire expertly parked the car in an empty slot and switched off the engine. She pointed to the huge wooden, hand-painted menu sign that featured everything from Boston coolers to burgers to onion rings to grilled cheese sandwiches. "My mom used to bring me here a few times every summer. The food's actually quite good."

Piper began whining, and that's when Ellie noticed the massive yard behind the building, which included picnic tables, benches, and a garden. "As much as I'd like to sit in the car and eat, I think Piper would love it if we took our food to one of those picnic tables." A true confession would have included Ellie's fear that she'd spill something in the car. And Claire didn't seem the type to take such accidents lightly.

"Excellent idea."

The carhop, a teenaged girl with a blond ponytail and a shy smile, took their order: a burger for Ellie, a chicken sandwich for Claire, and a shared order of fries.

"Can you come find us at one of those picnic tables?" Claire asked her.

"Certainly," the girl replied.

After she left, Claire said to Ellie, "Extra tip for her. Shall we go find a table?"

Ellie took Piper by the leash and they followed the stone pathway to the yard. Piper stopped for a pee on the nice, fluffy grass, while her nose continued to work overtime on all the smells other dogs had left behind. As an added bonus, there were the dropped crumbs of food that she quickly vacuumed up.

"I think Piper's in heaven," Claire said as they took a seat at a picnic table, Ellie tying the dog's leash to one of the table legs.

"I think I kind of am too."

Claire passed her a look that was unreadable at first before it yielded to one of unmistakable pleasure. To Ellie, it looked like a giant exhale of relief. "Good. I'm happy to be here too. It was always one of my favorite places as a kid."

Piper continued to sniff around, but Ellie made sure the leash remained tied. It would take awhile to rebuild trust after the cat-chasing, wandering-off fiasco. She forced her eyes to her dog because looking at Claire in her sleeveless top was giving her goose bumps. The good kind. And that was very, very bad.

"Ellie?"

Ellie snapped to attention and her heart thumped like a bass drum. Had Claire caught her looking at her shirt? No, that wasn't it, because there was no sign in her expression that she was about to admonish her. On the contrary, she was looking at her with something bordering on nervousness. Chewing her bottom lip was a dead giveaway. Oh my god, was Claire about to ask her out on, like, a real date or something? "Y-yes?"

"Do I…I mean, did I used to scare you?"

Laughter, nervous laughter, bubbled from Ellie's throat and out of her mouth. She'd been a ridiculous fool thinking Claire was about to ask her out on a date. Of *course* Claire would never do that. *Dumb ass!*

"Um. I wasn't actually trying to be funny."

"Sorry." Ellie's hand briefly went to her mouth to cover her mortification. "I didn't mean to laugh. I was laughing at myself, believe it or not, because that wasn't what I was expecting you to ask me."

"Um, okay. What were you expecting me to ask you?"

Ellie's imagination caught fire as she pictured herself having the guts to say to Claire, "To go on a hot date with you that ended in even hotter kissing. With maybe a little hand action thrown in." *Oh god.* Conjuring that kind of fantasy meant she wasn't going to be able to get that image out of her mind now, the one of them kissing. She was pretty sure her face was about fourteen shades of red and not from the sun.

"Um…" *Oh, fucking hell. Think fast.* "I, ah…"

"It's okay." Claire winked at her and Ellie almost died right there, because if Claire had read her mind, she'd never be able to look her in the eye again. "You can go ahead and answer my original question."

Whew. "Well, honestly, you did scare me a little when I was working for you."

"Hmm. I do seem to have that effect sometimes." There was that tiny furrow in the middle of Claire's brow as her eyes—eyes that matched the sky today—scanned the horizon. For all her cool detachment and her tough exterior, it was surprising—and charming—that she really did care what other people thought.

Ellie fought the urge to touch Claire's arm, because while she could be a little too tactile at times, Claire seemed to be the opposite. And the vulnerable vibes from Claire were definitely unleashing Ellie's protective nature. "I mean, sort of, but it wasn't in a bad way. It's that you have, like, really high standards. You're a perfectionist, and I admire that. But at the newspaper, I knew I could never live up to those standards. And so it made me feel like I was constantly disappointing you." How familiar was *that* theme in her life. She'd already experienced a whole lifetime of disappointing people.

Claire's gaze settled back on Ellie. "Thank you for being honest with me."

"I'm not sure I know how not to be. It's kind of my nature. And kind of my downfall."

"No, don't say that. Your type of honesty is a good thing. It's when others can't handle honesty that's the problem." She dropped her voice, and the warm tone pimpled Ellie's flesh again. "Don't change. And I'm…really sorry I made you feel like you disappointed me."

Ellie instinctively understood that the apology was a big moment for Claire, and her default nature was to soothe. "Okay. I mean, you didn't. Not really. I mean, that's pretty much…the disappointing thing…my issue, not yours." Ellie swallowed loudly. "I'm working on it."

Their server navigated her way toward them, holding a tray full of food on her shoulder. When she arrived and handed over the goods, Ellie couldn't help but lick her lips in anticipation. She was starving, and so, it seemed, was Piper, who whined and stood on her back legs until Ellie corrected her, then rewarded her with a fry.

Claire popped one into her mouth. "Oh these are good. I'd forgotten *how* good. Just as well or I'd be here every week." She took another fry and held it aloft. "Piper can have another one, can't she?"

Ellie smiled at this little show of endearment toward her dog. Claire's supposed aversion to dogs was so obviously an act, or at least an act in transition, and Ellie wondered what other things turned Claire into such a softie. "She would love another one, I'm sure."

Delicately, Claire offered it to Piper, and just as delicately, Piper accepted it.

"Good dog." Claire patted Piper on the head, awkwardly at first, then her hand settled into a smooth, sure stroke.

"Claire?"

"Yes?"

"Are we becoming friends?"

"I'm not sure. Are we?"

"Yes. I think we definitely are."

Claire smiled but didn't say more. They ate the rest of their meal in companionable silence, listening to the birds in the nearby trees and the muted conversations from other tables.

CHAPTER NINE

Love Is Like An Itching In My Heart

Claire did a double take at the sign outside the city's animal shelter. She'd been running errands and hadn't realized she was passing the shelter until the billboard blinked its intriguing message. "Check out adoptees 4 chance 2 win $200 gift cert. at local Ford dealer." The Mustang could use an oil change, and her winter vehicle, a Ford SUV, would need new winter tires this fall. What could it hurt, stopping in? Not only would it not hurt, but she might win that damned gift card, and Claire was never one to turn down an opportunity to win something. She'd gotten that from her mother, who entered every contest, every giveaway, and counted every coupon. They once won a trip for two to the Dominican Republic when Claire was a teenager. It was the only vacation they ever took together.

Claire was greeted by the distant barking of dogs and the faint smell of cat litter and antiseptic as she walked through the door. The place looked clean and was air-conditioned. With luck she wouldn't have to look at any animals and could simply stuff her name into the ballot box or whatever it was.

"Well, hello there," said an overly cheerful woman with long silver hair tied in a ponytail. Her apron read, *For the best seat in the house, you'll have to move the dog.* Cute. "Have you come to check out the pets we have up for adoption?"

"Ah…" Guilt momentarily washed over Claire, but not for long. "Actually, I saw your sign and thought I'd enter my name in the Ford gift certificate contest."

"I see." The cheery smile disappeared. As in, so you're one of *those* people. "Well, we can certainly enter your name in the draw. But only after you look at our lovely animals that so desperately need a home." Syrup was firmly back in the woman's smile and in her voice.

"I see. Well, in that case…" *I'll leave before I waste any more time here*, Claire thought, and started slowly backpedaling toward the door.

"Honestly, it will only take a second, er…Sorry, what's your name, love?"

"Um, Claire."

"Lovely name. So what's your preference, Claire, dogs or cats?"

"I don't really have one." As in, she preferred neither, which she was too polite to say.

The woman, whose nametag said Linda, quirked her head as if she hadn't heard correctly. "Come now, *everybody* has a preference. You look like a dog woman to me, and trust me, I know my dog people. Come on, dear, follow me."

The woman didn't understand people at all if she thought Claire was a dog person. But Claire found herself putting one foot in front of the other and following Linda, her curiosity piqued…not that it took much to spark curiosity in a journalist. She wished Ellie were here with her. Ellie who loved dogs, who had a gentle ease with dogs that was so natural, so straight from her heart, so genuine. Ellie would be talking this woman Linda's head off about dogs, bubbling over with enthusiasm, and the thought brought a smile to Claire's lips. Linda noticed, smiled back, and nodded triumphantly like she'd pulled off something impossible. *Great.* Now Linda thought for sure she was interested in adopting a pet.

"So, ah, how many dogs do you have up for adoption right now?" Claire asked as they wound their way through a labyrinth of hallways. The barking grew louder, as did the antiseptic smell of washed floors and cages.

"Thirty-six. We're bursting at the seams right now, which is why we're running the promotional campaign."

"Wow. That sounds like a lot of dogs. How come so many right now?"

"The storms down south, that's why."

Right. A swath of tornadoes and deadly storms had cut across the American Midwest a couple of weeks ago, leveling at least three towns and flooding a few more. Thousands of people and their pets had been left homeless. Linda explained that typically after natural disasters, many pets get separated from their owners and are never reclaimed. They end up in shelters all over North America, she said, in need of new homes. This shelter, which had a no-kill policy, tried hard to rescue animals from shelters in the States that had a kill policy, Linda explained.

Now Claire felt like a total ass, coming in only to try to win a gift certificate. But there might be a story here, as there often was when you least expected it. Maybe she could assign to a reporter a story about all these dogs in need of adoption. That would surely help.

They paused in front of a cage, then another. Sad eyes stared out at her from one. Hopeful, playful eyes from another. She tried to harden her heart, to turn away, but she couldn't quite manage it. Especially when she thought about Ellie and Piper. Or Ellie with Mrs. Gartner's Lab, Maggie. God, how could people like Linda stand being around these poor dogs all day, knowing they needed a home?

"So what happens to them if you don't find them a home, since you have a no-kill policy?"

"Eventually, the ones who aren't adopted will be shunted around from shelter to shelter. Some of them end up months or years in a shelter, unfortunately."

How awful! But it was an academic thought until Claire stopped in front of a cage with a long-haired dachshund, its fur a medium brown except for its ears, which were a deep, dark chocolate color. Eyes, the biggest, wettest, brownest eyes Claire had ever seen on a small dog, looked up at her and held her gaze. The tip of the dog's tail, also a darker brown than the rest of its coat, wagged ever so slightly, as though it were afraid to expect too much.

She knew it was a mistake, but she asked anyway. "What's this one's name?"

"Oh, she didn't come with a name, but because of her color, we call her Rolo. You know, like the candy?"

"Hi, Rolo." Claire touched the cage. "You have a very cute name, Rolo. And very sweet eyes." It was only another second before a small, pink tongue darted out and licked her fingers. Which Claire immediately recognized as trouble. Trouble that was only compounded by her reaching in further and stroking Rolo's ear, because Rolo then nuzzled her hand. Dammit, this little dog was reaching in and grabbing hold of her heart. You've got the wrong person, she wanted to say to it. *It's someone like Ellie Kirkland you want, little girl.*

"She likes you," Linda said. "She's about three years old, far as we can tell, and she—"

"Oh no, that's okay, I'm not interested in adopting a dog."

"That's fine, dear, but I was going to say that she loves music. She'll roll over on her back and wiggle around if the radio is left on."

Great, Claire thought. *She's probably a Motown fan.*

"She's a very easygoing dog. Totally house trained and healthy as a horse."

Claire peered more closely into the cage. "Okay, Rolo. Do you know who Smokey Robinson is? Stevie Wonder?" The dog quirked its head, its soft wet eyes boring deeply into hers. "No? How about Diana Ross?"

The dog seemed to grin, if that were possible. Not exactly a taunting grin, but it was as if it knew exactly what game Claire was playing. And losing.

"I've never had a dog," Claire mumbled. "I don't really know what you do with them."

Linda looked at her like she'd grown two heads. "You simply love them. That's all you really need to do, aside from the basics."

Claire panicked. Her mother never wanted a dog because she said it would be too expensive for them to keep one. "And there are books on these so-called basics, right?"

"Tons of them. And the Internet too. I'm sure you have friends or relatives who have dogs and who would only be too happy to give you advice."

Ellie. Ellie knew everything about dogs. "Um, well, I'm not really sure I—"

"I'll get Rolo's paperwork for you to sign off on."

Linda was gone before Claire could raise another protest. What the fuck was she doing? No, scratch that. She knew exactly what she was doing. She was getting soft in her old age. Soft in the head too. She leveled what she hoped was a warning glare at Rolo, but Rolo only wagged her tail harder. And, Claire could swear, smiled that stupid grin at her again.

Oh, for the love of god.

* * *

"So, when are you going to see her again?"

"See who?" Playing dumb with Erin never worked, but Ellie went for it anyway.

"Your hot cougar."

She'd returned from her afternoon with Claire in the Mustang unable to wipe the smile from her face. The heat in her cheeks wouldn't go away either, and it wasn't simply from the sun. Claire made her feel…attractive. Fun to be around. Worthy. Worth listening to. It wasn't often that people a decade older or more made her feel valued, yet when Claire looked at her, quirked her head like she couldn't wait to hear what Ellie said next, Ellie felt little hesitation in saying whatever was on her mind. Claire was about the last person she'd expected to feel safe with, and yet she did. Perhaps it was because Claire too had chosen to trust Ellie enough to display some of her own vulnerabilities.

"If you're referring to Claire Melbourne, I have no idea when I'm seeing her again. Probably never." The thought was killer depressing but probably true. They'd parted with a friendly good-bye, a meaningless "See you later," nothing more. Maybe they'd see each other in passing at the café or when Ellie walked Mrs. Gartner's dog. Who knew?

"But you like her, don't you?"

They sat on Adirondack chairs on the back patio, Ellie drinking a glass of wine as the evening wound down, Erin drinking iced tea. "I think *you're* the one who likes her," Ellie said.

"Nah. I'm not on the market, remember?"

"Wait, I thought you said you and Shelly aren't together anymore?"

"We're not." Erin's cheeks began to pink. "But I'm…you know, taking a break from dating."

"*You*? The great Erin Kirkland with the trail of brokenhearted ladies is taking a break from dating? Be serious."

"I am. It's, I don't know, time to focus more on my studies, on my future."

"But you completed four years of med school and never let that put a damper on your dating life."

"Yeah, well…things change."

It was weird, this new, mysterious Erin. "Are you going to tell me why you're camped out on my couch instead of staying at home, where you always stay when you're in town? And our moms are going to find out any minute that you're in town and not staying at the house, and then you're going to bring down the wrath of god on you or something. Or at least the wrath of Emily and Elaine Kirkland. And believe me, you don't want that."

"That's exactly why I'm giving myself a break from them."

"Yeah, except you're never the one who's the subject of their wrath."

"Look, I need a little break, a little stress-free time out from family stuff. Is that okay with you?"

Whoa! Erin sounded like she was about to crack, which was very unlike her. Erin could handle anything and look good doing it. "Um, all right. Fine. But, like, is everything okay with you?"

"Everything's fine with me." Erin pasted on a smile that Ellie didn't buy, but she let it ride. If Erin had anything important to tell her, she'd do it eventually. And besides, it was probably the pressure of having finished her final exams for medical school that had her so uptight. Her sister was allowed the occasional chink in her armor, Ellie supposed.

"So." Erin brightened, her attention on Ellie like a hot and unforgiving spotlight. "I can tell you're attracted to her, you know, so don't even try to deny it. And don't ask me again who the hell I'm talking about."

"Why do you even care if I'm attracted to her? It's not like anything's going to happen." She had a better chance of hopping a ride to outer space. And what was with the interrogation over Claire anyway? And why the hell was Erin imagining things that weren't there? Or maybe they were there, but deeply buried with no chance of seeing the light of day.

"Why shouldn't something happen?" Erin pressed.

"Because she's…a lot older and…I don't know, she's so much more together than I am. I mean, she has a career, her own home, a classic car that's to die for, while I have…sweet fuck all. Okay, wait, not sweet fuck all. I have a cute dog whom I love very much." Ellie sipped her wine, having done a bang-up job of making herself feel like shit.

"I hate it when you knock yourself like that."

"Well, it's true."

"It's not true. You're the kindest, most honest person I know, Ellie. Any woman would be lucky to have you, and I'm sorry if I haven't said that to you enough."

Ellie sucked in a sharp breath of surprise. *Wow.* "Um, okay, thanks. But it doesn't change anything with Claire. We're sort of…becoming friends, I think, nothing more." She was downplaying things and she knew it. At the Dairy Freez, while eating their lunch, she'd seen Claire's eyes run up and down her body in the briefest of glances. Felt it too, because it was like a thousand tiny jolts of electricity running through her body. But a little bit of friendly flirting was a hell of a long way from anything romantic. Like, a giant leap of delusion. In fact, there was little point in even thinking about anything happening with Claire, never mind talking about it.

"Well, don't sell yourself short, babe. Phone her up and ask her out."

"What?" Ellie nearly choked on her wine. She couldn't imagine doing something so ballsy, especially with Claire. Claire would laugh before verbally chewing her up and spitting her out.

"Put it out there. Ball in her court and everything. What have you got to lose?"

"Um, my pride?"

It occurred to her she'd never told Erin it was Claire who'd fired her. And she'd keep on keeping that secret, because she didn't need Erin to start hating Claire. Marissa already did a good job of that.

Erin passed her a look that reminded her that she hadn't much pride left, working in Café au Chocolat and walking dogs for a living. Ellie felt her face flush until her ringing cell phone saved her. She didn't recognize the number, but she picked up anyway, grateful for the distraction.

"Ellie? It's Claire. Claire Melbourne."

Ellie's stomach fluttered like a million butterflies had suddenly taken up residence there. Holy shit, had Claire somehow known they were talking about her? "Oh, hi!" She fumbled with the phone, nearly dropping it. "I…how are you?"

"I'm okay, I think."

"I didn't leave anything behind in your car, did I?" And then a horrifying thought occurred to her. "Oh no, Piper didn't damage anything, did she?"

"No, no, not at all. Listen, I could use a bit of advice. Er, some help maybe too."

Now that was interesting. Claire Melbourne was asking *her* for help. "Okay, sure. What's up?"

"You see, I've done something either really stupid or really brilliant. Are you free to come over tomorrow night? After I'm done at work?"

Ellie sat up straighter, stole a glance at her sister's grinning face, and gripped her phone tighter. "Um, sure, yes. I can come over."

"Perfect. I'll text you when I'm home. And Ellie?"

"Yes?"

"You're really saving my ass here."

Ellie did a little dance in her chair. "Okay. Good."

She could hear the smile in Claire's voice. "Tell you what. Join me for dinner. I'll bring home takeout."

Eavesdropping Erin flashed her a thumbs-up.

"You've got yourself a date, er, deal."

CHAPTER TEN

It Takes Two

The look on Ellie's face as she squealed and petted Rolo made Claire's stomach do a pleasant little flip. Clearly it was love at first sight, as Ellie, down on her hands and knees, murmured to Rolo in baby talk. Rolo lapped it up, hopping around with her nails clicking on the hardwood floor in a crazy tap dance, licking Ellie's face. *Love should be so pure, so uncomplicated*, Claire thought. Humans sure made a mess of it.

"Who's a good girl?" Ellie said, staring into Rolo's eyes and grinning. Rolo, Claire was certain, was grinning right back. "You are, Rolo. You're a good girl, aren't you? Good dog. Can you sit?"

Rolo's little behind plunked down on the floor.

"Good, good dog, Rolo. That's a very good girl." Ellie dug a small dog biscuit from the cargo pocket of her pressed shorts and gently placed it between Rolo's teeth.

"With small dogs, people are tempted to pick them up all the time," Ellie said. "Don't. Rolo here looks like she has a big personality. Which means she won't want to be treated like a delicate little puppy or something. She thinks she's a big dog, so you'll want to treat her like one."

"Um, okay. What about food? The shelter gave me a couple of days' worth, but I need to go shopping for more tomorrow."

"I can give you some recommendations." Ellie remained on the floor, tickling Rolo's chest and talking sweetly to her. It was endearing watching the two bond, but also a little unnerving because Claire worried that her dog might end up liking Ellie better than her. An unreasonable concern, but she was such a novice at this, she was sure Rolo would pick up on her inferior dog mommy skills and want to punish her for it.

"My first advice," Ellie continued, "is don't cheap out on dog food. It can save a lot of health problems if you use the good quality kind. And make sure it's not made in China."

"Hey, I've got an idea," Claire said, wondering why it hadn't occurred to her earlier. "What if I hired you to come and walk her once a day while I'm at work?"

Ellie shot her an indecipherable look.

"What?"

"This isn't guilt over firing me, is it?"

"No. Absolutely not. No guilt from me. Such things are not in my DNA, remember?"

Ellie got to her feet and laughed. "Right. Claire Melbourne's as tough as they come. I'm glad you reminded me of that, because I was beginning to forget."

"I have an image to protect, you know."

"Hmm. An image you shattered by rescuing a dog from the pound. I still can't believe you did that. What inspired you?"

"You mean, what the hell was I thinking?" Claire led the way to the kitchen, where she pulled down plates and glasses from the cupboards. "I'm thinking I must have fallen and hit my head somewhere, because I honestly have no idea." Spontaneity was something she imagined was more up Ellie's alley. Certainly any spontaneity involving a dog.

"Well, I'm really proud of you, Claire. I hope you know you did a really great thing. Rolo's a lucky dog, and I'd be happy to come and walk her."

"Thank you, Ellie." Claire fumbled the Styrofoam container of Szechuan chicken and rice. She couldn't remember the last time someone had told her they were proud of her. Her mom, most likely, and it was probably at university graduation. She and her mom hadn't often spoken to each other from the heart. Or at least, not in a positive way. Claire, especially in her adolescent and young adult years, had lashed out with plenty of criticism and judgment. The hard shell of her implacability also meant she'd been unable to accept compliments, to let light into her heart. She regretted it now.

In a voice trembling with emotion she desperately tried to control, she said, "I sure hope Rolo decides she likes me enough. And that she forgives my rookie mistakes. The breakfast bar okay? Or do you want to eat in the dining room?"

"Oh, I'm all for casual. Breakfast bar it is."

Casual, huh? Young people were casual about everything these days. The company they kept, the clothes they wore, even jobs. But sex was probably the biggest, as it had been for at least three generations now. Ellie, with her big heart, seemed too wholesome for casual sex, but she was young, and sex was what young people did, Claire supposed. Yet the thought of her sleeping around left her with a completely unsettling effect. She felt protective suddenly. And…wait…something else too. Surely that was not the hot knife of jealousy in her belly. Getting a grip would be a fantastic idea, so Claire told herself that Ellie could have a hundred girlfriends for all she cared. No, make it a thousand and it would make zero difference. She resumed her task of setting out the food along with the cutlery and plates.

"This smells great," Ellie said. "Especially to someone like me who doesn't cook much. Do you cook, Claire?"

"When I have time, which is only three or four times a week. Plus, you know, it's not much fun cooking for one." *Great. Go ahead and remind her of the fact that you've been single forever.* "Wine? Or something non-alcoholic?"

"Wine would be nice, actually. White if you have it."

Claire poured them each a glass from the half full bottle in the fridge and took a seat beside Ellie. "Rolo behaves remarkably well, don't you think?" The dog was curled up on the floor, her eyes half closed. "Or are they all like this?"

Ellie laughed, rolled her eyes. "Oh no. Believe me, most dogs behave much worse than this, especially when there's food around. Piper is a complete pain around food. She's a huge pig. Sometimes I have to put her in the other room if we have company for dinner."

Claire ate her rice and chicken and talked more with Ellie about dogs. It was nice, having someone to chat with over food. She hadn't eaten dinner with anyone since her incredibly boring date with Sandy a month ago, and it was no competition. She'd take a casual dinner with Ellie any day. "Oh! Before I forget, I have a giant favor to ask. Would you by chance be free this Friday night to come and feed Rolo her dinner?"

"Working late?"

"Actually…" Claire's shoulders slumped a little. She wanted to take back her agreement with Jacks that she'd try one more blind date, and only after making him promise never to set her up again, that this was the absolute last time. He swore the date wasn't with Sandy and it wasn't with somebody boring or nuts or anything else that was going to piss her off. In fact, he said, the woman in question was quite hot. And very nice. To which Claire deadpanned, "then why would she want to go out with me?" She turned toward Ellie. "I know I'm going to regret it, but for some inexplicable reason I agreed to go out again on one of Jacks's blind dates."

"Ooh, it's not Sandy again, is it?"

"For his sake, it better not be."

"That reminds me. I'm supposed to have a date that night too. My sister begged me to go on some sort of double date with her, so I'm afraid I won't be able to come over and feed Rolo."

"That's okay." *Damn. Ellie has a date?* "I'll slide home after work and feed her before I go out." Wait, was that a look of displeasure in Ellie's eyes? Hesitation, at least? "You look like you're not all that happy to be going on a date. Or am I misreading things?"

"No, you're not."

Claire exhaled her relief, then rearranged her face into something neutral before Ellie could notice.

"So, how come?" Claire placed their plates in the sink, ran water over them.

"Sorry?"

"How come you're not happy about going on a date? Isn't that what people your age do?"

A curl of annoyance made Ellie bite the inside of her cheek. She hated it when people lumped her in with everybody else, especially based something as inconsequential as age. As if all people in their twenties were rabidly in search of sex or finding someone to couple with. "I'm not against dating, but I'd rather not waste my time with someone I don't click with simply for the sake of dating. I'd rather get to know a woman first, I guess. Which must sound really, really nerdish. Or super old-fashioned or something."

"Not at all. It's refreshing, actually. I thought only old farts like me felt that way about dating."

"You're not an old fart, Claire. You could have a hundred women lining up at your door right now if that's what you wanted." *With me at the front of the line.*

Claire shook her head, her disbelief obvious. Why was it so hard for her to see that she was desirable? A great catch? "I think I've gotten quite good at being alone."

That was hardly an answer. "So how come you're going on another blind date if you don't mind being alone?"

Claire shrugged lightly, took a sip of wine, and Ellie imagined it was hard for her to be so open about a subject so personal. "Being good at living alone doesn't necessarily mean you want it to be that way forever. Maybe I'm finally at that stage in my life where I wouldn't mind sharing it with someone, I don't know. But not with just anybody. I'd rather go on being alone than date women like Sandy."

Ellie giggled a little. Boring Sandy. Not-in-Claire's-league Sandy. "Well, then I hope for your sake that your date Friday night is someone much more enticing than Sandy."

Mischief flared in Claire's eyes, and Ellie felt it ripple right through her stomach. "Care to place a friendly wager on that?"

"Ooh, yes! Ten dollars for you if she's another Sandy. Ten for me if she's someone you'd go on a second date with."

Claire threw her head back and laughed, exposing a neck that looked impossibly soft and smooth and something else Ellie didn't want to allow herself to consider. "You're on, Ellie. Your turn now. How come you're going on a blind date when you'd really rather get to know a woman first?"

"That's easy. I'm doing it because Erin asked me to. She's been acting kind of weird lately. Not herself. So I'm hoping this gets her out of her funk."

"I'll bet she doesn't have any trouble finding women to date."

Ah yes, perfect Erin, who possessed the brains, the better looks (well, as much as that was possible for an identical twin), and whatever thing it was that women couldn't seem to resist. Erin had an aura about her that was like a big neon sign that said, "I'm special." Ellie didn't want to guess what her own aura announced. "You're right, she doesn't." Ellie sipped her wine and slumped under the emotional weight descending on her, the one she'd been carrying around all her life. It was the invisible anvil over her head that said she'd never measure up to Erin, never measure up to their mothers' expectations, nor to those of the outside world. Words deserted her, and so she smiled instead, because smiling was better than crying.

"In my experience," Claire said softly as she returned to sit next to Ellie, "the people who seem to have it all, or seem to have it all together, most often don't. There's an old saying I've come to admire, one from the Deep South I think, that says 'you never know what's boiling in someone else's pot.' I sometimes forget that myself. No, not sometimes. Way too often I forget that. In my line of work, I've seen a lot of people, a lot of situations, that aren't what they seem at first blush."

Ellie thought about boiling pots as she finished her glass of wine. She liked that Claire had said it without sanctimony or even without the tone of someone older and wiser giving life advice to someone younger and not so wise. She sounded like she was saying it as much to herself. Ellie resisted the temptation to reach out and touch Claire, to thank her for offering comfort. "You're right. I'm not being fair to Erin, acting like she's the chosen one. I forget that with that golden crown comes a lot of pressure and expectations."

"From your mom and dad?"

"From our mothers."

Claire arched an eyebrow in surprise but said nothing.

"They're both overachievers, both physicians. Like Erin." She propped her chin on the palm of her hand and said wistfully, "I've always been the underachiever in the family. And that's the nice way of putting it. I usually refer to myself as the black sheep. In fact, I'd think I was adopted if it weren't for the fact that I have a twin."

"You're awfully hard on yourself."

Ellie shrugged. Self-deprecation was second nature. Which, default or not, probably wasn't a very appealing trait.

"Is this what you meant the other day, at the drive-in restaurant, when you said something about having an issue with feeling like you disappoint people?"

Ellie was unused to talking about such personal things with someone who wasn't a family member—like Erin or Marissa. But Claire looked at her with such understanding, such earnestness, that Ellie felt the pull to tell her everything. She wouldn't, though, mostly because it hurt too much. And the last thing she wanted to do was to cry in front of the redoubtable Claire Melbourne.

She shrugged lightly. "Erin's a pretty tough act to try and keep up to, that's all."

"But with all that pressure on her, that frees you up to do whatever you want, doesn't it?"

"That's part of the problem. I seem compelled to try everything under the sun for a career choice. I can't seem to find the one that fits." She remembered the moment in high school when she told her mothers she was most definitely not going into medicine and how they refused to believe her. Total denial.

And then they tried bribery, which was even worse. Then came the silent treatment that lasted about three weeks.

"So what's wrong with trying a few different things?"

"Everything. I mean, answer me this, Claire. When did you first know you wanted to be a journalist?"

Claire's face colored slightly. "When I was about fourteen."

"That's exactly my point. I'm too old to still be trying to figure this out."

Claire laughed. *Laughed*, for god's sake, and Ellie's stomach tightened in response. And right when she thought Claire was on her side.

Her face must have registered her disappointment because Claire held up a forestalling hand. "No, wait, please. What I mean is, twenty-six is not too old for anything. It's exactly the time in your life to explore things, to sample a bit of everything, rather than get stuck in some job or career you can't stand. It's more important to find something you're passionate about and that you're good at than to stick to some kind of imposed timeline or expectation that might not be right for you. You'll find something, Ellie. As soon as you stop worrying about whether your choice pleases other people first."

Ellie stood because she couldn't speak right away, took her empty wineglass to the sink, and rinsed it. Such simple advice, yet so damned accurate. Why couldn't her mothers have told her the same thing? It would have saved years of heartache, years of frustration.

She looked at Claire. So fierce, intense, stalwart. On the outside, so much like a plant that grows on a rock, not needing much water or nutrients. And yet she wasn't like that at all. She was kind, sensitive, even vulnerable. Things she wouldn't have believed about Claire if she hadn't seen it for herself. And although Claire was right in her advice, this was something Ellie needed to figure out—to come to believe—on her own. When she found her voice again, she said, "How about we take Rolo for a walk before I head home?"

"I think Rolo and I would like that very much."

After a twenty-minute stroll through the neighborhood, Claire handed Ellie a key to her house. "You sure you can work in a visit with Rolo once a day? Or every other day, if that's too much? And, like, you could bill me once a month or something?"

"Absolutely. I work in my dog duties around my schedule at the café."

"You're a lifesaver, Ellie."

Ellie's heart lifted because Claire needed something from her. And whether it was because she was trying to make amends for firing her or because she really did want Rolo to get some fresh air and stimulation while she was at work, Ellie didn't care. She had something to offer Claire. Something she was good at. "I'm happy to do it, Claire."

The acknowledgment, the trust, in Claire's eyes started a slow, pleasurable burn in Ellie. Claire trusted her and needed her and respected her. And listened to her. With a wild need she couldn't contain, she rushed into Claire's arms and hugged her. Hard. And oh, how incredible it felt. Claire was soft where Ellie wanted her to be soft, solid where she needed her to be solid. She could shelter like this for hours, losing herself in the sensation of being pressed up against Claire.

Claire rocked back on her heels a little but eventually relaxed her posture until she was almost, but not quite, hugging Ellie back.

"Wow," Claire said thickly. "What was that for?"

"Nothing. Everything." Ellie grinned and said, "Good luck with your date on Friday night."

"Thanks. You too."

It occurred to Ellie as she walked to her car that there hadn't much enthusiasm from either with their parting words.

CHAPTER ELEVEN

What Does It Take (To Win Your Love)

Claire's table for two was tucked away in a corner of the basement restaurant, which had the feel and the cool dampness of a cavern with its stucco, exposed brick and thick, oak ceiling beams. The décor was old and worn, but it was the food that drew people to The Cook's Shop, which was primarily Italian fare and one of the best downtown restaurants in Windsor. Claire gazed coolly around the space or what she could see of it anyway, which wasn't a lot in the dim lighting.

It would help if she knew what this mystery woman looked like. Or what her damned name was. Jacks had been more evasive than usual, and Claire raised her eyes to every woman who entered, but so far none of them had been alone and none of them glanced in her direction. She snuck another button loose on her blouse. Not that she was expecting her mystery woman to look, really, but it didn't hurt to be worth looking at.

For a distraction rather than out of any sense of urgency, she plucked her phone from her handbag. She quickly checked for texts, then emails. Nothing. She resisted—barely—the urge to text Jackson and demand—again—who the hell this woman was. But she knew her friend well. He'd text her back some stupid emoji or a sassy remark. She should never have let herself get talked into this, especially after the last failed attempt. And yet…Something lately made her not want to be so alone. No, not alone. Lonely. And it wasn't a some*thing* but a some*one* who'd ignited this yearning deep in her soul lately. It was Ellie Kirkland with her easy-to-talk-to demeanor, her cheerfulness that was really a facade for something much deeper and so alluringly complicated, that made Claire realize that being single, being alone, wasn't so much fun anymore. Talking with Ellie, spending time with her, sharing whatever it was that seemed to pass between them without words, without labels, made her forget herself. It was *easy* with Ellie, and it had never been easy with anyone before.

"Claire? Hi! What are you doing here?"

Claire fumbled to put her phone back in her bag, raised her eyes, and found herself looking straight into Ellie's surprised face. *What the hell?* "I-I'm here waiting for my date. What are *you*…wait, you and your sister brought your dates here too?" Not really an unusual coincidence, since it was such a great restaurant.

An adorable shade of red stained Ellie's cheeks, visible even in the dim lighting. "Oh no. Claire, I think I see what's happened here."

Ellie was making no sense. "What do you mean?"

"I don't know whether to laugh or cry." She ran her hands hurriedly through her thick hair.

"Either's fine with me. Why don't you sit down and tell me what's going on? At least until my date arrives."

"See, that's the thing." Ellie sat down with a hard thump. It was a table for two, with a nice little candle in the middle that made Ellie's brown eyes glow almost golden. Eyes that, at the moment, looked more than a little panicked.

"You look like you're about to deliver bad news." Ah, now it was becoming clear. Her date was a no-show and for some strange reason, Ellie had been tasked with breaking the news to her. Could this be any more embarrassing? "It's okay, I can save you the trouble. My blind date has bailed on me."

"Um, not exactly."

What? This was growing more confusing by the minute. She was about to ask Ellie what the hell was going on when the waiter inserted himself and asked them if they'd like to order something to drink.

Claire said to him, "The young lady won't be staying, but I'd like to order a bottle of something once my dinner companion arrives."

"If I may interrupt," Ellie said sheepishly, turning to the waiter. "As a matter of fact, I *am* staying."

The waiter furrowed his brow at them and said he'd be back once they figured out who was staying and who was leaving.

"I don't understand," Claire said, feeling thick and like she was the butt of a not-so-funny joke. She could use that damned drink about now. *Come back*, her eyes pleaded to the waiter across the room, *and bring the entire wine cellar*! "I'm supposed to be waiting for my date and you're supposed to be…double dating with your sister." She cast around but saw no sign of Erin.

"I think we've both been played. No, I *know* we've both been played. Dammit, I should have known something was up when Erin suggested a double date. Erin who's been telling me she's off the market and not interested in dating." Ellie huffed and mumbled to herself, "not that I really believed her."

"What do you mean, played?"

"By my sister. And Jackson. They've ganged up on us."

Claire's blood pounded in her ears. "They've played a practical joke on us?"

"I don't think it was meant to be a joke, no. I think they were deadly serious." Ellie's eyes narrowed. "Meaning, they're both in big, big trouble."

"You mean they arranged this? For you and I to be each other's blind *date*?" *Are you fucking kidding me*?

"That's exactly what's happened." Ellie explained how her sister had told her they were meeting their dates at the restaurant. As soon as they were in the door, Erin said cryptically that she couldn't stay but that Ellie's date was here, that she was the only woman sitting alone ("so you won't even have to look too hard!"). Erin was gone before Ellie could protest. Or slap the shit out of her. "I swear, I knew *nothing* about this. And I promise you, I'm going to kill Erin when I get home."

A rush of emotions flooded Claire: embarrassment, anger, undeniable relief. Okay, Jacks was a dead man. Fixing her up with Ellie on a bona fide date, without either woman knowing, was not cool. But at least the upside was she wouldn't have to put up with another Sandy for the next couple of hours.

"Well." The look on Ellie's face—exasperated, slightly annoyed—gave Claire an idea. "I think the best revenge is to have a good time tonight. What do you say?"

"You mean…treat this like a real date?"

Claire ignored the fact she was holding her breath. Where her courage to suggest the idea had come from, she had no idea. She hadn't had a drop of alcohol yet, so perhaps it was temporary insanity, because she didn't normally chase women, especially younger women who were former employees. Yet Ellie's answer seemed suddenly to be the most important thing in the world. She really, *really* wanted Ellie to say yes. "Yes. Like a real date. Why not?"

Ellie took only a second to break into a grin that soared right up into her eyes. "I think that's a marvelous idea. We'll show them."

She said yes! Claire did a little fist pump under the table. And then she almost giggled because it was like something forbidden had been placed right under her nose with a big go-for-it sign attached to it. Well, not really, but it was a nice thought. Sanity be damned. "We will." She signaled to the waiter that they were ready to order a drink. "And the first order of business is a toast. What do you say to sharing a bottle of wine?"

"I say absolutely. And Claire?"

"Yes?"

Gone was any sarcasm as Ellie fixed her with a serious gaze. "Thank you for agreeing to make the best of this…awkward situation."

Ellie took a sip of wine and silently thanked her lucky stars. She wasn't upset that she and Claire had been tricked into a date, because frankly, it was the only way she'd ever end up on a date with Claire Melbourne. Left to their own devices, they would never have ended up here together, so she made a mental note to thank Erin later, but only after giving her shit first. This was all a little unfathomable, and she tried to take a nice, calming breath. Lucky. She felt lucky right now. Oh, she'd noticed the many times Claire's eyes had raked pleasurably over her. And she'd not missed the way Claire smiled at her in a way that felt pure, that felt private and special, like she was the only one Claire smiled at in that way. And Claire certainly seemed to take a genuine interest in her when they talked about personal things, but that didn't mean she considered Ellie dating material. Still. It was a nice fantasy that she planned to take full advantage of.

She searched Claire's face for a clue. Was pretending this was a real date simply a little bit of fun for Claire? Some sweet revenge for the dating game Jackson and Erin had manipulated them into? Maybe, but Ellie would show Claire that she wasn't a kid, that she wasn't a flake who lacked ambition, that she was worthy of being on a date with, because Claire, it was pretty obvious, wasn't the type to waste her time on someone who wasn't smart, mature, ambitious, together.

Ellie took another sip of wine and then another. One way or another, she'd figure out how to prove she deserved to be Claire's date, as soon as she stopped being so damned nervous. Claire smiled at her and topped up her glass. *Great. Now she's going to think I'm an alcoholic or something.*

"I'm driving, so I don't plan on splitting this bottle evenly with you."

"I…"

Claire leaned over the table, her eyes riveted to Ellie's, her cleavage swelling beneath her blouse and acting as a magnet for Ellie's eyes. "There's no need to be nervous. Take a deep breath. I'm not going to bite, you know. We're friends on a… date. That's all."

Ellie swallowed and forced her eyes up. She'd been caught looking, surely, but then, wouldn't a real girlfriend have done the same thing? "All right. As long as this is a real date."

"Yes. A real date." The blue in Claire's eyes softened to the shade of a robin's egg, which reassured Ellie, but only for a moment. Her nervousness refused to be wrestled into submission.

"You look lovely tonight, by the way," Ellie said, remembering her manners. And Claire did, wearing black slacks, stylish ankle boots, and a lavender blouse that hugged her in all the right places. She smelled divine too, something faint that was fresh and natural and sort of minty, vaguely reminding Ellie of the mojitos she'd drunk with Claire at Jackson's barbecue.

"Thank you. You look beautiful, Ellie." Was that a blush infusing Claire's cheeks? Or was it only the candlelight? Ellie knew which she hoped for.

"Thanks. And, um, just so you know up front?" Ellie lowered her voice to a whisper. Might as well get this part over with and the faster the better. "I don't believe in sex on the first date."

Claire burst into laughter so deep, she shook with it. A couple of other diners looked their way and smiled.

Aw fuck. Ellie wanted to crawl under the table. She hadn't meant it as a joke. She was serious, because it was exactly the thing she said on first dates. Put it out there, no illusions, that the evening would not end in sex. It took the pressure off, in her experience. Saved embarrassment later, too, when the date ended and neither was sure if she should invite the other in for a drink and what it would mean if there was no invitation, or if the invited woman didn't want to come in for a nightcap, or she did, and then what? It was a sorry mess, is what it was, and Ellie liked knowing where the cards were going to fall before they, well, fell. But as Claire's laughter began to mercifully subside, Ellie's face burned fiercely, and there wasn't enough damned wine left in the bottle to make her feel not mortified. Unmortified? Was that a word?

"No, wait," Claire said, finally acknowledging Ellie's horror. "I'm so sorry, I'm..." She took a deep breath and apologized. Again. "I don't mean to laugh. I promise, I'm not laughing at what you said, I—"

"No, it's okay, I was being stupid. I wasn't…wasn't thinking. It stupidly came out because it's what I say on first dates." *Like Claire would ever fucking go on a real date with me anyway.* What the hell had she been thinking, stoking this little fantasy in her head?

"No, I'm glad you said what you said. Because this *is* a real date, remember? It…caught me off guard. I wasn't…expecting that."

"Right." *Wrong.* Ellie was no longer buying this real date thing, as much as Claire tried to assure her. She studied Claire with eyes that were like polished gems and a smile that was so much more dazzling than she'd ever shown in the workplace. The effect transformed her into a different person—someone softer, someone fun, someone charming, someone…incredibly sexy. Ellie's eyes strayed to Claire's shoulders, which were strong and erect. God. She loved the bold way Claire dressed and the way she carried herself with such confidence. She was a woman who knew exactly what she wanted and how to go about getting it. Which was a huge turn-on. But it also meant it couldn't be more obvious that she was only being nice and didn't mean any of this real date crap. Ellie sighed her disappointment. What she wouldn't give for a woman like Claire—no, not a woman *like* Claire, but Claire herself—to want her.

"What?" Claire asked.

"Sorry?"

"You sighed out loud. Are you disappointed that you ended up with me tonight and not someone…I don't know…else? A real life Princess Charming, perhaps?"

As much as Claire's tone sounded facetious, the tight expression on her face said she was serious. "Are you kidding right now?"

"Actually I'm not. Because if I'm being honest, the reason I laughed earlier is because I'm pretty sure there's no way you'd ever actually date someone sixteen years older. Oh, and let's not forget that same someone was once your boss and fired you not that long ago." Claire shook her head dismissively, like she'd already made up her mind about it. "Ellie, it's okay if you want to leave. We can skip all this and I can take you home. You don't have to humor me, you know."

"You think I'm humoring you?" Wow, where was this coming from? Beneath the fearless veneer, Claire was…insecure?

"Yes, I do. Because I'm no Princess Charming. Trust me."

Ellie shrugged off her own self-doubts as easily as slipping off a coat. Claire's honesty and vulnerability were doing things to her. Things that made her want to touch her, to kiss her, to reassure her. Hell, to take her to bed. *Jesus*. She had to momentarily remove her eyes from Claire to gather herself. "You think I'm looking for a Princess Charming to rescue me?"

It was a direct challenge, and Claire happily rose to it.

"No, actually, I don't. First of all, now that I've gotten to know you better, I can see you don't need to be rescued, and if you did, you're more than capable of rescuing yourself. I only meant…"

"Yes?" Ellie leaned forward, not only because she was dying for Claire to finish her thought, but because she wanted to tempt her with her own little cleavage show. Turnabout was fair play, as she felt her sleeveless blouse open a little more.

"I…um…only meant…" Sure enough, Claire's gaze slid to Ellie's chest. More satisfying was that her chest was making it hard for Claire to put words together. *Oh yes!* "Um, that I'm pretty sure your fantasy woman wouldn't look anything like me."

Emboldened by the wine she'd drunk, Ellie said, "I think you should let me be the judge of what my fantasy woman does or does not look like."

Claire nodded her head in acquiescence. "Good point."

"The truth is," Ellie continued, "I think every damned person in this restaurant is wondering how I got so lucky as to be your date."

Claire took a sip of wine and shook her head. "Ha, good one."

"Trust me, I am not joking." Ellie winked exaggeratedly, clutching onto her last strands of bravery for dear life. "My Princess Charming."

Claire laughed, and any residual tension between them evaporated. "My chariot is red. And a convertible."

"Ooh, I know. Your chariot, your highness, makes me swoon, in case you haven't noticed."

"I sort of have. And I like it when you swoon."

Oh, there were so many things Ellie could do with that declaration, but their food arrived. It was mixed grill spiedino for Ellie, spaghetti carbonara for Claire, and it all smelled delicious. Now that they'd both unpacked some of their hang-ups, Ellie's appetite returned with a vengeance.

Over dinner Claire confessed that it was only her second time on a date in over a year (the infamous Sandy being the other one), while Ellie admitted it was her third during the same period. Ellie had made it plain in their earlier conversation that she didn't date much, but seeing her like this tonight—her eyes bright with anticipation, her smiles generous, her humor lightning quick, conversation that was utterly guileless, and then of course her state of sexiness—made Claire think, *what a waste*. Ellie could have any woman she wanted, and clearly, it was their loss, these faceless, nameless, single lesbians.

"So," Claire finally said. "How come you haven't found someone yet that you click with?"

"Funny story, that. I seem to have a knack for attracting strange women. It makes my mothers crazy, which is about the only upside to it."

"Strange how?" Claire finished the wine in her glass. Two glasses was plenty when she had to drive, but Ellie was taking full advantage of not needing to watch how much she drank. The wine was flattening her nervous energy, ripping away any inhibitions she might have—not that she was saddled with a lot of them, as far as Claire could tell. No. Ellie was refreshingly honest, utterly without pretenses, and gorgeous too in a way that bordered on naïve. She wasn't at all like Claire thought a twenty-six-year-old would be or was supposed to be. *Damn*. Falling for Ellie, that wasn't part of the bargain tonight. No way.

Ellie shook her head, smiling at a memory. "One woman I went on a couple of dates with had a collection of hamsters."

"Hamsters?"

"Yeah, cages of them. Like, fourteen of the little buggers in total. Those noisy little wheels would go on all night long."

Claire had to avert her eyes, afraid they'd give her away. If Ellie knew all about the hamster wheels at night, did that mean she'd slept with this woman? Not on the first date, obviously. But on the second date? The third? Exactly when did she believe sex should occur? *Okay, wait*, she told herself. It wasn't like she and Ellie would ever be having a second date with the sex thing becoming a, well, *thing*. Her curiosity was purely academic. Yes, that's what it was, a hypothetical interest.

"And then there was the know-it-all. I made the mistake of taking her home to meet my moms and all she did was tell them how they could improve the meal they'd cooked and how they could decorate their house much nicer. She even proceeded to tell them how much more money they could make if they were surgeons or gynecologists than family physicians." Ellie's hand brushed her mouth as she giggled. "It was actually worth the price of admission bringing her home. Though my mothers have never forgiven me for it. They almost had heart attacks on the spot."

"I'll bet. So they haven't exactly approved of your dating choices?"

"You can say that again. They think my judgment's about as good with women as it is with my career choices."

Ouch. They sounded like mothers from hell, but then, it also sounded like Ellie sometimes got a kick out of pushing their buttons. "And what would they think of me? Of us being on a date?" It occurred to her that Ellie could easily use her—a woman sixteen years older—as a way to goad her mothers. She hoped Ellie would never do that to her, but then, she had no intention of ever getting in the middle of a dysfunctional family drama.

"More wine? Coffee? Dessert?" The waiter was back.

"Coffee for me," Claire said.

"Ooh, I see your dessert special tonight is a red velvet cake with vanilla fondant icing." Ellie was licking her lips hungrily, an act that was akin to striking a match to Claire's overactive imagination. Her tongue should be considered a lethal weapon. How could she be so innocently seductive? Did she not understand the power she possessed? *Stop it, Claire, just stop it. You're being an old perv.*

"Two pieces?" The waiter raised his significant eyebrows at Claire.

"No thanks. Not unless I'm walking home."

"We'll share a piece," Ellie supplied.

When the waiter departed, Claire said, "Thank you, Ellie. I love red velvet but my waistline doesn't."

"Your waistline is perfect."

"For someone a dozen pounds overweight, it is." Her job didn't leave much time for working out and pursuing active hobbies. Taking Rolo out for regular walks was something she looked forward to now, but that was about as athletic as she got. Oh, plus golfing a couple of times a year with Jacks, which was an excuse for him to drink wine coolers while making her drive him around in the power cart.

"Why are you putting yourself down?"

Because you're young and gorgeous and my body can't hold a candle to yours, Claire wished she could say out loud. She shouldn't have blurted out as much as she already had. She never talked about her body with anyone, not even Jacks.

Ellie continued on, oblivious to Claire's internal fat shaming. "If I brought you home, I think my moms might actually approve for once. Huh." She seemed to be thinking, or visualizing, something as she stared off toward the ceiling. "That's not a bad idea, actually. What are you doing later next week?"

"Oh no, you're not throwing me into that shark tank. They actually scare me, and I don't scare easily."

Ellie laughed, settling her gaze on Claire, and it felt like a warm, soft blanket falling around her shoulders. Ellie made her feel young, alive, like every nerve ending was on fire, and at the same time restful, at ease, as though she had nothing to prove. It was like taking off and landing at the same time.

"You're right. I don't want to scare you off yet."

Yet? Did that mean she wanted to see her again? Claire's throat tightened with want; she cleared it roughly. She was imagining things, letting her mind go to places that were far, far out of bounds. "What about your sister? Does she have more luck bringing girlfriends home?"

"Erin's girlfriends are always a big hit with our moms. They fawn over them like they're going to become a future daughter-in-law or something. Which of course drives Erin nuts because she likes to play the field. I think the longest she's dated anyone is three or four months."

Claire kept her mouth shut, because her conclusions about Erin weren't exactly complimentary. Ellie's twin seemed to go around acting like the sun shone out of her ass. Which was how she was brought up, of course, so no surprise there. The twin-with-it-all seemed to take a lot for granted—her looks, her charms, her brains, her privileged upbringing. To Claire it was Ellie who was the enticing one, the complex one. Ellie worked for the things she wanted, eschewed handouts, lived a life of simple pleasures with her love for dogs, for vintage music. Even if she did sometimes come across as directionless, her refusal to put on airs or to be shoved into a box was gratifying. Ellie was real. She was genuine. She was, Claire realized with a gasp, stunning in every possible way.

"You okay?" Ellie peered at her with concern.

Claire fanned herself. "Sure. A little warm, that's all." She cringed in horror at her mistake. *What if Ellie thinks I'm having a hot flash or something?*

The waiter returned, carefully placed the plate of cake between them with two forks, as well as coffee for Claire and a dessert liqueur for Ellie.

"Oh, I didn't order this," Ellie said of the small glass of what smelled like crème de menthe and something like vanilla.

"On the house for the young lady," he said and slid Claire an almost imperceptible wink.

Hmm, somebody wants me to get lucky, Claire thought. *Or he wants a good tip, more like.*

"Come on," Ellie urged, passing the second fork to Claire. "Dig in."

"I shouldn't."

Ellie did that thing again where she licked her lips, driving Claire a little insane. And then her eyes began sizing Claire up like *she* was the cake. *Oh shit.* This was going to be trouble. And not of the terrible variety.

It was a warm evening and the top was down on the Mustang. Ellie turned her face to the breeze, exulting in the freedom the car offered. That, combined with the alcohol she'd consumed, was making her feel tingly and warm and gravity-less, like she was swimming in a tropical pool with a gorgeous woman by her side. Before getting to know Claire better these last few weeks, Ellie had been immune to the attraction, the seductive power, of an older, established woman who walked with the air of someone who knew she would be followed, who talked with distinct confidence and security in her knowledge and in her authority. Claire listened, she spoke in measured tones, she knew what she wanted and what she didn't want and made no apologies for either. *I want to* be *her*, Ellie thought. *No, wait. I want to be* with *her*. And yet the idea of being with Claire seemed as unlikely as a fantastic job suddenly tapping her on the shoulder. Because while Claire might be physically attracted to her, and Ellie was pretty sure she was, at least a little, and seemed to enjoy her company, there'd been nothing to indicate that tonight was anything more than a one-off. What Ellie did understand implicitly was that Claire would never make the first move.

"Mind if I turn on some music?" Ellie asked, because it might keep her from saying something she'd instantly regret, like, mind if I break my no-sex-on-a-first-date rule tonight?

"Sure." Claire hit the power button.

Motown music poured out; Ellie clapped with glee as the Supremes sang "You Keep Me Hanging On." She ignored the big stop sign flashing in her head, the one that usually appeared when she thought about singing in front of others. To hell with it. Tonight was fucking perfect and she wanted to sing her lungs out. "You don't really love me, you just keep me hanging on," she sang into the endless, star-filled sky. She knew the words by heart, as she did with most Motown songs, which made her extremely weird because nobody else her age knew these songs like they were on last month's billboard chart. *Fuck it.* This was pure bliss. "…and set me free…wooooooooo."

When the song ended, Claire was looking at her like she'd grown two heads, and her voice was full of awe. "Wow. Your voice…it's lovely. I didn't know you could sing like that."

"Neither does anybody else. Except Erin and Marissa."

"Seriously? You should be up on a stage somewhere."

"Ha. Becoming a singer would definitely give my mothers an aneurysm." She laughed at the thought.

"You care an awful lot about what they think for someone who's twenty-six years old."

The wind and a distant car horn garbled some of Claire's words. "Sorry?"

"You…never mind."

"Claire?"

"Yes?"

"I don't want to go home yet." There was nothing about this night that she wanted to end…the music, driving with the breeze ruffling her hair and face, and most of all, the woman sitting beside her.

"Okay. Where do you want to go?"

"Anywhere. Somewhere." Anyplace they could be alone.

"It is a gorgeous evening." Claire checked her mirrors, then cranked the 'Stang into a U-turn, pointing its nose back toward the Detroit River. She parked in the public lot at the bottom of Ouellette Avenue, came around to Ellie's side, and opened the door for her. "Care for a walk along the river?"

"Perfect. I'd love to."

The lights from the Detroit skyscrapers winked at them, reflecting off the dark water in ripples of shimmery gold. There was another couple walking some distance ahead of them, but otherwise they were alone. Ellie took Claire's arm for support. The alcohol was making her a little wobbly, especially in her heels, which fell a touch short of matching her height to Claire's.

"Thank you, Claire."

"For what?"

"For being such a good listener. I can always use more of those in my life. What especially means a lot to me is that you encourage me without judgment."

"I do?"

"You do."

"Well." Claire grinned at her, setting off the kind of elation in Ellie that made her feel like a teenager again. A teenager with an insufferable crush on an older woman. "I think I'm beginning to mellow in my old age. Or at least, outside of work, I'm beginning to mellow in my old age because I enjoy listening to you. And talking with you. And I'm really enjoying tonight."

"I'm enjoying this too. Like crazy. But who's old? Nobody around here."

"Well, as a matter of fact, I'm—"

"Shh." Ellie halted them and angled her body to face Claire. "I promise to stop talking about my hard-ass mothers and my inability to stand up to them if you stop talking about being old and overweight. Deal?"

An eyebrow lifted in surprise. And was that a tiny smirk of amusement at the corner of Claire's lips? "All right. Deal. And Ellie? Since we're being honest…"

"Yes?" Ellie slid her hands into Claire's. The touch of her fingers heated her from the inside, leaving a trail of fluttering through her chest. She wanted to trail her fingertips all the way up Claire's arms, feel the soft cotton of her blouse against her skin.

"You…" Claire's eyes got soft in that surprising, amazing way that only women who are supposed to be invulnerable can do.

"Yes?"

"I'm kind of glad you don't have sex on the first date."

"You are?" *For you I could make an exception. All you have to do is ask.*

"Yes, but only because I imagine you've probably had lots of first dates since, well, you were old enough to date. And, I know it's completely selfish, but I'm kind of hoping there haven't been a lot of second or third dates with women."

Ellie's heart leapt into her throat. A little tap dance on the spot would have been inappropriate, but it was fun to imagine doing it, because with that simple declaration, Claire was stating her intentions. Well, maybe that was going too far, but she was certainly suggesting that she liked Ellie as more than a friend.

"Claire." *Okay, now for the scary part.* The part that could either see this moment turn into magic or a steaming pile of shit, depending on what she said next. And how Claire reacted. *Here goes.* "I want another date with you. And a third one. And a fourth one. Because you're not like anyone I've ever met. And I don't want this to end tonight." Ellie could barely breathe right now.

"Ellie, you flatter me, but—"

Ellie stepped into Claire and crushed her lips against hers. She let everything around them fade to black as she gave herself to Claire's mouth, lost in the haze from the alcohol, from the warm night, and from the spark of interest in Claire's eyes, from the magic in her words. And oh, dear god, Claire might tell her to go to hell, but this felt so good, so powerful, so fucking amazing. It took all her strength to ignore her stampeding heart, to guide the kiss with tenderness and sweetness, to take her time, to refrain from begging Claire to take her home with her. She somehow managed to barely flinch in surprise when Claire full out began returning the kiss. Bravely, she planted her hands on Claire's waist, loving the way they felt there, and oh, how she ached to touch her all over, to be touched by her. The truth was catching up to her at the speed of her galloping heart, and with the tiniest leap, she knew she was falling for someone who was so damned good at throwing up roadblocks, who seemed on the one hand to want her too, and on the other, to push her away. It was dangerous, this little cat and mouse game that might very well end with a broken heart. *But I can't stop, dammit. I can't, I can't...*

Claire's mouth moved expertly against hers, like that of someone who'd done a lot of kissing and knew exactly how to do it. Her hands slid up Ellie's back, caressing lightly, patiently. There was no urgency in ending the kiss, nor in expanding it into something more, even though Ellie was hungry for everything. She wanted to melt into Claire right on the spot, revel in the softness of her curves, which were so refreshingly real and so mercifully unlike the size fours she'd dated in the past. Claire was by far the sexiest woman she'd ever kissed, and Ellie's center throbbed, all hot and wet and demanding release. It occurred to her that if they weren't someplace public, her first date rule would definitely be out the window.

It was Claire who broke the kiss, and the combination in her eyes of need, fear, desire, hesitation, nearly brought Ellie to her knees.

"I think I better take you home now," Claire said in an uneven voice. Her eyes said something completely different.

Minutes later, after Claire eased the car to a stop in front of Ellie's townhouse, she fished around in her handbag and held out a ten-dollar bill.

"What's that for?" Ellie asked.

"For not being anything at all like Sandy." Her wink was slow and scorching and hinted at something that looked a lot like hope.

CHAPTER TWELVE

I Heard It Through The Grapevine

"Hey, boss." Jackson poked his head inside Claire's office.

"Jackson." Claire tossed her reading glasses onto her desk. She'd started needing the damned things a few months ago.

Jackson slipped inside and shut the door behind him. Claire usually sat out in the newsroom at the span of copyediting desks, but today she felt like hiding in her corner office. Hiding because she worried the shame of what she'd done would show on her face. She'd been dying a slow death of embarrassment all weekend, ever since her big *date* Friday night with Ellie. She'd almost considered calling in sick today so she wouldn't have to face Jacks. Because Jacks would take one look at her and *know* she'd kissed the hell out of Ellie. And enjoyed every second of it.

"Okay, spill it," he said, crossing his arms over his chest, hovering over her desk like he was *her* boss.

"Look, I'm kind of busy today, so you'll—"

"Oh no you don't. You can't avoid me forever, Claire Bear! And don't you dare pretend you don't know what I'm talking about." He gave her his death stare, which wasn't anywhere near as diabolical as he imagined. He looked like a cartoon character, and Claire had to bite her bottom lip to keep from smiling. "So...your date with Ellie, how did it go? And I'm guessing it was either great or a disaster, judging by the fact that I didn't hear from you all weekend."

She'd pointedly ignored his texts asking, then demanding, then begging, how her date with Ellie had gone. She would make him wait at least a little longer.

"Come on, you can't leave me hanging like this." He crumpled into the chair across from her desk, his tough act forgotten. He looked like a five-year-old boy who'd learned Santa Claus didn't exist. Well, Claire thought with a sliver of irritation, he deserved the silent treatment because he had no business setting her and Ellie up like that. It was sneaky, manipulative, underhanded. And so what if she'd enjoyed it? That wasn't the point, dammit.

"Look," he pleaded, his hands up. "It wasn't even my idea. It was Erin's. I swear to god."

"Throwing her under the bus, eh? How chivalrous of you."

He looked like he was going to cry, so she took pity on him. Sort of. "That was not cool, what you two did. You couldn't have embarrassed the two of us any more if you'd tried."

"Embarrassed? We weren't trying to embarrass either of you. Our intentions were good, honest. We were trying to do you two a favor."

"A favor?" Oh, that was rich. "Look, Jacks, stay out of my love life from now on, okay? No more introducing me to women, no more blind dates, nothing. And I'm deadly serious. One more little stunt and I'm going to tell Julian about that guy at The Red Zone who tried to give you his number."

"Don't you dare!" Jackson sprang to attention like a human antennae. "Julian would have a fit. And I don't need the third degree over something that amounted to nothing."

Claire waved her hand to show her threat was empty. Jackson's relationship with Julian was the longest one he'd ever had, and she wanted it to work out between them. "I mean it about the little dating games. No more."

"So it was that bad, huh?" He sat down, resuming his defeated pose. He was kind of cute when he sulked.

Claire schooled her expression because she didn't want to let Jackson off the hook quite yet, though it was becoming a herculean effort to continue hiding her true emotions. The date had been...exciting. Ellie was delightful. A very good conversationalist, funny as hell. And, well, ridiculously attractive. To the point where Claire assumed strangers would never have guessed they were on a date because Ellie was young and hot and Claire was...well...not. Not that she considered herself unattractive, but she was most definitely not in Ellie's league. Ellie looked like she'd walked off the pages of *Vogue* or something.

"Wait. Wait just a minute." Jackson was nearly levitating out of his chair with the triumphant look of someone who'd scored the game-winning touchdown. Or solved the JFK assassination. "I know that look. You had a wonderful date with Ellie, didn't you?"

Claire's cheeks were so hot they were probably melting right off her face. "I...it was fine, okay?"

"Oh no. It was much better than fine judging by the nice shade of red working its way up your face." He clapped his hands in glee. "Oh, I knew it! I knew you two would hit it off marvelously on a real date. A little nudge was all that was needed. Julian told me to butt out, but when Erin suggested it, I *knew* it was the right thing to do. Oh, I'm so happy." He reached across the desk to pinch her cheek but she managed to swat his hand away in time. She hated—really hated—when her best friend was right. Hated even more that smug, satisfied look on his face. *Fine.* But let him *try* to get anything else out of her.

"So, my dearest friend." That stupid grin again. "Tell me more. Did you sleep with her?"

"Jackson!" A quick glance through the large glass window of her office told her others had heard her outburst. Quietly, she implored, "Are you nuts?"

"What? Why?"

"Because I'm...she's...oh, forget it."

"So you didn't sleep with her. That's okay. I mean it was only the first date. But you did kiss her, right?"

"Okay, you know what, mister? I don't have time for this, and neither do you if—"

"Aha! You did kiss her. Thank god. I was beginning to worry about you, Claire."

The kiss, every glorious second of it, flooded Claire's memory. She'd been so surprised when Ellie pressed herself against her and kissed the living daylights out of her. Not that she hadn't wanted Ellie to kiss her. More like, it seemed such an impossibility that she'd given up on the idea. And then it was happening, and the kiss was so soft, so tender, so mouthwateringly exquisite that it nearly made Claire's knees buckle like something right out of a 1950s romance movie. And when Ellie's hands moved to her waist, her heart had thumped so loudly that she was sure Ellie could hear it. She only ended the kiss because it had begun to frighten her. Not the kiss, but the feelings that accompanied the kiss. Kissing Ellie had had the slow, terrifying power of undoing her. Of turning everything in her life upside down. And Claire didn't allow herself to do things that might blow up her life. Ever.

"You look like somebody ran over your cat. If you had a cat. Come on, the kiss couldn't have been *that* bad."

"It…" *Jesus.* She couldn't get the kiss out of her mind, replaying it all weekend, and it was driving her crazy. How could she possibly have so many warring emotions over such a simple act? Doubt, fear, guilt, exhilaration, arousal, joy. She was a jumble of confusion. A hot mess. And she was so, so typically never a hot mess over anything. Cautious, plodding, pragmatic, yes. Spontaneous, reckless, adventurous, never. After a long, steadying breath, she told Jackson all about their *date*.

"So that's great, Claire, it's awesome. You were both into it. Which means you've asked her out on another one, right?"

"Wrong."

"What? Why not?"

"She's practically a kid. And I'm practically…I don't know, old enough to be her mother?" Not really, but it sounded more dramatic, and Jacks liked drama.

"Give me a break. She's twenty-six and you're forty-two. I've dated guys that much younger than me. It's no big deal. Everyone's an adult. Nobody's getting hurt."

Except this old heart of mine, Claire thought. That damned kiss had underscored the fact that she'd never felt so unsettled, so blown away, so out-of-control, so crazily turned on, from any of the countless other kisses she'd shared with women over the years. Ellie and her pink-lipsticked lips had set Claire's world on fire. Even now, she could still taste her.

"This thing…" She halted. What was it exactly they were doing? And how could she possibly explain it? "It would never work. We're from different worlds. We're…there's too many differences, too many obstacles. It's pointless to even start anything."

Take, for instance, the differences in their general outlook on life. Ellie somehow managed to be happy, despite not having much of a clue about what the future held. That was a talent. Claire, on the other hand, tended to look at the future and decide, based on a formula of probabilities, whether to be optimistic or pessimistic.

Jackson rose in silence, paced the room, his head bowed in thought. Then he rounded on Claire with his square jaw all granite hard and his eyes impatient and accusatory. "This is not the Claire Melbourne I know and love. What did you do with her? 'Cause this Claire Melbourne is a fucking wimp. A coward. Somebody who should be teaching kindergarten kids, not running a bloody newsroom. Jesus, Claire, would you get your head out of your ass?"

It took another moment for her to close her mouth, which she had to pick up off the floor first. Jackson rarely spoke to her so bluntly or at least not *this* bluntly. He was her ally, her best friend. A brother, if she had one. What the hell had she done to deserve *this*?

"That's right. You heard me and I'm not sorry I said it." But his temper was fading, the storm of his emotions nearly spent. "Look, Claire. I've seen you march right through police lines to get a story. Christ, you've interviewed killers before. Skewered that pedophile priest with that investigative piece you did years ago, remember that? So why are you letting this thing with Ellie scare you so much?"

Claire wished she had a simple answer for him. The more complicated one probably had something to do with the fact that she was a cynic when it came to relationships. She'd never really seen a healthy one, not one that actually worked for any length of time. Throw in a few complications like their age gap, Ellie's uncertain career future, and Claire's aversion to relationships, and *voilá*. A recipe for failure to launch. She was doing both herself and Ellie a favor by not seeking a second date.

"I'm sparing myself and Ellie from something that won't work, all right? And I don't want to talk about this anymore." Her friend was right that when it came to her job, she was fearless. But this was different. This was her heart. And she didn't want the bullshit of having it broken. "Now, would you please leave? I've got work to do."

Jackson smiled at her, made the chin-up motion with his hand. "You deserve to be happy, Claire. Think about that, would you?"

She watched as he clicked the door shut behind him and thought about his parting words. Everybody deserved to be happy. So what. Life didn't come with a guarantee for happiness.

* * *

"You still mad at me for conspiring to set you up on that blind date with Claire?"

Ellie and Erin had cycled the six kilometers or so to Jackson Park, then through the park and to the outdoor tennis courts, where they stopped to watch two guys lazily bat a tennis ball around. Ellie could have kept going, but Erin looked a little wan.

"Who said anything about being mad?"

"You've been moping around ever since."

"Have not."

"Have so."

If she was moping, it was because she hadn't heard from Claire since their date, other than trading a couple of texts confirming her usual noon hour visit and walk with Rolo each day. It was her day off from the café, so she and Erin, who was still bunking at her house, agreed to spend the afternoon together.

Ellie sighed louder than she intended, earning a look of scrutiny from Erin. Erin, who could write a how-to book about dating women. "All right. Look. I'm not mad. And you're right, I'm attracted to Claire and I needed that little kick in the butt from you. But as honorable as your intention was, our first date is also going to be our last."

"No way. I don't believe you."

Ellie shrugged. "It's obvious she's not into me, okay?" She replayed the kiss in her mind, in all its mind-blowing sweetness. She hadn't foreseen the surge of emotions that had accompanied it—the mutual tenderness, the undercurrent of want swirling fiercely beneath the surface. Claire had most definitely been into it too. And then she sort of freaked out, which Ellie knew would happen. *Knew* it! "Story of my life."

"Come on, it's not the story of your life."

"Erin, don't even!" She did not need her sister's pity or a lecture or whatever the hell she was gearing up for.

"So you think my life is perfect? Is that it?"

"Like, hello. You've just graduated from medical school *and* you've always gotten any woman you want. Without any seeming effort, I might add." How in the hell could they have the exact same DNA?

For a long time Erin didn't speak. Which was unlike her. She was rarely at a loss for words, always sharing an opinion or an observation. Her witty comebacks were legendary. But not today. They watched the two teenaged boys bat the ball around with their rackets, ignoring rules and hitting out of bounds as often as they pleased, never bothering to chase the ball down when they missed.

"All right, I'm sorry," Ellie mumbled. "Your life's not perfect. I get that."

There was the glisten of unshed tears when Erin turned to look at her. What the hell was going on with her? Since her return a couple of weeks ago, she was still mostly avoiding their mothers, her mood was all over the map, and she uncharacteristically sat around like a lump half the time. Erin was always the one who'd clean up after the last person left a party and then be the first one up in the morning. When it came to studying, she'd stay up half the night without any visible adverse effects the next day. She was the most energetic, happy-go-lucky person Ellie knew.

"Okay, look, you're scaring me." Ellie put her arm around her sister's shoulders, surprised by the trembling beneath her fingers. "What's going on with you, Er?"

Erin waved her hand in dismissal, looked away, and in that moment Ellie pledged to herself that she was not letting her sister off the hook this time. Something was going on and she was damned well going to root it out. "So," she ventured. "Looking forward to your move to Toronto next month?" Soon Erin would embark on her residency, the next big step after medical school, when her hard work would pay off with more responsibility.

"I guess."

"You guess? Last semester it was all you could talk about." Erin couldn't wait to finish med school and get into *real* doctoring, as she called it.

Erin stared at the two tennis players, though it was generous to call them that.

"All right, that's it."

"What?"

"We're not leaving here until you tell me what the hell is wrong."

Erin's eyes were dry again, her recalcitrant demeanor back in place. "Who said anything is wrong? Besides, I thought we were talking about your love life."

"We were, except I think it's time we had a talk about *your* life. You're not yourself, Erin. You look like shit. You're still avoiding our moms, you—"

"Am not. I had lunch with them yesterday."

"Fine. And did they ride you about why you're not staying with them?"

"Not really. I told them I didn't want to feel like a teenager again, staying in my old room. I'm used to being on my own now."

"Fine. But this is me. What's the real reason you're hiding from everybody? And not tripping over yourself with excitement to start your residency?"

"Just…don't push this, all right? Please?"

Erin was near tears again, and Ellie's stomach bottomed out; something was desperately wrong. "No. Not an option. My life is always an open book to you, which means you're not allowed to keep secrets from me. Just because we haven't been around each other much the last seven years does not mean you get to—"

"All right, all right. Fine."

Ellie heaved an inward sigh of relief. Her next drastic measure was going to be threatening Erin that she couldn't stay with her and Marissa any longer if she didn't confide in her. It would have been an empty threat, of course, but desperate times called for desperate measures.

Another couple of minutes ticked by.

"I'm pregnant."

"*What?*" Was this a fucking joke?

The look on Erin's face said it was not. She'd gone white, and a fine bead of sweat sprouted on her hairline.

"Nine weeks, and don't ask me if I'm sure."

Ellie waited for her brain to fully absorb Erin's bombshell and for her heart to stop doing its impression of a jackhammer. It didn't make any sense. Erin was as gay as she was. Neither had ever slept with a guy before and had never wanted to. So how…? "How did this happen?"

"The usual way."

Ellie studied her sister. The sister she thought hadn't a straight bone in her body. "But…why? I mean, what the *hell*, Er? You slept with a *guy*?" She couldn't keep the shock and disappointment from her tone.

Erin rolled her eyes at her. "Yes, I slept with a guy. We used birth control but it…failed, obviously."

Questions, so many of them, piled up one after another. "So you're not gay? Or you were, but now you're not? I don't freaking understand this at all. I mean, you went on and on at Jackson's barbecue about how hot you thought Claire was. Plus you've *always* dated women. Was that for show? I mean, I thought you were dating some woman named Shelly and that you broke up with her because she was nuts or something. Were you *lying* to me all this time? About everything?"

Erin couldn't meet Ellie's eyes. "There was no Shelly. Only a Greg. I lied about the name and the gender, okay? But nothing else."

Ellie scrubbed her cheeks with her hands. A huge headache had begun to throb at her temples. "In about five seconds I'm going to scream if you don't tell me everything that's going on." God, not only was her sister not gay or not entirely gay (sort of gay?), but she was going to have a baby too? Had she lost her mind or something? Fallen and hit her head? Suffered amnesia?

"I'm…Shit, I hate labels. When we were kids, I knew I liked girls, okay? Same as you. But when I went away to university, I wasn't so sure anymore. I started to think about guys…that way. A little. I didn't do anything about it until I met Greg six months ago. He was a classmate. We sort of started dating."

"So you're…bisexual?"

"Yes. I think so. I don't know."

Hard as she tried, Ellie couldn't quite come to grips with this new information. "So does this mean—"

"Dammit, I don't know what it means! Look. I'm sorry. I went with it, okay? I don't know whether I'll date another guy in the future or not. Anyway, Greg and I aren't together anymore."

"What? He left you?"

"Not exactly. I dumped him right before I came back here. I liked him but not enough to be tied down to him for the rest of my life or anything. He wasn't meant to be a long-term thing, you know? He was…sort of an experiment. I don't know, I don't have all the answers."

"So he doesn't know about the baby?"

"No. And he's not going to. At least not any time soon. My body, my life, my baby. Period."

"Okay. What are you going to do?"

Erin's face crumpled. Tears, hot and sloppy, streaked down her face.

Ellie pulled her sister into a hug, let her wipe her tears against her T-shirt. "We'll figure this out together, okay? It's going to be okay."

Erin nodded mutely into Ellie's shirt.

"Oh shit. Do our moms know about this?"

Erin shook her head. And it occurred to Ellie that this was the first time in their lives Erin had ever done anything shameful, anything to overtly disappoint their mothers. Perfect angel Erin, anointed with all the family's hopes and dreams, a perfect carbon copy of Emily and Elaine, wasn't so perfect after all. And while she and Erin would figure out a way through this no matter how big a fit their mothers threw (and they would!), Ellie did a silent little fist pump behind her back. Because her sister was human after all.

CHAPTER THIRTEEN

Baby I'm For Real

Claire clipped Rolo's leash to her collar, popped one earbud into her ear, and cranked her iPod to some contemporary blues music. It was a muggy evening, as summer evenings often were in the Midwest—all that hot air pulling up moisture from the Great Lakes and creating a sauna. It was dusk, though, so at least the sun wasn't an issue. On hot days like this, she'd instructed Ellie to keep Rolo's noon walks short. On reflection, she probably didn't need to specify such things in a note to Ellie, who was much more an expert at all of this than she was.

Ellie. It'd been exactly one week since their sort-of-real date, and the only contact they'd had since were the exchange of notes on Claire's kitchen counter and a few texts pertaining to Rolo. Claire knew she was being a coward. But what was she supposed to do? Say? They couldn't ignore the kiss, and yet how could they walk it back? Because going forward wasn't an option. She'd been foolish to get swept up, to think that slow roll in her stomach and the sparks behind her eyelids were something real, something to build on.

As if merely thinking of Ellie could summon her, there she was, in the flesh, up ahead walking Mrs. Gartner's dog, Maggie. Claire, in her newfound cowardice, gave serious thought to hiding behind a tree. But then Rolo, with her excellent eyesight, spotted Ellie and started popping wheelies and yipping like a crazy thing, each yip louder and louder until Ellie turned around. Even Rolo's tail got in on the act, wagging so vigorously it looked like it might spin right off her little body.

Ellie and Maggie did a U-turn and walked toward them. "Rolo! Hiya, baby girl!"

Dammit. Claire pulled the earbud from her ear and stuffed it into her pocket as Ellie got down on her hands and knees, petting Rolo and giving her a loud smooch on the top of her head.

"How's my good girl, huh?" Rolo ate it up, rolling onto her back for a belly rub.

"Hi," Claire said. Well, that was inventive.

"Hi." Ellie raised her eyes to Claire. Eyes that were sad. Or worried. Or something. Eyes that were definitely very un-Ellie like. Her inability to hide her feelings was one of the things Claire had come to enjoy about Ellie. Except when Claire was the cause of feelings that were sad or upset.

Great, she thought, *I've really gone and hurt her feelings by not following up after our date. I've treated her like crap. Again.* The guilt reminded her of her manners. "Would you, um, like to walk with us?"

"Sure."

The two dogs exchanged sniffs before the four of them began walking in silence. It was weird, unsettling, to see Ellie so quiet. *She must really be upset with me*, Claire thought.

"Rolo been okay for you this week?"

"Sure, yeah. She's great."

They walked another block in silence, and Claire couldn't take much more. Never before had she had to work this hard at having a conversation with Ellie. Ellie was always off and running with something to say, lighting up the world around her with her energy and cheerfulness. Not today. Definitely not today.

There was a bench up ahead, under a tree. Claire motioned for them to take a break. The dogs were panting and Claire was about to as well.

"Ellie…"

"Yes?"

God, those eyes. They were putting a crack right in the middle of Claire's heart, making it impossible to breathe. She blushed hotly, remembering the kiss. It was a good kiss. No, it was a great kiss. An epic kiss. And if it'd been with any other woman, Claire would have been blowing up her phone the next day asking for a second date. Which totally wasn't fair to Ellie.

"I…Look, I'm really sorry I haven't called you since our… our date. It's poor of me and I hate that I've been so rude about it all." Not really an explanation, but it was a start.

"Thank you." Ellie reached down to stroke the dogs, mumbled something pleasant to each of them. It was another minute before she turned back to Claire. "So how come you haven't?"

"Haven't what?" Claire swallowed. She was being pathetic. A pathetic coward.

"Haven't wanted to talk to me."

"I'm sorry, Ellie."

"You already said that."

Claire's shoulders slumped heavily. "You're right, I did." She reached down and petted Rolo behind the ears, holding onto every last second she could because she wasn't sure what to say next. She thought of trying to throw Ellie off track with some lame excuse or distraction, but then she stole another look at her face and saw the confusion, the sadness playing over her lovely features. That did it. "The reason is because I wasn't sure what to say, or do, about…you know, what happened."

"You mean our kiss?"

How could this young woman possibly be twenty times braver than she was? Oh, right. It was because she wasn't a middle-aged fool like Claire. "Yes. The kiss. It…surprised me. I…On reflection, I'm not sure I was ready for it."

A spark momentarily returned to Ellie's eyes. "You, um, seemed ready. At the time, I mean."

"Okay. Right. I guess I was ready at the time but not ready afterward." *Jesus, I'm not even making sense to myself!*

"So that means what? That you regret it?"

"No. It…means I got scared. I guess." A six-year-old had a better vocabulary.

"So I scare you?" Ellie playfully bumped shoulders with her. "That's turning the tables."

Understatement of the year. "Okay, but don't get ahead of yourself. It was more *me* that I was scared of, not you."

Ellie's brow furrowed, and the expression was so cute that Claire was tempted to smooth it out with her thumb. "You're scared that you want to do it again. Am I right?"

Claire laughed shortly. "Am I that obvious? I guess the whole mysterious-older-woman thing isn't working for me."

Ellie smiled, and the relief Claire felt was instant. "I don't want you to be a mystery, Claire. I…want us to be ourselves. To be honest with one another. I miss talking to you and I sooo need to…" Her chin trembled and her breath hitched.

"Ellie, what's wrong?"

"Nothing. Everything."

"Can you start with one thing?"

Ellie spoke so fast that Claire almost didn't catch it all. "The application window closes at the college next week and I'm thinking of going back to school full time for the two-year veterinary technician program. And my sister's suddenly bisexual. Oh, and she's pregnant."

"Wait. What?"

Ellie began repeating herself, slower this time. It was adorable, but Claire made her stop. From her reporting experience, she knew enough to let people ramble, but she also knew enough to pluck out the most urgent thing first. "Erin is pregnant?"

"Nine weeks, well, almost ten now, I guess. It's, I mean, I *never* saw this coming. Ever. Erin had her whole life planned out, and now this. I'm scared for her. I don't know how she's going to manage, what she's going to do."

"Is she keeping it?"

"Yes. And please don't tell anyone. I shouldn't have—"

"No, it's okay. I won't tell anyone. What about her career?"

"She's going to drop her residency. I mean, postpone it a year. She's not sure if she's going to stay around here or not, but I don't see how she can move away, not now. We...I...can help her."

"And how do you feel about her being bisexual?"

Ellie shrugged. "I was sort of upset at first, mostly because there was a time we told each other everything. But...she's her own person and I'm my own person. So whatever makes her happy. We're joking now that her dating pool is twice as big as mine."

"Do your mothers know about all of this?"

Ellie snorted. "No, but they will tomorrow. I'm going with Erin to break the news to them."

Good luck with that one, Claire thought, silently wishing the two sisters would show their mothers some backbone. As in, lots of it. "I'm guessing they probably won't take it very well?"

"Nope. Erin's their golden child. She's supposed to have a stellar start to her career and only *then* maybe give them a grandchild. And you know what I feel the worst about?"

Claire resisted the urge to take Ellie's hand. It was such a powerful urge that she had to practically sit on her hand. "What's that?"

"Honestly? Part of me is happy to see Erin disappoint our mothers for, like, the first time ever. And that's pretty shitty of me. I'm a shitty sister."

"You're not. You're human. And the important thing is your actions, not your private thoughts. You're supporting Erin. And she needs that right now, I assume."

"She does." Ellie swept her gaze over Claire and something pleasurable fluttered through her stomach. It felt like a swarm of invisible butterflies. "Thank you, Claire," she whispered hoarsely.

"For what?"

"Listening. Giving good advice. And...for not running away from me a few minutes ago. You thought about it, didn't you? Except Rolo wouldn't let you."

Busted. "I did. But I'm glad I decided to be an adult about it."

"Me too."

"So what's this about going back to college for the vet tech program?"

"I'm thinking about it."

"You love animals, so it makes sense."

"It does. Piper, Maggie, Rolo. They make me want to work with dogs, to have a career working with pets. I've always loved animals. It never really occurred to me before that I should pursue that kind of career. But…"

"What's making you hesitate?"

Ellie looked skyward. "My mothers won't approve. A two-year college program won't be prestigious enough for them. And the earnings from a career like that aren't lucrative. I mean, enough to live on, but not much more."

"Well, if it's what you really want to do, does the rest matter?"

Ellie shook her head.

It had taken Claire years, decades, to accept that money and the opinions of strangers meant almost nothing in the grand scheme of things. She wasn't proud of how long it'd taken her to learn those lessons or what she'd lost along the way. "Let me ask you this, Ellie. Whose life are you living? Yours or theirs?"

Ellie looked at her so long that Claire feared she'd put her foot in it. And then Ellie smiled crookedly. "You're right. I need to live my own life. And so does Erin." Her hand crept onto Claire's arm and she gave it a squeeze. And then her voice was so soft, so full of meaning, that it made Claire's mouth go dry. "Thanks for this, Claire. You have no idea what your friendship means to me."

"Ellie?"

"Yes?"

What am I doing what am I doing what am I doing? "Would you like to bring Piper and join Rolo and me Sunday afternoon for a picnic?"

"I'd love to! I mean, Piper and I would love to. But on one condition."

"What's that?"

"That we consider it our second date. And another thing."

Claire's breath got caught up in her throat. When had Ellie begun to have that kind of power over her? "Yes?"

"That we also finish the conversation you probably thought you'd evaded. The one about our kiss that has you so…okay, I'm not going to say scared. How about frazzled? Confused? Agitated? Worried?" A raised eyebrow underscored the humor in her question. "I can whip out my pocket thesaurus if you'd like."

Claire laughed. There was no pulling the wool over this one's eyes. And that was a good thing. She knew she'd never respect a woman who didn't call her on her shit, who wouldn't stand up to her. *I want a woman who's a handful.* Funny how at one time she thought Ellie was anything but, and it was no wonder she hadn't respected her during her time at the newspaper. "All right. You've got a deal."

* * *

Ellie and Erin sat at the kitchen table drinking iced tea. Ellie had poured a shot of whiskey in hers because they—well, *she*—needed a little bolstering before heading over to their mothers' house this afternoon. It was going to be ugly, but she wouldn't dream of letting Erin go alone. Erin, who didn't have a clue what it was like to be on the receiving end of their moms' wrath, was going to need someone in her corner.

Marissa thumped down the stairs, yawning, her hair a mess. She'd worked most of the night and was finally emerging.

"Coffee," she mumbled, her arms straight out in a zombie impression as she made her way to the coffee pod machine. It wasn't until she'd poured a cup and taken her first sip that her eyes landed on the twins. "What's with the long faces, you two?"

Ellie and Erin traded a look. Marissa had been working tons lately, what with coworkers being away for summer holidays, so they hadn't seen much of her. "Well? Spill it. And don't tell me it's nothing, because it's me. Your cousin. The one who witnessed you both growing up. And you were both lousy at keeping secrets. And I love you guys no matter what. So there."

Marissa. Ellie smiled. What would she do without her?

Erin grew flushed, but she managed to look Marissa straight in the eye. "I'm pregnant."

"You're *what*? Wait a minute." She took a gulp of coffee, then another. "Okay, I think I heard wrong. Tell me again. I'm awake now, I promise."

Erin rolled her eyes. "Pregnant. As in, going to have a baby in about six months."

Marissa's mouth formed a perfect O. "You're kidding." She looked at Ellie for confirmation. "She's joking, right?"

"Nope."

"So, like, you went to a sperm bank or something because for some weird, inexplicable reason you decided you wanted to become a mom right after finishing med school?"

Erin winced. "Not quite."

"You mean you slept with a *guy*?" Marissa posed the question exactly as Ellie had done, then relaxed her tone. "I mean, it's cool, don't get me wrong. I'm surprised, is all. Hell, I've even slept with a couple of guys."

It was Ellie's turn to be shocked. "You have?" Was she the only one around here who hadn't sampled the other side?

Marissa shrugged, took another sip of coffee. "Whatever. So," she continued pointedly, "don't tell me this pregnancy was planned?"

Ellie answered for her sister. "Of course not. And no, our mothers don't know, but they will in another hour or two."

Marissa shook her head slowly back and forth. "Jesus. They're going to have a freaking fit. You know that, right?"

Ellie pointed at her drink. "Why do you think I have whiskey in my iced tea?"

"Can I come? Just to watch? I promise I won't say anything."

"Absolutely not!" Ellie glowered at her cousin. "This isn't some sporting event, you know."

"Oh, yes it is. It's going to be a bloodbath. Like an MMA fight or something."

Erin rolled her eyes. "Sheesh, you guys. It won't be that bad."

Ellie and Marissa shared a secret smile. Yes. It would be exactly that bad.

"Anyway," Erin continued, "I'm trying to convince Ellie to do a little diversionary tactic and tell them at the same time that she's dating Claire."

"Wait." Marissa clutched her heart as if she'd been given too much shocking news in one sitting. "You're officially dating the woman who fired you? How come I miss everything?"

"She fired you?" Erin stared open-mouthed at Ellie.

God, how she loved/hated her family. "Yes, she fired me. And then offered to rehire me, but I said no."

"Really?" Erin said. "Why didn't you want to go back?"

"Long story." Which, come to think of it, was even longer now that she was sort of dating Claire. An intern dating her boss would most definitely be frowned upon. "Come on," she said to her sister. "We'd better get a move on. They're expecting us any time."

Minutes later, as they headed out the door, Marissa called out, "Good luck!"

* * *

"It's so nice to have our two daughters sitting here together for a change," Emily said, drawing in an exaggerated breath as though she were breathing in a bouquet of flowers. It was rare these days, but not *that* rare. "Don't you agree, Elaine? Hasn't it been forever?"

The four of them sat around a table on the covered patio. The swimming pool, a massive infinity one with a built-in waterfall, sat yards away, sparkling in the sunshine. It had cost a small fortune and was hardly ever used.

"It has," Elaine answered, intertwining her fingers with her wife's. They were always doing little things like that to express affection, and it gave Ellie a warm feeling inside knowing her moms had an almost perfect relationship and that they remained in love after thirty years. They each anticipated the other's needs, finished one another's thoughts, they were like poured concrete that levels itself. They were so good at this marriage thing that they were setting an awfully high mark, one that Ellie feared she'd never be able to match.

Iced tea had been poured all around, and a tray laden with grapes, apple slices, watermelon, and pineapple chunks sat untouched in the middle of the table. Ellie snatched a grape and popped it into her mouth, waiting for Erin to come out with her news. This could be awhile, she thought, as she reached next for a chunk of pineapple.

"So," Emily said to break the silence. "Ellie, it's almost August. What are your plans for the fall?"

"Uh…what do you mean?" No way was she going to tell them she was considering the vet tech program at St. Clair College. She was still thinking seriously on the idea. And still thinking about how she was going to break it to them if she decided to enroll.

"Well," said Elaine. "Part-time work at that…that *café* isn't going to get you through the winter."

It was all Ellie could do to keep from rolling her eyes. She almost blurted out that she didn't only work at the café, that she walked dogs too. Like *that* would appease her mothers. *Right.*

Erin gave her a look of commiseration before clearing her throat loudly. "Actually, there's something I need to discuss with you both."

Two sets of eyes bursting with pride turned to Erin. It was nauseating, the way the light switched onto Erin. "Yes, dear?" the mothers said in eager unison, and Ellie wanted to gag. They were probably expecting fantastic news, like Erin had decided to specialize in neurosurgery, or something exotic like biochemical genetics. Under the table she patted her sister's knee. They were a team and they'd get through this.

Erin began to speak, closed her mouth again, until Ellie gave her a little pinch of encouragement. "You see, the thing is…what I wanted to tell you is…" Erin swallowed visibly, and Ellie finally appreciated that her sister was about to step off a huge precipice for the first time in her life. That not only was she risking serious rebuke from their mothers, but she might lose their support, their respect, forever. "I'm…I'm going to have a baby."

It was as if a black curtain had come down on the patio, and Ellie could swear the sun was actually eclipsed for a moment. There was no audible sound either. And then the words poured out loud and in torrents from Emily and Elaine. Shock and disbelief segued into loud and obnoxious protests, as if utilizing that tactic could change Erin's confession into something completely different. Questions came next.

"How could this possibly have happened?" Emily demanded, and Erin told them about her brief relationship with Greg.

"But...you're a lesbian," Elaine sputtered. "Like the rest of us. This is...this is...unfathomable. What changed?"

"I don't..." Erin took a deep breath. How hard it must be for her sister to admit to a family of lesbians that she was different, that for once in her life, she wasn't like any of them. "I've come to realize that I'm bisexual," she finally said, and in a tone that did not invite further examination, further criticism, to be accurate.

"And when did you decide that?" Emily's tone dripped with condemnation.

Erin huffed. "I'm not debating my sexuality with either of you, all right? I'm twenty-six years old and I can sleep with whomever I please."

Hear hear, Ellie thought. She'd remember that line for when or if she ever told them about Claire, because they'd most certainly have a similar, reproachful reaction to her dating someone sixteen years older.

"All right, fine. Sleeping with somebody is one thing." Elaine's tone was knife sharp. "But to get pregnant? What were you *thinking*?"

"Or not thinking," Emily grumbled.

Ellie watched as Erin sat stone still, her posture rigid against the onslaught. And an onslaught it was. Their mothers continued to level myriad questions at her about what she planned to do, all while getting in their little digs about what a stupid thing it was to get herself pregnant and right after medical school. Ellie could swear a catastrophic natural disaster wouldn't rate this high on their moms' outrage meter.

Time to step up to the plate and take some of the body blows. "Look," Ellie said, having to raise her voice to be heard. "Erin will work things out. This is not the end of the world. She'll still be a doctor, and a great one, but with a little timeout to have a baby. And I, for one, plan to do whatever I can to help. I expect you both will as well because that's what families do for one another." She raised a challenging eyebrow at her parents.

Was that a flash of shame on their faces? Well, maybe not quite, but there was definitely a relaxing of the facial muscles that suggested a little bit of a reset. Her mothers could be incredibly supportive, generous, loving. When they chose to be. But all too often, that support and generosity came with so many strings, they could start a symphony orchestra.

"Oh, and by the way?" Ellie felt a smirk twisting the corners of her mouth, even as her heartbeat thundered in her ears. "I'm dating a woman sixteen years older than me."

CHAPTER FOURTEEN

Just To See Her

The dogs yipped happily, bumping each other until they ended up rolling around together on the grass, a tangle of tails and legs. Rolo, Claire was relieved to see, loved other dogs, and Piper, who had probably thirty pounds on Rolo, was gentle with her yet didn't let her off the hook when Rolo chomped a little too hard at one point. Piper was only too happy to throw Rolo on her back to teach her a lesson.

It was a doggie play session, Claire kept telling herself. Ellie could call it a date all she wanted, but it didn't make it so.

"I saw the article in the paper yesterday about the pets rescued from the big storm and that they're still more than a dozen here that need adopting." Ellie took the turkey sandwich laced with Swiss cheese and lettuce that Claire handed her from the picnic basket and licked her lips hungrily. "By the way this looks fantastic, Claire, thank you." She took a bite and rolled her eyes heavenward. "You made these?"

"I did."

"Well, if you ever need a second job, I'm pretty sure I can get you in at the café." Ellie teased her with a wink. "So, the story in the paper. That was your doing?"

Claire tried to hide her sheepishness but failed miserably as heat flooded her cheeks. A year ago—hell, three months ago—she would never have authorized a reporter to write such a soft story. It was Rolo's fault, and Ellie's, that her edges were becoming less sharp, less defined, and her gray areas were getting grayer and more fluid. All of which weren't really very helpful for a newspaper editor. Her boss, the paper's managing editor, had begun looking at her recently like she was losing her touch. Which, she supposed, she was. But dammit, she was getting so tired of being a pit bull so much of the time. It was exhausting. All those years she thought she had to be so strident, ferocious, callous, because that was the job and that was the way she was taught and that was what she was rewarded for. Well, perhaps that line of thinking was plain wrong. Or antiquated, at the very least.

"It was my doing," she said on a sigh. "I can't help but think that if I hadn't stopped in at the pound on a whim, Rolo would still be there, looking for a home."

"Well, I think it's awesome. You did good, and I'll bet tomorrow when the shelter opens its doors, there'll be a lineup of people wanting to adopt these guys." She reached out and stroked Rolo's back. The dogs were staying close now that food was being consumed, their noses in the air, their tongues darting out dangerously close to any crumbs.

"I'm not so sure, but thanks." Claire hoped the results would be worth her sticking her neck out.

"Don't let anybody try to tell you that these homeless dogs aren't worth the ink in your newspaper. They so are. They need a champion, exactly like humans sometimes do."

Claire let Ellie's compliment ignite something warm and reassuring in her. Her boss wouldn't be happy with her tomorrow, but tomorrow was tomorrow. Today she was sitting with a gorgeous young woman who was looking at her like she was some kind of superhero.

"So tell me about this place." Claire followed Ellie's gaze to the fort's rolling hills that acted as a defense fortification to the Detroit River and beyond. "I mean, I think I was here on a school trip when I was about eight, but I don't remember much about it. History wasn't, isn't, really my thing." She smiled adorably in apology. And it worked. Normally Claire found a lack of basic knowledge about the area's history irritating, but in Ellie's presence, weird things happened to her. It was as though she became someone entirely different—someone more patient, more considerate, more thoughtful, even empathetic. And the really weird part? It felt kind of good.

"Well, let's see. Fort Malden was built right before the War of 1812. British troops stayed here. Just beyond there…" Claire pointed to the river. "The British captured an American schooner at the start of the war, and that's when the fight was on. The Americans crossed the river and took the town of Sandwich, not far from here. The first British fatalities of the war were two soldiers from this fort when the Americans captured it. The British took the fort back a few months later and conducted their own incursion across the river into Detroit. Ultimately the British torched and abandoned this fort in 1813 with the Americans hot on their heels."

"I'm impressed. You know a lot about this stuff."

"I'm a nerd, what can I say."

Ellie leaned across the picnic blanket, her face inches from Claire. "I find nerds incredibly sexy. Did you know that?"

The air crackled with something vibrant and almost forbidden, and Claire wanted to kiss Ellie. Badly. Her mouth watered at the thought, yet as she looked into Ellie's eyes, the soulfulness in them struck her. There was so much more to this woman than her youthful exuberance, her fresh honesty, the uncomplicated and unpretentious way she presented herself. She was so much deeper than all of that. *I want to know you*, Claire thought. *All of you*. There was an old saying that still waters run deep. Ellie wasn't still, but she did run deep.

Claire drew closer until she could smell the soap on Ellie's skin—cucumber and something minty—and dropped a kiss beneath Ellie's ear. A soft, barely-there kiss that brought an immediate ache to her chest. As if sensing that Claire wanted much more, Ellie angled her head toward her mouth and kissed her on the lips. The heat was instantaneous, the tingling rioting down Claire's jaw and straight into her spine. It was so much like the first time she'd ever kissed a girl—that racing feeling where your heart and your head are miles ahead of you, and your body, well, your body is warm and numb and slowly melting into what you're sure is a puddle of warm liquid. More than that, kissing Ellie was like an amalgamation of all the kisses she'd ever shared with women, leading to this single apex where everything felt so right, so perfect—a single moment that seemed to erase all the moments that had ever come before, so flawless was it. Ellie deepened the kiss, moaning quietly against Claire's mouth. With each passing second they lost themselves in the kiss, Claire unraveling a little more until her control was soon dangling by a very tenuous thread. This wasn't a kiss soaked in too much wine or inspired by a romantic evening walk along the river. No. This was broad daylight. This was completely sober. This was…serious.

Claire pulled back from the kiss but continued to look at Ellie until her eyes fluttered open.

"Everything okay?" Ellie whispered, and there was that fine little furrow between her eyes that would one day be as deeply engraved as the one between Claire's eyes. *Don't be like me*, Claire thought. *Stay the way you are forever.*

She almost whispered it to Ellie, but instead, she said, "Yes, everything's fine, I promise." She backed away a little, putting space between them. "So tell me about your visit with your mothers yesterday."

Ellie recounted every detail of her parents' shock and disappointment at Erin's news, and how at the end, they'd hugged their daughters good-bye but something had shifted. There was a distance, a perceptible detachment between them.

"It'll take time," Claire said, "to absorb the news."

"I guess. But I keep thinking what you said to me before. About whose life I'm living, mine or theirs. And the same goes for Erin. And you're absolutely right, Claire. If they don't accept the decisions Erin and I make, maybe we need to consider that it's time to cut the umbilical cord."

"That's a big step. You're prepared to do that?"

Ellie looked away, her gaze drifting to the river where a freighter lumbered slowly and quietly past. "I think I am. No. I know I am, if it comes to that."

"All right. Are you frightened?"

"Terrified."

Claire reached out and took Ellie's hand in hers, and it felt like the most natural thing in the world. "You'll be fine."

A small flash of hope registered in Ellie's eyes. "I hope so. And now, there's something I've wanted to do since the minute I got here."

Claire's heart leapt into her throat. They'd already kissed, so what else could she have in mind? Before she could guess, Ellie sprinted for the rolling embankment that led straight down to what looked like a moat surrounding the fort, except it was dry and grassy. She dropped and disappeared from sight.

"Ellie? What are you doing?" Claire followed. "Are you all right?"

Ellie was rolling down the embankment, laughing and squealing all the way. After hitting bottom, she got to her knees, brushed the blades of grass from her chest and her hair, her smile as big as the horizon.

Piper's leash in her hand, Ellie led the dog out of Claire's car. "Good girl, Piper. You've been a good girl today. Would you like to come in, Claire?" *Please say yes.*

"I'd better get Rolo home, but thanks. I enjoyed today, Ellie."

"Me too. Like, a lot." She leaned carefully against the driver's side door, so close she could feel the day's sunshine and heat from Claire's skin. She took a deep, slow breath to buy another minute. The hardest part was keeping her nervousness from edging into her voice, leaving it high-pitched and childish. She felt like a kid, scared and lacking confidence, and she hated feeling that way. "I...I'd really like to go on another date with you." She swallowed, ran her fingertips over Claire's tanned forearm. "I want to see you, Claire." She remembered the term she and her friends used when they were about ten years old. Going steady. Yes, that's what she wanted to do with Claire. Go steady with her. Date her exclusively, intimately. See where things went. She'd always been good about not having expectations early on, which meant she was rarely disappointed. And if she was, it made it easier to move on.

"I'm not so sure that's a good idea."

"Why not?"

Claire looked away, and in that instant Ellie could see she wasn't nearly as confident as she usually projected. Claire was scared. "It's...Look, the odds of something working out between us are pretty slim. I mean, we're so different, we're—"

"Two women who have a great time together, who enjoy one another's company. That's it. That's all I'm asking for. Please?"

"Ellie..."

At the risk of pushing Claire further away, Ellie went for it anyway. "Claire, what are you afraid of?"

A long moment of silence passed. Piper was growing antsy, tugging on her leash. Ellie ached for those baby blues to swing her way, to settle on her softly, warmly, slowly. Finally they did. "I'm not sure. I think...I don't know why being with you scares me, but it does."

Ellie's stomach dropped from her throat mercifully back to its rightful place. "I'm scared too. But you know what? I hate letting fears paralyze me. And I'm tired of that voice in my head that dooms me before I even try something." It was her mothers' voices, in large part, and it was time to silence them. "Let's throw caution to the wind and do it. Let's go on another date, which, you know, isn't exactly a marriage proposal."

Claire's mouth twisted into a smile. "I'll think about it. We'll talk later this week. How's that?"

"Wimpy, but I guess it'll do for now." Ellie gave Claire's arm a final squeeze. "Bye, Claire. Bye, Rolo."

Marissa was waiting for her inside the foyer, pretending she hadn't been looking out the window at them. Ellie had seen the blinds move.

"Hmm, no good-bye kiss? Does that mean this little experiment with your mean boss is over?"

"She's not mean and she's not my boss. Hasn't been in almost two months." Ellie removed Piper's collar and leash, then filled a water bowl for her.

"What, hasn't been mean in almost two months or hasn't been your boss in almost two months?"

"Ha ha, very funny."

Marissa followed her into the kitchen and retrieved two wineglasses from the cupboard. "I need a drink and I don't want to drink alone. You in?"

"Sure." Maybe a drink would help dislodge the memory of that hot kiss with Claire today at the fort. Well, more like temporarily tuck it away so she could obsess over it later.

Marissa poured them each a glass of Chardonnay from a chilled bottle in the fridge. "So, are you going out with her again?" She handed Ellie her glass and the two hoisted themselves up to sit on the counter. There was a perfectly empty, functional table and chairs to use, but what the hell.

"Maybe. Where's Erin?"

"At some pregnant ladies yoga class. And you're evading the question."

"No, I didn't, I answered it. Mmm, this wine's good. Where's it from?"

"New Zealand, and 'maybe' isn't much of an answer."

Ellie considered shutting the conversation down, but Marissa had supplied the wine and it was amazingly good. She figured she sort of owed her one. "I want to see her again, but she's not sure."

Marissa arched an eyebrow. "*She's* not sure? What, is she nuts?"

"I appreciate the vote of confidence." Ellie's throat ached. "I'm pretty sure it's the age difference."

"Well, you're not even close to jailbait, so what's the problem?"

"I don't know. I wasn't around before the Internet. You know, like they're two different worlds. Pre-Internet and Post-Internet, and never the twain shall meet."

Wine sputtered from Marissa's lips as she exploded into laughter. "You're kidding me, right?"

"Yes. No. I don't know." Claire hadn't really explained her hesitation very well. It was like she was grasping at any old excuse to keep Ellie at a safe distance. And yet Claire was the one who'd asked her on the picnic. And it was Claire who'd initiated today's kiss. Sort of. Maybe there was hope.

"Are you serious about her?"

Seriously attracted to her, check. Seriously wanting to get to know her better, check. Seriously wanting to kiss her again, check. She was serious about all of those things, and then she thought about the way her skin tingled whenever Claire touched her or she touched Claire. The way her chest ached when Claire's gaze settled on her. The way she couldn't stop thinking about her when she lay in bed at night. And it wasn't only because she was a sucker for the woman's eyes or for her shapely ass or for her breasts that looked like heaven. Her attraction to Claire was all of those things, but it was so much more. She loved the way the two of them could pretty much puzzle anything out in such a calm, reasonable manner and the way Claire made her feel like she could do anything she set her mind to, that her previous mistakes and choices didn't matter so long as they eventually led her to the right choices. Claire was so grounded, so centered. She was a rock, and Ellie needed a rock in her life.

The breath she drew in as she thought about all these things nearly choked her. "Yes," she croaked. "I'm more serious about her than I've ever been about anyone in my life."

"Well, you're good at going after things you're serious about. So why are you holding back, letting Claire dictate what should or shouldn't happen?"

Marissa was right. Claire needed a shove, because her indecisiveness was a major buzz kill. Ellie made a mental note to call her tomorrow and nail down a third date. *Oh yeah.* Claire wasn't going to know what hit her. "You're absolutely right. I'll call her tomorrow. Now, tell me why you needed a drink. Bad day at work today?"

"You could say that. I mean…" Marissa shook her head and looked skyward. "What is *wrong* with people, you know?"

Ellie laughed. "Now that's a loaded question. Are you really talking about a specific person or is this your way of saying the whole world is going to shit?"

Marissa waved a hand in the air. "Yes to both." She was a news junkie who was always going on about the political mayhem in the United States and other countries or about the latest stupid, dangerous craze that people were doing, like last year's laundry detergent pod challenge.

"All right," Ellie said. "Why don't you tell me what specifically is bothering you today." She didn't think she was up to another rant about Donald Trump at the moment. Mostly because she'd heard them all a million times and they depressed the shit out of her.

Marissa began telling her about a seventeen-year-old girl who'd had an abortion a couple of days ago at the hospital. Normally, since she worked in the ER, she didn't concern herself with what went on in OB-GYN, but the girl had been brought back to the ER because of complications.

"Was it rape? Incest?"

"No, no, nothing like that."

Ellie had watched her cousin's face redden in anger as she told the story. "So what's got you so upset?"

"I shouldn't be telling you this. I mean, you know, confidentiality and all that, but I'm so freaking *mad*!"

"I don't want you to get into trouble, Riss. Maybe you better not tell me."

"No. I have to tell somebody." She took a long gulp of her wine. "You know that bombastic redneck congresswoman from Michigan? Barbara Harrison?"

Ellie rolled her eyes. Oh god, not another political rant. "Yes. The one who basically said all non-white immigrants should be sent back to where they came from?"

"That's the one. And she's like all super anti-abortion and anti-women's rights. I mean, Christ, does she not know she's a woman? That she wouldn't even be a congresswoman without all the hard work feminists put in over the last century? Anyway, the girl who had the abortion? It was her daughter."

"What? Why would her daughter have an abortion over here in Canada?"

Marissa's gaze pierced her. "Why do you think?"

Ellie wondered if it was because universal health care in Canada meant people didn't have to pay out-of-pocket for care. But the Harrisons weren't poor, so that couldn't be it. Then it dawned on her. "Oh, I get it. They're trying to avoid media attention by slipping over the border and having it done here, right?"

"Bingo. Can you imagine how Congresswoman Harrison would be publicly skewered for her anti-abortion stance if her constituents knew her own daughter had one?"

"Jesus. But wait a second. How would they qualify to have the procedure done here? Don't you have to be a Canadian citizen or at least a permanent resident?"

"Yes, unless they had their private health insurer pay for it, which I doubt they would do because they wouldn't want the word getting out. I heard somewhere that the congresswoman's husband is Canadian, so maybe if the daughter has dual citizenship, they did it that way."

"But you'd still have to reside here for a period of time. I remember my moms talking about how there's a lot of fraud over our public health insurance by Americans, like fraudulent copies of the insurance cards made so they can come over here and get free health care."

Marissa shrugged, hopped off the counter, and opened the fridge. "Beats me how they did it. The hypocrisy though! I mean, seriously, people. El, you want a top up?"

"Only if you are."

"Damn right I am."

Ellie sipped her wine and settled in for a long rant from her cousin about American politics.

CHAPTER FIFTEEN

Ooh Baby Baby

Bob Tanner was a no-bullshit guy who'd taken over as managing editor three years ago, making him Claire's direct boss. He had good newspaper creds, and Claire respected him. As she took a seat across from his desk, she knew by the look on his face that this was no social call. She decided to preempt whatever bad news was coming. "What's on your mind, Bob?"

Tanner picked up last Saturday's edition, which featured the story about the animal shelter and the dogs that needed homes after the terrible storms down south. "I want to talk to you about this." He held up the paper like he was holding a dirty diaper.

Ah yes, of course, the soft story on the homeless dogs. Claire bit the inside of her cheek to keep from smiling, because she refused to take his bait. He could be pissed off about the story all he wanted, but the story had struck at the hearts of readers, and feedback had been positive.

"As a matter of fact, we're working on a follow-up story. I'm hearing that our story led directly to six adoptions, so we'll freshen it up today, give ourselves a little pat on the back, remind readers that a few more dogs need homes."

Tanner had yet to crack a smile. Or show any expression other than displeasure. "I'm disappointed in you, Claire. You know this sort of feel-good drivel doesn't sell papers. Well, not enough, anyway. And I don't need to tell you our circulation is continuing to drop. Is this…" he pointed the newspaper at her accusingly, "really the best use of our shrinking resources and the best way to attract readers and advertisers?"

"At the time, yes." Claire refused to be cowed. She was no rookie at this stuff; she had almost as many years in the business as he did. "Readers occasionally want stories they can rally around, feel good about. And they've responded well to it."

"You know as well as I do that since we blew that story on the kickbacks two months ago, our reputation took a huge hit. And now we're looking goddamned soft with stories like these." He set the newspaper facedown on his desk. "We need to sell newspapers, Claire. Badly. We need to stand out from our competitors. If we don't…"

He let the threat hang in the air. Newsrooms had been gutted in recent years because of declining revenue that could be directly linked to the Internet. Readers wanted their information for free and businesses didn't want to have to pay to advertise. It was a vicious circle. Tanner could stomp his feet in frustration all he wanted, but a couple of controversial stories weren't going to save the newspaper business.

Claire hardened her jaw. "Happy stories, positive stories, sell newspapers too. Readers want a break from all the terrorist attacks and mass shootings and the latest Trump nonsense. I'm talking about balance, not dog rescue stories *instead* of stories on corruption or whatever. We need to cover all the stories in our community, both good and bad."

Tanner ran his hand roughly over his fashionable two-day-old stubble. "I know, I know. It's…head office is breathing down my neck lately. We need something good, something juicy. We need…" His eyes pinned Claire's. "We need to redeem ourselves for dropping the ball on the kickbacks story about the deputy mayor. That's what I'm saying. Something to give us a little shot in the arm, and yes, I know it's a temporary solution, but it would at least get the bean counters off my back for a while."

Heat rushed up Claire's neck at his reference to Ellie's mistake, which had happened on her watch. And now in so many words, Tanner was saying she'd better redeem herself, and soon. No need to spell out the repercussions if she didn't. Quite possibly more layoffs or even Claire's job. "I understand. Anything else?"

"No, that's it." He managed to look a little chagrined, but only a little. She understood the pressure he was under, but goddammit, what about a little loyalty to her? "I'm glad you understand."

Boy, did she ever. Asses were on the line if she and her team didn't come up with something good soon. She slinked back to her desk. She knew a good story when she saw one, wasn't afraid to go after controversy, but she'd meant it when she told him readers sometimes needed a break from the daily diet of negative news. She'd never really thought about how much she herself had needed a break from the constant stress of her job, from the harsh realities of the world, until she'd begun spending time with Ellie. Because whenever she was with Ellie, she managed to take a deep breath, to look around, to enjoy the moment. With Ellie she'd come to know peace, contentment— things she'd not allowed herself to feel very often.

Oh, shit. Ellie. Claire glanced at the wall clock. She had to get home to prepare for her date with her.

"Hot date?" Jackson called after her as she gathered her leather messenger bag and hurried through the newsroom. She scowled at him over her shoulder. Fortunately she'd already bought the groceries she needed to make tonight's dinner, but she didn't want Ellie walking in on a disorganized mess.

On the drive home, the roof down, Motown music blaring, Claire gradually shed the tension in her shoulders. Being with Ellie would make her forget, for a few hours at least, this crap with her job. She couldn't wait. She laughed as she remembered the phone call from Ellie yesterday suggesting dinner. More like demanding dinner with her and not taking no for an answer. She'd even joked that since she had a key to Claire's house, she would bring dinner over, leaving Claire no choice in the matter, and it was more a threat than a joke. Claire quickly acquiesced, offering to cook dinner for them, and while it might or might not be considered a date, she resolved *not* to kiss Ellie like she'd done at the picnic. She'd keep things friendly, platonic. Which meant not sneaking looks at Ellie's sumptuous body and her very kissable lips and everything else about her that was adorable. Nope. It was dinner. What could be simpler than that?

When Claire opened the door to her, Ellie rose on her toes and launched herself into a hug before Claire had the chance to back away or squirm out of it. She knew Claire wasn't much of a hugger, but too bad. Ellie was a hugger and she wanted to hug Claire, and dammit, she was going to.

The thrill of seeing the faint blush on Claire's cheeks streaked through Ellie. While Claire might not want to verbalize how she felt right now, her feelings were, quite literally, written all over her face. *Deny what's between us all you want*, Ellie thought, *but you'll be lying to yourself.* "I brought wine," she said, producing a bottle of chardonnay.

"Oh, thank you, you didn't have to do that."

"No, but then, you didn't have to invite me to dinner."

Claire laughed as she led Ellie toward the kitchen. "I think you pretty much invited yourself."

"Hmm, good point. In that case, the wine is my way of apologizing."

"No need for that. I enjoy your company. It's just…" Claire reached for the half-empty glass of wine on the counter she'd gotten a head start on.

"I know, I know. It's not really a date, right?" *Crap*, Ellie thought. *No kissing, no making out, no talking about kissing or talking about making out.* But there would be wine. *Hallelujah!*

"Right." Claire retrieved a corkscrew from a drawer and opened the chardonnay. "Can I pour you a glass?"

"Absolutely, thank you." Rolo bounded into the kitchen, her whole body in full wiggle mode. "Hi, baby! How are you? Who's my good girl, huh?" Ellie dropped to her knees to give Rolo some welcome belly rubs and chin strokes.

"I think my dog likes you better than she likes me."

"Nah. Like most dogs, they live in the moment. So basically the next person through the door is their new best friend. Though she does seem to especially enjoy my belly rubs. Don't you, Rolo baby?" Ellie got to her feet and accepted the glass of wine, her fingers brushing Claire's, and from there a warmth spread up her arm and straight into her chest. She was so tempted to jokingly ask Claire whether she wanted a belly rub too but decided it was best not to freak her out this early into their date. Or non-date.

"Okay if we sit on the patio? I've got some chicken and veggie kebabs on the grill."

"Sounds lovely."

Rolo followed them outside. The yard was fenced, and it wasn't long before the dog had forgotten her new best friend and embarked on a sniffing adventure. Ellie and Claire sat side by side on the sliding rocker for two, and it felt so comfortable, so familiar, as though this were a pre-dinner ritual they'd shared hundreds of time. Have a drink, sit together on the patio, and discuss their day while dinner grilled a few steps away. Ellie would trade the raucous music and dancing at The Red Zone any day for this. Because this was perfection.

"How was your day?" Ellie asked.

"Oh, the usual."

"Nothing newsworthy in the city today?"

"Not especially. Why?"

"You look a little tired, is all." Stressed, more like.

Claire sipped her wine silently, contemplatively. Something was bothering her, but in any case, she wasn't talking about it. She stretched her neck, reached up, and rubbed the back of it.

"Let me do that," Ellie said, setting her drink down on the side table.

"I'm fine, really, it's—"

"I won't bite, Claire, I promise. Well, unless you want me to."

Something hot flamed in the blue of Claire's eyes, and Ellie didn't wait for further resistance. She reached behind Claire with one hand and began to massage the back of her neck and shoulders. It took a few moments for the muscles under her fingers to loosen. She could swear she heard a moan. "You okay?"

Claire's eyes closed, and Ellie wanted to kiss each eyelid. "I, yes, it…this feels good. Thank you."

Ellie moved closer, faintly touching her lips to Claire's neck, the muscles there tightening at the contact. What she really wanted was to kiss Claire into submission, turn all those resistant muscles into jelly. Oh wait, was that kind of kissing against the rules? And if so, what else was against Claire's rules? And what wasn't? *Fuck it*, Ellie decided. She needed to kiss Claire. Her lips grazed Claire's earlobe, and she jumped like she'd stuck her wet finger in an electrical socket.

"Jeez, Ellie, wait. We can't…this isn't a date, okay?"

It was shocking that a mere touch from her could nearly make Claire jump out of her skin. Shocking but also rewarding. "Claire," Ellie said in a low whisper, and she didn't bother trying to disguise the want in it. "I can't be this close to you and not want to kiss you. You're so beautiful and—"

"No, I'm not. Ellie, I appreciate you trying to make me feel good, but—"

"Make you feel good? Is that what you think I'm doing?"

Claire stood up abruptly, a little shakily, and strode to the gas barbecue. She lifted the lid and rotated the contents on the grill. "I…I'm not really sure what you're doing, to be honest." The irritation in her voice was hard to miss, and Ellie couldn't help but wonder if she'd blown things.

She joined Claire at the grill, placed her hand contritely at the small of Claire's back. "What I'm doing is falling for you. Since we're being honest."

"Ellie, no."

"Claire, yes." Placing her hands directly on Claire's arms, Ellie turned Claire to face her. Someone had to take control here and fast, because she was not going to lose this woman over pride or fear or whatever the hell kept coming between them. "Tell me, please, what you're so afraid of."

"Ellie—"

"Please?" She'd keep begging if she had to.

"It's...Look, we're so different, okay? You're cheerful, you're kind, you give people the benefit of the doubt. I'm none of those things. I don't see the world as a very nice place. Where you look at someone in trouble and feel empathy, I wonder what their agenda is. Don't you see how different we are?"

"What's wrong with having differences? Why should we all be cookie-cutter images of each other?"

"That's not what I'm saying. I'm—"

The urge to touch Claire was irresistible and she raised her hand to her cheek, lightly cupping it. And then she raised her mouth to Claire's and began kissing her thoroughly, intently, because, quite simply, she couldn't be this close to Claire and not kiss her. And with luck, the kiss would dissolve whatever differences between them Claire thought were so damned important. Because this, right here, the way their bodies and their mouths fit together, the way this kiss made everything else seem so inconsequential, was what mattered. Clearly, Claire was having an epiphany too, because her hands moved to frame Ellie's face and she was kissing her back with sweet abandon.

"Um...Claire?" Ellie murmured against her mouth.

"Yes?" Claire's mouth had its own ideas and trailed to Ellie's earlobe, where it began a delicious exploration.

"I...I..." Everything felt so damned good, so *hot*, and she didn't want it to stop, but... "I think something's burning."

"Oh crap!" Claire spun around and popped the lid open on the gas grill. Scooping up a pair of tongs with one hand, she tossed the kebabs on the upper grill, then reached for the temperature knob. "Whew, that was close. I think that means dinner is ready."

Something else was sizzling too, Ellie decided. Namely, the fire raging in her crotch.

So much for her resolve not to kiss Ellie tonight. It'd gone up in smoke the way dinner almost had, but she'd rescued it in the nick of time. The dinner, that is. As for the kiss, there was no going back from that. She'd lost that battle at the very first challenge. Ah, well. It's not like there was some mystery to it. Her attraction to Ellie was inescapable and had the power to smash her resistance in a nanosecond. She was powerless against it. A weakling. A goner. At least there were far worse things to be defenseless against than a beautiful woman.

At the patio table, they ate kebabs of chicken, cheese, peppers and zucchinis, along with garlic bread, and killed most of the bottle of chardonnay while Rolo watched with saucer-sized eyes and waited quietly for table scraps.

"That was delicious, Claire. Thank you. You're almost as good a cook as my moms."

"Then I'm flattered. Thank you."

After dinner, it was Ellie's idea that they should take Rolo for a walk. Returning as twilight crept upon them, Claire knew what inviting Ellie back in might mean. No, *would* mean. More kissing for sure and possibly a lot more, but before any of that, they needed to talk. That is, if Claire could gain a little self-control over her lips. When Ellie looked at her with that smoky, dark desire in her eyes or touched her with that tantalizing blend of tenderness and want, Claire lost her mind.

She spoke before she had time to reconsider. "Ellie, would you like to come in?"

"Yes, absolutely!"

Oh, help, Claire thought. She poured them each a glass of wine and suggested the living room because the mosquitoes would feast on them if they stayed outdoors. Rolo curled up on her little bed in the corner, zonked from her walk and all the attention Ellie had lavished on her throughout the evening.

"She really is a great dog," Claire said, nodding in her direction. "It's like she knew I'm not an experienced dog owner, so she's been taking it easy on me. She—"

"Claire?" Ellie patted the cushion beside her on the couch. Compounding Claire's dilemma was the twinkle in Ellie's eye and the curl of her upper lip that Claire had come to recognize as trouble.

Oh shit.

Her mom had brought her up to be polite, so she sat.

"It kind of feels," Ellie said, setting her wineglass down on the coffee table so she could use her hands to express herself (could she be any more adorable?), "like we keep ignoring the elephant in the room. Don't you think?"

"There's an elephant in the room?" Okay, that was a lame attempt at a joke. Claire dropped her smile.

"There is. I went out on a limb and told you I'm falling for you, that I want to be with you. And you're leaving me out on that limb all by myself. Your words say one thing, and then your body says another. Which is it, Claire? Do you want me or don't you?"

Claire considered evading, she was getting good at it or thought she was, but Ellie's patience had clearly expired. And she didn't blame her. She hated the way her conflicting feelings kept tripping them up on this new path they were forging, and yet she couldn't help it. This was all so new, so unexpected, so frightening.

Ellie persisted. "We're attracted to each other, we enjoy each other's company. You're not going to deny that, are you?"

"No."

"I don't care that we're different in a lot of ways. I enjoy the fact that we're different. I want to explore this…whatever it is we have going on…further. But I can't if you keep throwing up roadblocks. And I'd really like it if you would tell me what keeps holding you back because I'm really not that scary a person."

"You're not, eh?" Claire felt a smile tug at the corners of her mouth.

Ellie scooted closer. "Nope. In fact, when you fired me, I'm pretty sure it was you who was the scary one."

Claire winced. "Ouch. I deserved that." She reached for her glass and took a bolstering drink before setting it back down. How the hell could she adequately explain that Ellie was way, *way* out of her league? That people would think she was—

"Claire, stop."

"What?"

"Whatever self-flagellation you're doing right now."

"Okay, here's the thing," Claire said, because to hell with it, it was time to come clean. "You're twenty-six, Ellie. You have your whole life ahead of you, while I'm sort of halfway stuck between looking forward and looking backward. I've done most of what I've set out to do in life. I mean, other than maybe travel some more, and maybe write a book one day." And perhaps fall in love, but she wasn't about to be *that* honest. "And then there's…"

"What?"

Okay, here goes. "You've got model good looks and the body to go with it. You're drop-dead gorgeous, Ellie. Which begs the question, what would you want with me?"

Ellie's mouth fell open. It took her a moment, but then her eyes darkened from brown to black. "Claire Melbourne, when are you going to get the fact that I'm incredibly, unequivocally, irrevocably, insanely attracted to you. *All* of you. Your sense of humor. Your very smart brain." Ellie rose onto her knees and scooted toward Claire.

Oh god, what is she doing?

"And your stunning eyes." And then Ellie was straddling Claire's lap, her hands on Claire's shoulders and her eyes doing that smoky seduction thing that turned Claire's brain to mush. "And your very kissable mouth. And your long, very strong legs. Oh and your ass is like the sexiest thing I've ever seen, did you know that?"

Claire shivered as Ellie's words echoed in every cell of her body. The cynical side of her brain didn't want to believe any of it, and yet she knew Ellie meant it. Every. Single. Word. Because the emotions in her face betrayed her.

"And Claire, your breasts…are amazing." Ellie's gaze dropped, her tongue darting out to lick her lips, and it was about the sexiest damned thing Claire had ever witnessed.

"Claire, you know what I'd really like?" Ellie traced her finger along Claire's jawline until she felt the muscles there contract and relax. "I'd like it if you stopped resisting. If you'd trust me."

She closed the gap with her mouth and settled her lips on Claire's, tasting the sweetness of the wine there. Her hands moved to Claire's hair, so soft and fine, and she let it sift through her fingers like warm sand. She quickened the pace of the kiss, felt Claire respond in kind. She gasped lightly as Claire's hands found her ass, cupped her cheeks, and she pushed further into Claire's body, needing the solid contact and the warmth. She moaned, and arousal flamed to life in her belly, a curl of heat slowly unfurling and spreading outward. Claire wanted her every bit as much, and the confirmation gave Ellie exactly the permission she needed to continue. She sucked Claire's bottom lip into her mouth, nipped it gently, before she entered Claire's mouth with her tongue. It was a sweet exploration, one that Claire returned until her lips trailed hotly down to Ellie's throat. Ellie arched her neck to grant better access, moaned as teeth grazed her hot skin.

Ellie was on fire. Her hips had begun a slow rocking motion, and oh how she wished Claire's hands would move a little further inward, right between her thighs. To hell with it, she wouldn't wait for Claire to make the next move. She dropped her hands to Claire's shirt, near the buttons that needed to be undone, like, right now. But first she traced a finger down the V of the shirt, toyed with the silky fabric. One button, then the next, then the next, slowly. She watched Claire's chest rise and fall, each breath growing more rapid with every button that succumbed to her mission. She was almost there, almost home free, when Claire's hand suddenly put a halt to her progress.

"Ellie, wait." Claire's voice was husky, halting. Was there anything about this woman that wasn't a turn-on? Oh, right, the constant stop signs. Those were most definitely not turning her on. "We should…"

"It's okay," Ellie whispered. "I want to make love to you. But this isn't just sex. I want to spend time with you. I want to date you. I want us to see what we have together because I'm really, *really* liking what I see so far. Please say yes."

The blue of Claire's eyes lightened, like the sun had come out, and she smiled. "Ellie Kirkland, has anyone told you what an incredible woman you are?"

Ellie rested her forehead against Claire's, smiled against Claire's skin. "Not today, no." She cleared her throat, nervous suddenly, because it was time—well, past time, actually—to define what the hell it was they were doing. "Claire Melbourne, will you date me? As in, officially date me?"

Claire was grinning—definitely a good sign. "Okay. But on one condition."

"Okay, name it." Really, she hadn't meant to answer so eagerly.

"That we go slow. In the...you know...department."

Ellie couldn't help herself. She placed her mouth next to Claire's ear and whispered, "Sex? In the sex department?"

A shiver greeted her in response. "Yes."

"This is our third date, you know." She was pushing the envelope, but only to be mischievous. It was fun seeing Claire flustered and knowing she was responsible for it.

"Ellie—"

"I know, I know. I'm only playing with you." She climbed off Claire, though it was almost painful to do so. "Fine. But I do have a question for you. About our next date."

One eyebrow lifted. "Yes?"

"Will you come for dinner with me to my parents'?"

"Um, wait, are you sure you want that to be our fourth date?"

"I do. I'm going to tell them about enrolling in the vet tech program."

"What? You've enrolled? Officially?"

"Yup."

"Wow, good for you. I think that's awesome!"

"See? I need you there for a little moral support. And, well, I'd kind of like to show you off."

"Hmm. Not use me to needle them, I hope?"

"Absolutely not." Ellie reached for Claire's hand on the couch between them and intertwined their fingers. "It's time my mothers got to know what makes me tick, what's important to me, and *you* are important to me. They need to accept me, which means accepting my decisions, without judgment and condemnation. To treat me like an adult. And if they can't do that..." It was too painful to complete her thought, but Ellie was fully aware of what the next step was.

"Well, I can't disagree with you. So, yes, if it's okay with them, I'd love to be your date for a meet-the-parents night. Even though it kinda scares the hell out of me."

"Oh, my brave one." Ellie leaned over and gave Claire another kiss. And then another, deeper one.

"Um," Claire said, ending the kiss with a smile. She reached for the television remote and clicked it on. "Boy, I sure don't want to miss the news tonight, what do you say?"

Ellie laughed. God, Claire was so transparent. "No, we couldn't possibly miss the news."

A picture of the Michigan congresswoman, the one Marissa had told her about, was on the screen. "Can you turn that up please?" Ellie asked.

"Ha, now who wants to watch the news?" Claire teased before turning her attention to the television. "I wonder what that kook is up to now? Man, that woman is a piece of work."

"Boy, is she ever. You wouldn't believe what Marissa told me the other day."

CHAPTER SIXTEEN

The Hunter Gets Captured By The Game

"Now remember," Ellie said to Claire, peering over her sunglasses at her. "Let's try to avoid talking about Erin tonight. My moms are both still acting weird about her being pregnant and postponing her residency."

"Gotcha. And how is Erin doing?"

Claire had decided to let Ellie drive the Mustang, not only because it was simpler for her to drive since she knew the way to her childhood home, but because, truth be told, she found Ellie sexy as hell behind the wheel of this vintage beauty. She liked how Ellie handled the car with grace and confidence, her hands tight on the wheel except when she needed to shift gears. The shifter and the clutch she handled smoothly, and Claire couldn't but wonder what else her hands were adept at.

"She's okay. A little depressed about having to put off her career for a while, I think. I'm not sure she's even processed yet how much her life is going to change."

"And what about you? Are you okay?"

Ellie's eyes swung briefly from the road to Claire. "Of course, why wouldn't I be?"

"Well. You're going to be an aunt, and a very involved aunt, I'm sure. And for another thing, you're starting school again in a couple of weeks."

"And thirdly," Ellie said, her eyes back on the road, a smile tugging at her lips, "I'm officially dating a very hot, older woman."

Claire laughed. "Well, I'm not sure about the *hot* part of that equation, but you're sure you're okay with this older woman meeting your parents?"

"Are you kidding? I can't wait. Dating you makes me feel like, finally, I've been given my adult card or something. It's like…" Ellie took her hands off the wheel to elaborate, but Claire quickly thrust them back into place. Ellie laughed. "Okay, okay, I'll be careful with your precious Mustang."

"You'd better, or you'll have to answer to my mother's ghost. Now what were you about to say before I saved you from crashing my car?"

"You mean before you so rudely interrupted me?"

"Yeah, something like that." Claire loved their easy banter, the gentle but intelligent teasing. She'd never really gotten it when people talked about clicking with another person; she was beginning to understand it now.

"I was going to say…" Ellie's voice wavered with emotion. "That I finally feel like an important part of my life is slotting into place. Like I was looking at a jigsaw puzzle sitting there in a million pieces, and now all of a sudden it's making sense, and I can see how all the pieces are supposed to fit together, you know? And it feels amazing, Claire. It feels like I'm not… lost anymore." She slid her hand across the console and onto Claire's thigh.

"I'm so glad, Ellie." There had been only two times Claire had ever felt completely lost in her life. The first was when her father left and the second was when her mother died. School, then work helped fill the void, pushing her forward. Those two things had been her salvation, and she couldn't imagine what it would have been like for her had she not possessed such a ferocious determination to be a journalist. And oh god, that hand on her thigh right now was making her twitch in the most deliciously painful way. A few more inches and she'd command Ellie to pull over to the side of the road.

"Good, because you're a big part of why I'm feeling the way I am. Having such a strong woman believe in me…"

The wind swallowed the rest of Ellie's declaration, which Claire was grateful for, because she wasn't ready to take the conversation to the next level. Mostly because she and Ellie had agreed to take things slow, though she supposed going slow probably didn't entail meeting your girlfriend's parents so soon. *Girlfriend.* Had that descriptor really popped into her head? Yup, it had. And it felt okay. Better than okay. "Anyway," she said, signaling it was time to change the subject because, yeah, she was still a bit of a coward when it came to matters of the heart. "I'm still in shock over what you told me about Congresswoman Harrison the other night. I mean, the hypocrisy! She's publicly equated abortion with the work of the devil, and she sneaks her own kid over here to have an abortion? Un-fucking-believable."

"I know, right? I feel so bad for her daughter. Imagine growing up with that witch as your mother."

Claire had been quietly fuming ever since Ellie told her about Barbara Harrison and her daughter's secret abortion. There were far too many politicians and public officials who didn't come close to adhering to the values they preached for others to follow. It was so damned dishonest, and worse, it was dangerous. "If that woman's constituents only knew…"

"No." Ellie removed her hand from Claire's thigh and pulled the car to the curb. She peered at Claire over her sunglasses again. "Claire, you absolutely cannot do anything with the information I told you. You understand that, right?"

"Of course I understand that. But it's definitely a story in her home state, especially with the midterm elections coming this fall. You can't—"

"No!" Ellie said more forcefully. "Marissa would kill me. And it would be extremely disrespectful to the Harrisons' daughter. It's a private matter, Claire, not a public one. Not this time."

"I disagree. This kind of story has huge implications. There's a *responsibility* to—"

"A responsibility to the patient, to the Harrisons' daughter. That comes first."

Claire shook her head. It was unfortunate that the daughter could end up a pawn if the news got out, but there was a much bigger picture at stake. The congresswoman deserved to be held accountable, but it wasn't Claire's fight, nor was it the time to argue an academic point. "I suppose it's not a good idea to argue right before we meet your moms."

"You're right, it's not." Ellie grinned and leaned over the console. "So kiss me instead."

Ellie didn't know what she expected, but it wasn't this. Her mothers were actually being nice to Claire. Not exactly warm and effusive, but definitely not cool and distant and judgmental the way she had expected them to be. Elaine had even led Claire into the kitchen to talk about the special meatballs and sauce she'd made from scratch, and now as they ate dinner, Ellie shoved a forkful of spaghetti into her mouth and considered how she would break the news about going back to school. Claire seemed to sense her apprehension—of course, shoving food into her mouth like she hadn't eaten in days had probably given her away—and brushed her thigh against Ellie's in a show of support. Now was as good a time as any, she supposed.

She set her fork and knife down. "Um. There's something I need to tell you both."

Emily and Elaine exchanged a look before Emily turned on a bright smile. "You mean introducing us to Claire isn't your only reason for being here?"

Elaine reached for the bottle of chianti and hovered it over Claire's glass. "More wine, Claire?"

"Um, sure, thank you."

The two moms were going out of their way to be polite and charming to Claire, surprisingly so, although it might have a lot to do with relief, the skeptical side of Ellie concluded. Relief because it was only Erin who was bi or something altogether not entirely lesbian. Or maybe they thought Claire could take over their mothering role, make Ellie toe whatever crazy line they seemed to want to draw for her. Whatever the reason, it was weird not being the black sheep. The rebellious side of her wanted to push the envelope just to be sure.

"Actually, yes, I did want you both to meet the woman I'm dating." She gave Claire's thigh a gentle squeeze.

"Well," Elaine said, nodding at Claire, "we think you might be very good for our Ellie here."

"Oh?" Claire straightened and wiped her mouth with her napkin, and Ellie held her breath a little. "How so?"

"We assume," Emily said, "that you were the one who fired Ellie from the newspaper."

Oh shit. Ellie hadn't mentioned that little nugget to them, but they'd grilled Claire earlier about what she did for a living, and they'd undoubtedly put two and two together.

Claire didn't show any outward sign of discomfort, though Ellie noticed a tiny splotch of red forming on her neck. "That's right, I did," she said steadily. "I realized later that—"

"No, no, you probably did her a favor," Elaine interrupted. "We always expected Ellie to follow Emily and me, and her sister, into the health care field. We still do. And now she has a chance to start over again."

The self-satisfied look on her mothers' faces made Ellie's blood boil. When she first told them she'd been fired, they'd called her boss heartless. Now they were spinning it as a good thing, a chance for her to go back into a field the two of them could be proud of. This was un-fucking-real. What about what *she* wanted? Why couldn't they simply support her unconditionally for a change? Was that too much to ask? And as for dating Claire, they weren't fooling anyone by rolling out the red carpet for her. No, it was all about what kind of influence Claire could have on her, how she might change her into someone her mothers approved of. None of it came as a surprise, but it still hurt. Ellie's eyes stung hotly and she bit her bottom lip.

Claire's hand crept into her lap to give her hand a squeeze. Thank god Claire was here with her.

Pick your battles, she reminded herself. Now for the next bombshell. "The other news I wanted to tell you is that I'm going back to school in two weeks."

Emily clapped her hands in glee. "Oh, dear, that's wonderful news! I'm so happy to hear that. Something in health care I hope?"

"Actually, yes." Ellie bit her bottom lip again and glanced sideways at Claire, who gave her an almost imperceptible wink. "I'm taking the two-year vet tech program at the college."

Elaine's fork dropped to the table with a clatter. "Vet what?"

"Veterinary technician."

It was a couple of minutes before anyone spoke. Emily finally said, "That's...I don't know what to say because, frankly, I'm disappointed."

"What? Why?" Ellie knew exactly why, but she needed to hear it.

Elaine stated the obvious. "Ellie, it's a technical program. A trade, not a profession."

Ellie rolled her eyes. Okay, that was an immature thing to do, but too bad. "I know that. I already have a university degree in journalism, plus the time I spent in the pharmacology program before that. The college is going to let me skip a couple of classes because of my previous education."

"But..." Emily took a sip of her wine, then looked at her wife in a silent plea.

"It's beneath you," Elaine said, taking the bait and speaking for both of them, biting off her words. "You're smarter than that, Ellie, better than that. The job it'll qualify you for, it's only going to pay you, like, what, twenty dollars an hour or something? I mean, if you want to work with animals fine, but the least you could do is become a veterinarian."

Ellie had to swallow hard to keep her food from backing up her throat. They were so fucking pretentious sometimes. Money and appearances and prestige, were those really more important than doing something you had a passion for? They were being terribly unfair with Erin too, barely speaking to her right now, and all because they were so consumed, so preoccupied with everyone in their family having to be excellent in every damned way, every single damned minute.

Claire cleared her throat and jumped in. "I think it's very brave of you, Ellie. You're finally going to do something you have a huge passion for. And a gift for." Her eyes flicked to Elaine and Emily to include them. "She's very good with dogs, you know. They light up when they see her, and she—"

"So as I said, why not a veterinarian then, if you must work with...with...dogs and such?" Elaine said to Ellie, pointedly ignoring Claire.

"Maybe someday," Ellie said. "But not right now. This will get me in the field, working at a veterinarian's office, and then I can go from there. I might never want to become a vet, not if I'm enjoying being a technician." She didn't want to sugarcoat things, make them think that being a veterinarian was in her future when it might not be. "It's like saying, why become a nurse when you could become a doctor? Don't you think nursing is a valuable profession?"

"Of course," Elaine replied. "But you're comparing apples to oranges."

"Actually I'm not."

Elaine huffed, stood up and began noisily clearing the plates and cutlery. Emily still hadn't said much, but her jaw was so tightly clenched it looked like she might snap a ligament. Finally, she leveled steely eyes at Claire. "Claire, if you continue seeing Ellie, I hope you're prepared for the possibility of supporting her one day, because trust me, it'll be a very long time, if ever, before she'll be supporting herself."

Ellie gasped at her mother's cruel declaration. Her hand began to shake, and she had to stuff it under her leg to make it stop. "What did you say, Mom?"

Everyone looked at Emily, the silence reminding Ellie of a spinning ride that had come to a sudden and complete stop. "You heard me," Emily said, but far less forcefully this time.

Ellie glanced at Claire, who'd visibly recoiled in bewilderment and shock. "Come on, Claire." Ellie pushed her chair back and stood up. "I think we're done here."

"Wait," Elaine said, the tiniest note of desperation in her voice. "Let's have dessert and talk this out."

"You mean so you can try to convince me that I'm doing something stupid? Or better yet, so you can belittle me some more?" God, how stupid she'd been, thinking they might actually respect her decisions and start treating her like an adult.

Claire stood too, matching Ellie's rush to escape.

At the door, Emily tried to take back her words, but it was a pathetic attempt and too late anyway.

"I'll drive this time," Claire said calmly to Ellie, opening the passenger door for her. "Shall I take you home?"

"No."

"Okay." Claire started the car and slipped it into gear, eased it onto the road. "Would you like to stop somewhere for a drink?"

"No."

A minute or two later, Claire pulled the car into an empty parking lot. "I'm so sorry about what happened back there. Can you at least, like, give me a hint about where I should take you?"

Tears were like hot needles against the backs of Ellie's eyes. She didn't want to be out in public because at any moment she might dissolve into a blubbering heap of anger and hurt and despair. Going home only meant a million questions from Marissa and Erin, and she didn't want to face that either. Looking straight ahead and with a level voice, she said, "Can we go back to your place?"

CHAPTER SEVENTEEN

How Sweet It Is

Claire made a pot of tea, poured two cups, and carried the cups on a tray along with milk and sugar and two spoons to the living room, where Ellie waited on the sofa. She had to be devastated by her mothers' reaction—even to Claire, their comments had come as a shock. But Ellie seemed determined to do the stiff-upper-lip thing, refusing to discuss it further on the ride back. And once they'd arrived at Claire's, Rolo needed to be let out, and then Ellie had spent a good ten minutes on the floor with her, giving her belly rubs and talking sweetly to her. But Claire knew all about keeping feelings like anger and hurt inside until they ate away at you, hardening you on the one hand, but leaving you afraid and unsure on the other. She wasn't about to let that happen to Ellie.

"Thank you," Ellie said, grabbing for the cup of tea like it was a lifeline. Their fingers brushed, and Ellie glanced up at her with appreciation in her eyes.

Claire took a seat on the couch too but left most of a cushion between them. "Can we talk about what happened?"

A light shrug. "Not much to talk about. Same old, same old." But in her eyes was her despair, evidence of the pounding her pride and heart had taken at the hands of her moms. "I'm sorry I took you over there. I knew it was likely to go badly, and I should never have subjected you to that."

"No, don't apologize. You wanted me for support, to be a buffer between you and your parents. I get that. I wanted to do that for you." And she would do it again if Ellie asked.

The dam broke as Ellie convulsed into tears, her hands shaking so badly that Claire had to extract the mug of tea from them. Then she was next to Ellie, her arm pulling the younger woman into her shoulder, and she let Ellie's tears soak into her blouse. If she could, she would hold Ellie like this all night long. As much as she wished she'd told Ellie's mothers where to stick their tough love or whatever it was they were doing to their daughter, this was Ellie's fight, not Claire's. Because while Ellie might need her on certain levels, she didn't need her to rescue her, to be her savior, to be a surrogate mother. Ellie was much braver than she gave herself credit for.

"Listen," Claire said matter-of-factly. "Go ahead and be sad for what your mothers aren't giving you, for the way they treat you, because believe me, it's not fair. But you're a strong woman, Ellie. You will get through this. You can have a happy, rewarding life, with or without their approval." She stroked Ellie's back in small circles. "You don't have to give them the power to make you this miserable."

"But why can't they love me for who I am? Why do they always try to shove me into the box they've designed for me? Erin too, it's just that she's gone more willingly until now."

"I can't answer that. I don't even know if they could answer that."

"I should cut them out of my life." Ellie's voice was raw and rough from emotion, fierce too. "Have nothing more to do with them. That's what I should do. Stop subjecting myself to their criticism. Stop trying to please them. It pisses me off that I've let them get to me like this all these years. Especially when I've tried so hard to be independent. I haven't even taken any money from them in three years."

"You've done nothing wrong."

"Maybe. But in their books, I haven't done much right."

"It's a big step, cutting them out of your life, if that's what you choose to do." Claire had cut her father off when he left her and her mother. Of course, the estrangement was his fault too because he hadn't tried very hard to maintain their relationship. Now he was living out west somewhere with his second wife and their teenaged child, and she hadn't spoken with him in more than a decade. "It's hard to go back if you do that, and it's not the right choice for everyone. But if it comes to that, I'd advise keeping the lines of communication open. To not shut the door completely."

The younger you were, the easier it was to pick up the pieces and rebuild. But after a certain age, it was easier to wall off the damage and leave it there. She didn't want for Ellie the mistakes she herself had made.

Ellie sat back against the couch with a heavy sigh. Claire removed her arm, and Ellie seemed to flinch from the loss of contact. It was only a moment before she grasped Claire's hand and held it between them, warming Claire, sending a tiny electrical current up her arm.

"Do you miss your mom?"

The question was like a bucket of cold water on Claire, and she swallowed back the tide of emotions suddenly swamping her. She and her mother hadn't always gotten along, mostly because they were so different in temperament and personality, but they'd survived so much together, bonded like two castoffs on a life raft. Now she had no one. Well, no one except Jackson, but this realization that she was so utterly alone was a gaping hole the size of a massive canyon in front of her. It had mostly been a choice these last few years. Now it was starting to feel pathetic. Crippling.

"I…" Claire faltered, tried to corral her thoughts, but it was like trying to capture bubbles that burst as soon as you touched them.

"It's okay," Ellie whispered. "You don't have to answer. Just know that I want to be here for you as much as you've been here for me."

Claire slammed her eyes shut, trying to sort out the patchwork of feelings, when suddenly Ellie's lips were touching hers, so softly at first they were like butterfly wings against her skin. She didn't want to respond because dammit, she needed to puzzle out what she was feeling, step back a little, but things—deep, soul-shattering things—were shifting inside her, dissolving all her navigation signs, cutting her moorings. Ellie's hand was on her cheek, stroking tenderly, and Claire gave in to the powerful urge to abandon herself to the kiss. She deepened it, pressing back against Ellie's mouth, sliding her tongue along the contour of Ellie's bottom lip. Ellie moaned as she gave entry to Claire's tongue, and the sound, so full of want and need, undid Claire. Her hands cupped Ellie's face, slid up to her hair. God, her hair was so silky, so thick and full of waves that went on forever, and it was only now she realized that she'd wanted to run her hands through Ellie's hair since that day she'd returned Piper to her. Visions of that hair splayed across the spare pillow on her bed lit up her field of vision, and then there were more visions, naked visions, as Ellie's finger trailed an exquisite trail down her jaw, her neck. It was excruciatingly pleasurable. And so was the tingling between her legs, the warmth low in her belly, the hum of excitement that seemed to electrify every inch of her skin.

"Claire," Ellie said in a voice barely recognizable. "Make love to me."

Claire swallowed the ache in her throat, stilled the fingers that were right then freeing a button on her blouse. "Ellie." Oh God, was she really about to put the brakes on this? Yup, she was. "Not like this."

"Not like what?" Ellie's breath, minty and hot like the sun, brushed her ear. "Like this?" Her hand slipped inside Claire's blouse, lightly skimmed a nipple that had gone painfully erect, and Claire gasped. Goddammit, a couple more seconds and she was going to be past the point of saying no. She needed to slow this train down. Stilling the hand inside her shirt took every ounce of her willpower and, dammit, it sucked being the reasonable one right now.

"You're upset. We're both…emotional. This might not be the best time." There. She'd left the door open a crack because this needed to be Ellie's decision too.

"Claire." Ellie said in a voice solid, strong. Any evidence of her earlier pain and anger was gone. "I want you. So much. And I want to show you how much. I want to be with you, and not just tonight. But tonight would be…" Her mouth curved into a slow smile, her dimples like bright beacons in the dark. Yes, those dimples drove Claire nuts. And yes, she wanted to kiss them. "Amazing. An amazing start. Claire, you blow my mind. You touch me in a way no one else ever has, because you get me. And I don't want us to wait any longer."

Claire's desire to be involved with the argument fell away. Her eyes dropped to Ellie's chest, which rose and fell rapidly, then trailed back up to her mouth, her very kissable mouth, and then up to her eyes, which were dark and smoky and bottomless and oh, man, could she get lost in those eyes. As in, disappear forever.

Ellie reached up and stroked her face, her jawline—her touch commanding her, showing her who was boss. For once the sensation didn't frighten her. For once, she wanted to embrace it.

"Yes," she said simply, soberly, because any other alternative felt wrong. She needed to make love to Ellie. "Yes."

They lay side by side on Claire's bed, their clothes fully and frustratingly still intact, the bedside lamp dim but strong enough for Ellie to catch the deepening shade of Claire's eyes. There was caution there, desire too, same as there was in the way Claire stroked Ellie's neck, her shoulder, the top of her chest. When Ellie reached down and pulled her own top and bra over her head and tossed them to the floor, Claire's mouth opened in soundless approval.

It was a gamble, taking control so aggressively, but Ellie went with her gut feeling that if she waited on Claire, she'd be waiting a hell of a long time. "Claire, it's okay to be nervous."

"Ellie, I'm not…all right, how did you know?"

"Because I can see it in your eyes." Could feel it in her touch, too, the slight hesitation. Ellie lay back down beside Claire and faced her. She left a couple of inches of space between them. "Will you tell me why?" She tried not to worry that Claire might be having second thoughts not only about making love, but also about their relationship, about Ellie.

A clock ticked rhythmically in the distance. Claire's chest rose and fell smoothly, her eyes dropping to Ellie's breasts before lifting again. Ellie knew her tits were pretty irresistible, and the thought buoyed her.

"I…" Claire licked her lips. Lips Ellie would rather be kissing right now. "I haven't slept with anyone in a while and I—"

"Like, how long?" Not that it mattered, but Ellie was curious as hell.

"Almost two years."

Ellie grinned. Something about Claire's lengthy celibacy infinitely pleased her. "You're practically a virgin then."

Claire screwed up her face. "That's kind of what I'm afraid of."

"What do you mean?"

"All right, it's like this. I'm rusty as hell. And since I'm about a million years older than you, my body might not be what you're accustomed to."

Ellie tried—really tried—not to laugh, but failed miserably. And then instantly regretted it as Claire stiffened and turned her face away. *Shit.* "Claire, wait. I'm not laughing, I promise." She closed the distance between them, pressing her naked chest against Claire's side. If only Claire would look at her. "None of that stuff matters to me, I promise."

"But it might, if not now then tomorrow or next week or… who knows when."

"This isn't really about me, is it?"

Claire's eyes found hers again, and even in the dim light it was amazing to see the hue in them soften to the color of a cloudless, summer sky. "Why can't I hide anything from you?"

"Do you want to?"

"Yes. No. I…It's like this. I feel physically inadequate around you sometimes."

"And you think I don't?"

Claire's brows pinched together. "You do? Why?"

"Because…" How could she say this delicately? "For all I know you've had forty or fifty lovers by now. Which makes me not nearly as experienced as you."

Claire laughed, and it was like the pressure releasing from a valve. "I can assure you I have not had forty or fifty lovers. Or even twenty. Or…well, you get the idea."

"I don't actually." Ellie grinned and propped herself on her elbow, keenly aware that she was bare breasted and Claire was, well, annoyingly not. "Tell me. How many?"

An adorable blush crept into Claire's cheeks. "Would you think less of me if I said there've only been six all this time?"

"Six? Really?"

"I know, pathetic, isn't it?"

Ellie touched Claire's chin with her finger to keep her from turning away again. "No. I think six is perfect." With relish, she thought, *lucky seven for me.*

"And what about you?" Claire asked.

Ellie looked skyward and pretended to do a mental count. "Well, let's see. Hmm…" Then she silently counted out with her fingers, first on one hand, then another. It made her laugh when Claire's eyes widened as the count increased. "Okay, wait, I'm kidding! I've had a total of three lovers. So you see? That pretty much makes us even in the experience department. Whew."

That earned a smile before Claire's eyes grazed her face, her throat, swept down to her breasts again, where they lingered. Oh yes, Claire was into her breasts all right, and instantly her nipples tightened at the thought of Claire fixating on them, loving them. Ellie leaned closer and kissed her deeply, pressing her body more firmly into Claire's. She threw her arms around Claire's neck, locking the two of them even more tightly together. It came as a surprise when Claire squirmed loose and nervous eyes clamped onto hers.

"What's wrong?" Ellie whispered.

"I'm afraid you'll be disappointed in my body. It's…not like yours." Again Claire's eyes dropped to caress Ellie's breasts, and dammit, she wanted Claire's hands, her mouth, on her breasts. Her clit twitched at the thought.

Okay, fuck this bullshit. It was time to banish Claire's stupid, unfounded insecurities, because that was exactly what they were, stupid and unfounded. Claire was beautiful, and nothing could ever change Ellie's mind about that. She wanted Claire. Wanted to worship her body first with her hands, then with her mouth.

With the kind of determination she hadn't ever exhibited in bed with a woman, Ellie swiftly climbed on top of Claire, pinning her with her body and her hands as Claire's eyes widened in surprise. "I'll be the judge of your body," Ellie said, barely recognizing the heat in her own voice. "Starting right now, because I want your shirt off."

Oh good god. Claire could hardly breathe, so exquisite was Ellie's touch as she removed her shirt. Never had she been wanted so fiercely before, and it felt…liberating, euphoric. There was no longer a need to be the one in control, to act as the brake pedal. Ellie was being more than clear what the next few minutes, the next hours, held for them.

Ellie's hands moved to her breasts and cupped them, and oh, how she wanted the tattoos of Ellie's fingers on her skin, wanted little bruises branding her. She wanted to wake up tomorrow and see those little marks because they'd remind her this actually happened…was happening. They would be evidence of how much Ellie wanted her, because she couldn't quite banish the surprise that this gorgeous young woman wanted so much to make love to her. Ellie's mouth kissed an impatient trail down to her breasts, and this was exactly how Claire wanted things— urgent and primal and insatiable. As if Ellie had sensed her need, her mouth found Claire's nipple, and she began sucking and licking at a tempo that nearly shattered Claire. Already she was dangerously close to climaxing. She worried her long dry spell might make her come too quickly, when what she really wanted was to enjoy every thrilling, tormenting second for as long as she possibly could.

"Ellie, I…" She sucked in a long, ragged breath in an attempt to gather herself. She was so hard and so wet and so absolutely blind to everything but her need for Ellie to pleasure her. "Please."

"Please what," Ellie whispered hotly in her ear.

"Oh god, I need you inside me. I need you…everywhere."

Ellie hurriedly removed the rest of Claire's clothing, and then her own pants and underwear. As she resumed lying on top of Claire, her eyes roamed Claire's body, encompassing all of her.

Claire studied her eyes because eyes didn't lie and she needed the truth. There. Yes. Ellie was looking at her like a starving woman sizing up a feast. Relief flooded her.

"Jesus, you're beautiful," Ellie murmured. "So beautiful, I barely know where to start."

"I think…" It was so damned hard to breathe right now when every beat of her heart, every surge of her blood, demanded release. She wanted to savor every touch, every look, but not right now. Right now she needed Ellie to make her come. "I might need you to skip a few steps."

Ellie grinned, slipped her smooth, naked thigh between Claire's legs, and Claire rocked against her, so desperate was her need for friction. "You're everything I want, Claire, do you know that?"

"Show me," Claire said, her voice full of gravel, thick with desire.

And Ellie did. Her fingers found Claire and danced in her wetness. Claire opened wider, arched back into the pillow, displaying her need this time without any fear or shame. She could hear herself groaning, but it was almost as though she were apart from her body. And yet she wasn't because every nerve ending felt as if it were on fire. Ellie was doing that to her, making her want her so furiously. Her other lovers had not come anywhere close to igniting this kind of desire. And she knew exactly why. It was because she'd never really let herself go with anyone else, never let herself *be*. Never trusted enough, not only her sex partner, but herself too. With Ellie, she wanted to strip down everything to its raw, inviolate state, as frightening and thrilling as the prospect was. Because Ellie would keep her safe. Ellie *was* safe.

Ellie began whispering things, dirty, delicious things that pushed Claire further to the edge. Things like, "I want to fuck you, Claire, I want to fuck you so hard that you're going to beg me not to stop." And then, "I want to touch and taste every inch of you, baby, do you know that? I want to fuck you with every part of my body."

Claire begged with her voice. And begged with her trembling body. She felt Ellie slide down the length of her, a torment in itself because release couldn't come fast enough. When Ellie's mouth found her—teasing, licking, sucking, pulsing with rapid-fire strokes—it was a sweet torture that blew Claire apart. She wrapped her legs tightly around Ellie's waist, throbbed against her mouth until her orgasm plundered her, leaving her boneless and quivering and almost in tears. The rush of emotion came as a shock, and when Ellie slid up to hold her, the very look in her eyes—tenderness, affection, joy—Claire knew was mirrored in her own.

"You," Ellie said, "are an exceptional woman, Claire. And I loved doing that to you." She boldly traced her finger along Claire's jaw, down her throat, down the center of her chest, her gaze following the path made by her finger. "So much that I want to do it again and again and again."

Claire's breath stalled somewhere in her throat. Ellie was lovely. Ellie was beautiful. But the prospect of needing her so much, of needing Ellie in her bed and in her life, was all so new and quite a bit formidable. Because as much as she adored and cared for Ellie, she understood that sex could sometimes ignite emotions that wouldn't necessarily be there the next morning. She wanted to be sure neither of them regretted tonight, that taking their relationship to this next step had been—was—the right thing to do.

"Are you…is this okay?"

"*Okay?*" Ellie's smile was ravenous, intoxicating, with not a trace of regret anywhere. "Oh, Claire."

"What?"

"Can I?"

"Can you what?" Claire tripped over her thoughts. What she needed this second was to stop thinking so damned much. Thinking held her apart from the moment. All her life, too much thinking had kept much of her happiness a fraction away. And Christ, she was tired of keeping a fucking lid on everything all the time. This unspooling of her body was such bliss. She could admit that she didn't want it to stop.

"Do it. Do you. Again and again." A wicked smile and a naughty tongue darted out from between Ellie's teeth.

Claire thrummed with desire again. "Stay the night?"

"I thought you'd never ask." Ellie kissed her before moving away. She sat up and reached for her phone. "Sorry, I need to text Marissa and Erin to let them know. And to make sure they can look after Piper."

Claire reveled in the picture before her of a naked Ellie sitting on the edge of her bed, her back to her, thumbing the keypad on her phone. She swept her eyes over her, breathed in deeply. *My lover*, she thought. *My much younger lover*. Her pulse quickened, her arousal coursing thickly through her again. "Come here," she said, her voice husky with sex. She wanted this woman. *So* much.

Ellie slammed her eyes shut, threw an arm across her face. God, she couldn't let Claire see her this way. See how much in love with her she was. Because she was never any good at disguising such things, and this was *not* the time. She could hold her sex, yes she could, like a seasoned drinker could hold their liquor, even though what she really wanted was to nestle against Claire, wrap herself around her, right here in this bed, and never wake up again. Or rather, wake up exactly like this, with Claire, every morning.

Claire was inside her, stroking deep and slow. And Ellie rode her, let the sensations take her higher and higher, until it felt like a wave about to crest and crash all over her, pulverizing her beneath its sheer power. She moaned, urged Claire to go harder and faster. When she felt Claire's mouth on her, she flew completely apart.

"Oh, I'm coming. You're making me come so hard, Claire. Oh, god!"

Her world exploded in a swirl of hot colors as her body clenched, shuddered. She surfed the waves of it as long as she could, wringing every last drop from her orgasm because she didn't want to waste a single second of it. When she came back to herself, Claire was on her elbows smiling up at her.

"Okay?"

"Much, much more than okay. Come here, baby."

Claire scooted into the crook of her shoulder. "Are you sleepy?"

"Nope. Not even close. You?"

Claire's eyes sparked, hot like the lick of a blue flame. A flame that shot straight to Ellie's center. "Nope, not tired. You make me feel like I could stay awake for a hundred years, if this is what staying awake entails."

Ellie stroked Claire's arm. She would need all night to get enough of this woman, and even then…

CHAPTER EIGHTEEN

If I Could Build My Whole World Around You

Claire carried their plates into the living room. So engrossed was Ellie in examining her LP collection (well, most of it had belonged to her mother) that Claire could only imagine the protestations if she suggested they eat in the kitchen.

"Oh, I'm so sorry," Ellie said, accepting her plate. "I wasn't paying attention. God, this looks amazing." She inhaled deeply with a moan of satisfaction, her eyes closed, and Claire was reminded of her face last night while she'd loved her, pleasured her. It was the same look of rapture and hungry anticipation, and for a moment Claire's knees nearly buckled.

"I thought we could eat in here on our laps, if that's okay."

"Mmm, more than okay. I'm starving. How did you know?"

Claire blushed hotly, remembering their insatiable kisses, their anxious hands and mouths. How many times had they made love last night and early this morning? Was it four? Five? Claire was a teenager again, relentlessly turned on, miraculously uninhibited. She'd never given and taken so much in one night with anyone before, and she would be happy to do it all over again if not for the muscles she didn't even know she had screaming at her. "I, um, kind of figured we worked up a bit of an appetite."

"I'll say. Wow, is this feta cheese in the scrambled eggs?"

"Yes. Chives too. My own creation."

Ellie arched a playful eyebrow. "I love your creations, by the way."

Claire cinched her robe tighter. In the light of day, she worried Ellie would notice her wrinkles and the bit of flab around her waist and find her, well, not the same as last night, when she hadn't been able to get enough of her. Time for a diversionary tactic. "The records you were looking at, which ones are your favorites?"

"I'm always a sucker for the Supremes. And the Temptations. But you've got some real Marvin Gaye gems in there. Smokey Robinson, too. Do you play them often?"

"No, not much. Well, unless I confess something to you."

Ellie's grin was adorable and infectious. "Ooh, what?"

"It's kind of embarrassing."

"Confessions are supposed to be."

She would never dream of telling anyone, not even Jacks, but there was something about Ellie—her honesty, the mischievous gleam in her eyes that somehow managed to look innocent—that knocked down her defenses. She wasn't quite sure when it had begun, this desire to want to share things with Ellie. "Strange as it sounds, Rolo happens to love Motown music. Discovered by me quite by accident. So we, ah, you know, sometimes put on the old records and listen to them together."

Ellie clapped her hands in glee. "Oh my god, seriously? I love that! Can the three of us do that sometime? Play your Motown records and dance? Oh, and Piper too."

Words deserted her, so Claire smiled instead. Ellie had described a scene of such domestic bliss that for a moment it made Claire's head spin. Not out of shock, but rather at the perfection and the joy it implied. Would their relationship progress to living together one day? Claire had never lived with another woman, which probably made her a bit of a freak. It was premature to even vaguely consider the idea, nor was she anxious to shake up that part of her life yet. But the sarcastic comment from Ellie's mom, Emily, continued to haunt her—the barbed insult about Ellie needing Claire to support her one day. It was a ridiculous comment, because first off, Ellie was independent and not the type of person who required a handout, and secondly, Claire wasn't the type to mother a grown woman. She never wanted Ellie to feel like she was a kept woman.

After their food was consumed over small talk, Claire set her empty plate on the coffee table and watched Ellie do the same. The air crackled with unexpected tension, and Claire could feel the weight of those soulful brown eyes on her.

"We should talk," Claire said. "About last night."

"All right. Should I be worried? Have I done something wrong?"

"No, you haven't." *Dear, beautiful Ellie.* Claire wasn't stupid; she knew damned well she'd begun falling for her, and long before last night's crazy sexed up date. But falling for a twenty-six-year-old felt like rolling the dice on her entire life, taking a gamble akin to switching careers out of the blue to something wild and risky and completely out of her comfort zone. Or quitting her job to travel the world or something. She'd never done anything so monumentally spontaneous, this crazy. But Ellie was freedom. Ellie was the unknown. But as exciting as it was, intoxicating too, she didn't know if she was strong enough to handle it. "I'm not sure I'm ready for last night to mean... everything."

Ellie's eyes searched hers. In them was a flare of panic, of wounded pride, and Claire regretted her choice of words instantly.

"Wait," Ellie said in a thin voice. "I was upset last night when we got here. My moms...Oh no! Last night wasn't pity sex, was it? Is that what you're trying to tell me?"

"No, I promise it's not that at all." She moved closer to Ellie on the couch but not too close. And though she ached to touch her, touching her made her lose her mind, made her want...so much. "I only want to be sure that—"

"I get it. You want to make sure you're not leading me on, that I'm not getting too serious too quickly." Ellie tried to smile, but it fell apart, her gaze falling to Claire's lips before darting back up. "Don't worry, I don't have a U-Haul parked outside or anything."

"No, it's not that." And it wasn't, not really. The truth was, Claire was so close to completely abandoning herself to Ellie, to handing Ellie her heart on a silver platter. And there was so much wrong with that, because her heart was fragile—a virgin in the love department, and Ellie had the power to squash it. Yes, she was a coward, but she also wasn't stupid enough to walk away from the most exciting woman she'd ever known. "I meant what I said earlier about needing us to go slow, to take things one date at a time, that's all. I've been on my own a long time, and…I'm not really sure how to do this." Tentatively, she touched Ellie's wrist. "You're lovely, Ellie." Her breath caught; she tried to disguise it with a cough. "And I've never been more scared of anything in my life." There, she'd been brave after all.

Ellie pulled her against her chest, wrapped her arms tightly around her, and it was almost too much for Claire. "Listen," Ellie whispered, planting a kiss on top of Claire's head. "We'll go slow. I promise. We'll be turtles, okay?"

Claire smiled into Ellie's T-shirt, which was one of Claire's and a couple of sizes too big for Ellie. "Turtles. I like that."

"Turtles who go on dates. And who, well, have sex sometimes?" The hope in her voice made Claire smile. The mention of sex, however, went straight to another part of her anatomy.

They'd had sex, lots of it, over the last ten hours. Claire could restrain herself, behave like a rational, responsible adult, and send Ellie on her way, get herself in the shower, and have a nice, quiet, rest of the day alone. Well, alone with Rolo because, after all, she and Ellie were taking things slow. *Right?*

Ellie's lips were on her throat, doing incredible things. Oh Jesus, when had that started? And why were those lips so soft? And so *good* at this? Claire didn't resist when Ellie's hands found their way inside her robe. A fresh flare of hunger surged through her as Ellie pulled her robe apart, laid her down on the sofa and climbed slowly on top of her.

Outside, the summer was rotting like the dried, curling leaves of a corn husk. Inside, Claire felt as ripe and sharp as new growth.

* * *

Piper nearly knocked Ellie over upon her return home. "Oh, my poor baby, mommy's sorry she was gone so long. How's my girl, eh?" She got down on her haunches and gave Piper the love she demanded, which could have gone on all day, the way Piper kept dancing and spinning and licking her face like a windup toy that wouldn't stop.

When Ellie looked up, her sister was leaning against the wall, arms folded in a matronly fashion across her chest, her expression landing somewhere between amused and scolding. "Long night? And morning? Seeing that it's past noon."

Ellie couldn't seem to halt the heat from creeping up her neck and into her face. She knew Erin wasn't truly scolding her, more like razzing her, but still. She hadn't been on a date that had lasted all night and half the next day in, like, never. "I, ah, kinda lost track of time."

"It was that good, eh?"

"It was." Ellie grinned. She was going to explode in a ball of crazy joy if she didn't talk about it.

"Then tell me all about it. As in, every last detail, especially since I have no dating life of my own and probably won't for at least the next two years." Erin rolled her eyes. "Who am I kidding. Probably the next eighteen years!"

"Come on, you will so."

"Yeah, right."

"Why don't we take Piper for a walk while we chat?" The dog was still going nuts, acting like she hadn't seen her master in a week. Ellie clipped the leash on her and grabbed a poop bag from a box in the front hall closet.

"Great idea."

It was cloudy, the threat of rain heavy in the air, but from Ellie's best guess, they had a couple of hours yet. Down drafts had begun cooling the hot, moist air.

So?" Erin bumped her shoulder playfully.

"So...it was pretty great."

"Well, duh! You wouldn't have been out with her all this time if it wasn't. So did you have an insane amount of sex or what?"

"Actually, yes."

Erin's eyes popped before a stupid grin split her face. "You *do* have it in you. Way to go, El!"

"You're not the only Cassanova in this family, you know."

"Yeah, well, look where that got me. So don't make me wait anymore. Tell me the truth."

"About...?"

"Are you totally in love with Claire Melbourne or what?"

Ellie stopped to let Piper sniff a pee spot on the grass from some other dog. "Maybe. I think so, yes." The full sensation in her chest confirmed it. "When I'm with her, I feel...good, you know? Great. Like I can do anything, be anything. The way she looks at me, like I matter, like what I say and think and do, matter to her. She treats me like an equal, even though I know she still has this huge problem with our age difference."

"If she treats you as well as you say, it sounds like her problem with the age gap is about her and not you."

"That's what I think too. I keep trying to tell her it doesn't matter to me, that I'm attracted to her in every way possible, exactly the way she is. And that our differences make us more interesting to each other."

"So give her some time to get used to the whole thing."

"I will. I'm pretty sure she's freaking out a little right now."

"Have you told her you're in love with her?"

"And send her running in the opposite direction? Absolutely not." They resumed walking after Piper tried to pee three times over the old pee spot. "She wants to go slow, and I've agreed."

Erin chortled. "Slow everywhere except in the bedroom?"

A rush of giddiness nearly overtook Ellie. "Something like that."

"So tell me all about your date from start to finish. Did you go to dinner? To a show? Did you go make out in that awesome car or wait until you got back to her place?"

"Actually, we had dinner with the E's." It was their nicknames for their mothers that they'd begun using around the time they turned ten.

"Seriously? You took your date to have dinner at our moms'? Are you *crazy*?"

"Yes. Well, not crazy, more like a glutton for punishment. They actually seemed to like Claire, I think, but they weren't so okay with me going back to school to become a vet tech. As a matter of fact, they said some pretty shitty things to me."

"Ellie, they're not going to change. Haven't you figured that out by now?"

"I guess I haven't. I mean, I have, but I keep hoping…"

"That makes you an optimist, but it doesn't make you right."

Her nature was to give people the benefit of the doubt. What she wasn't so good at was knowing when to pull the plug, when to stop putting up with something that wasn't working. Just like she should have walked away from journalism before she got fired, although, in her defense, she had successfully left pharmacology before she'd gotten too invested in it. "Have you been back to see them since you told them your news?"

"Nope. And they haven't contacted me, either."

Their pace slowed as their moods darkened. "Jesus Christ. That's so fucking wrong. You're carrying their grandchild. I don't understand how they could do this."

"Did they mention me at dinner last night?"

"Nope."

"See? There's no coming around, El, I'm telling you. If they could put me on an ice floe, they would."

"Come on, I refuse to believe they're that heartless. I'm hoping they need a little more time to get their heads around it, that's all."

Erin's eyes snapped to Ellie's. "Like they get their heads around your career choices? I guess you need them to shit on you a few more times before you believe they're not going to change."

Ellie's throat tightened. It was difficult to believe their parents didn't love them and wouldn't eventually support them. But her sister had a point, and it was the same point Claire had made. How long should she keep putting up with their crap? She didn't want to, had given herself plenty of pep talks that she'd stand up to them, but every time she thought about giving them an ultimatum, she chickened out. "You know what? Forget about me. It's you who needs their support." Erin would give birth in a few months. There wasn't much time left to sort things out before their family grew.

"I'll manage. I always have. All these years, I only let them think I followed their wishes because I was loyal and dutiful, but the truth is, I wanted to become a doctor not for them but for me. It's what I've always wanted to do. My wishes happened to align with theirs, that's all. I would have become a doctor with or without their influence."

"Maybe you should tell them that."

"I don't think they're in any mood to hear anything I have to say right now."

Ellie linked her free arm through Erin's. "You know what? The most important thing is that we have each other."

"I'll second that."

"But I still think we need to give them one more shot. It's only fair to give them a chance to realize what they might lose."

Erin's sigh was laden with the weight of the world. "Are you proposing we give them personality transplants so they'll suddenly become human? Not sure that's medically possible. In fact, if it was, I'd bottle it and sell it and become an instant billionaire."

"I'd be happy to be your partner in that endeavor." Ellie tried to picture what her life, and Erin's, might look like without their mothers in it. It was a scary prospect, because Emily and

Elaine had always been there, larger than life with their staunch opinions and their oversized ambitions. Egos too. But even when the first thing out of their mouths was criticism, they'd never abandoned their daughters. But being there physically wasn't enough anymore. The prospect of winning their approval was more and more remote and a hell of a lot of work. It was time she and Erin stood on their own two feet, and really, what was the worst that could happen? They had each other, they had Marissa, Ellie had Claire, and Erin would have a family of her own.

"I'm not sure how many more shots they deserve, El."

"No, you're right. I think it's time they realize once and for all that they either support our decisions and love us unconditionally or they lose us both. And their grandchild."

They walked in silence for a while before Erin whistled low. "That's about as ultimatum-ish as you can get. But I'll tell you one thing. I refuse to let my child grow up being treated as a second-class citizen by them. So, yeah. I'm in."

Nausea was like a fist to Ellie's stomach. This was a monumental step, but they weren't kids anymore. Erin was having a baby and Ellie was finding love for the first time in her life. Emotion thickened her voice. "You know what? I think we're finally growing up. And it feels fucking awesome!"

There was a smile in Erin's voice. "So tell me more about Claire. When's your next date?"

"She's got a busy few days coming up at work, and I've got to get ready for school. Oh and plus we're supposed to be going slow."

Erin scoffed. "Meaning sex three times a week instead of every night?"

"Oh stop! Believe it or not, it's not just sex." And it wasn't. Sex was merely the icing on the cake.

Gone was Erin's sarcasm as she fixed Ellie with a serious gaze. "I know it's not. I think Claire's the best thing that's happened to you since...well, growing up with me."

Ellie bumped her sister's shoulder playfully. "Oh, I so hope you're right."

CHAPTER NINETEEN

My World Is Empty Without You

Jackson scampered into Claire's office and closed the door, holding up his laptop like a trophy.

"Jesus, you startled me." Claire tossed her reading glasses on the desk. She'd been going through yet another email from her boss, Bob Tanner. He'd begun tossing story ideas at her—controversial, headline-grabbing stories, as if she couldn't come up with any on her own. How annoying. Insulting, actually.

Jacks sat down across from her and plunked his laptop on her desk, flipped it open, and powered it up before glancing at her. "Oh. My. God," he declared, his eyebrows nearly hitting the ceiling. "You did it, didn't you?"

"Did what?" Claire rubbed her eyes from too many hours spent staring at her computer.

"Come on, Ms. Coy. You got laid, didn't you? And loved it, by the look on your face."

"Excuse me?" *You ass, Jackson. Jesus.* Was she that transparent? God help her if she was.

"Sorry," he said, looking contrite. "I'll rephrase. You and Ellie made passionate love to soft music and the softer glow of candles. Ooh, or maybe it was under the stars, in the backseat of your Mustang. After a romantic dinner, of course. And you look exhausted, but in a good way."

"Are you reading romance novels on your lunch break again?"

"As if I'd need to do that. I get all the romance I want right at home."

"Well, good for you. Now, can we talk about whatever it is you're dying to show me on your laptop?"

"Priorities, my friend. And your love life is—excuse me, *was*—priority number one. Now that we've solved that little… Oh wait. Where are my manners? Was it totally lovely?"

"What?"

"With Ellie!"

Claire's cheeks burned.

"It was, wasn't it?"

Lovely was one word. Hot was another. Sweet, amazing, delicious all came to mind, not to mention magnificent. "All right, yes, it was wonderful. Now can we get on with whatever brought you in here? Besides my sex life, that is."

Jacks heaved a dramatic sigh. "Fine. Be that way. But the next time we go out for a drink, I want to hear all about it. Especially your wedding date. Do you need some help planning it, darling? Because I would *love* to help."

"You know, you really are too much. And with an imagination like yours, you should have gone into fiction writing, not journalism."

"I'm too happy for you to be insulted by your little comment. But speaking of journalism, I've been looking into Congresswoman Barbara Harrison and her teenaged daughter."

"Of course you have." She'd mentioned the secret abortion to Jackson over a drink, wanting to vent, because venting about it to Ellie wasn't an option. She hadn't asked Jackson to look into it as a possible story, but it would have been naïve of her to think otherwise. If the rumored abortion hadn't happened on Canadian soil, local soil, it would be total a non-starter for a Canadian newspaper. Even then, so what? Would her newspaper's readership really care that some American politician's kid had an abortion here? Claire was unconvinced.

"Look," she cautioned. "Don't get too far ahead of yourself. I'm not even close to being convinced it's a story. Or at least, a story for this newspaper to do." Like a lot of people, she was so sick of politicians who said one thing and privately did another, so disgusted by the self-righteous, right-wing blowhards who wanted to take away people's freedoms in the name of religion or misogyny. The emotional side of her wanted to punish Barbara Harrison and her kind. But it wasn't her job, or the duty of the newspaper, to punish anybody.

"I know that, boss, but this is some interesting shit. I was able to confirm that a seventeen-year-old girl had an abortion at the hospital on the date you specified, but the patient's last name wasn't Harrison. It was Benson. Angela Benson. Benson is the last name of Jim Harrison's mother, with Jim being Congresswoman Harrison's husband. He grew up in Windsor and his mom has lived here all her life."

"How do we know this Angela Benson is in fact Angela Harrison?"

"We don't, technically. But the address given for her is the same address belonging to Jim Harrison's mother, Irene Benson. Apparently she remarried when the congresswoman's husband was a teenager and she changed her name from Harrison to Benson."

So Ellie's information had been correct. Connecting the dots was where the real journalism work took place. "How did you manage to find all this out?"

"I, ah, happen to be friends with a guy in the hospital's finance department. I had to sweet talk him a little. And promise him a very expensive bottle of wine." Jackson was soon sporting a blush of his own, which only deepened when Claire pointedly raised her eyebrows at him. "All right, all right. He and I had a thing a few years back."

"Hmm. Guess it pays to be friends with your exes, huh?"

"Damn right it does."

"I don't know, Jacks. It's still idle gossip. Abortion isn't illegal in Canada, and our readers are Canadian. They don't care about Barbara Harrison and her politics because it doesn't affect them. She's a source of entertainment, I'll give you that, but we're not *The National Enquirer*."

"I know that." Jacks broke into a triumphant grin. "What I haven't told you yet is that Angela Benson/Harrison and her father, who accompanied her to the hospital for the procedure, used an Ontario government-issued insurance card."

"Does the kid have dual citizenship?"

"Yes."

"So what's the problem? I don't see anything shady there."

"That's where you're wrong. To qualify for an OHIP card, you have to be a citizen or landed immigrant *and* to have resided in Ontario for at least the past 153 days." Jacks called up the government website on his laptop and showed Claire.

Her heart pounded the way it always did when a good news story began to take shape. The adrenaline rush was one of the things she loved about journalism, and breaking a big story was the biggest adrenaline rush there was, but it was her job as editor to play devil's advocate and to do so calmly. "So maybe she's been staying here with her grandmother for the past few months?"

"I don't think so. I checked with the school board and she's not been enrolled in any schools here over the past year under Benson or Harrison."

"Homeschooled? A dropout?"

"Maybe but I doubt it. I snooped around the grandmother's neighborhood, asked a few neighbors if they've seen a young woman around Irene Benson's house and they all said no."

"All right, but that's not exactly concrete evidence if you're telling me you think they're defrauding our government by using our health care system when in fact they don't qualify for coverage."

"That's exactly what I think is happening and don't worry, I'll get more evidence."

If it was true, it was a one of the biggest scoops for the newspaper in years, in line with last year's scoop about a local doctor who'd defrauded the government of more than a million dollars over three years through false billing. Readers were incensed. This too, she was sure, would incense them, but there could be absolutely no shortcuts. The evidence would have to be compelling. "Have you tried to talk to Irene Benson yet? Or the kid? Or her parents?"

"No. I don't want to tip off the family yet. But I've filed requests under the Freedom of Information and Protection of Privacy Act to get a look at Angela Benson's Ontario Hospital Insurance Plan card and the family's application for the card. My next step is to prove that the kid has been living in Michigan full time and going to school there the past year, making her ineligible for this OHIP card they seem to have magically gained."

"What about the Ministry of Health? Have you talked to them yet?"

"Nope. I don't want to tip them off yet either, in case they decide to get busy covering their tracks. This could be incredibly embarrassing for the government. People will question whether the Harrisons bribed a government official, and even if they didn't, how many other people have illegally acquired health cards? Hundreds? Thousands? I don't know about you, but I'm not so keen on our universal health care system helping people who don't pay taxes here. These are my tax dollars, Claire. And yours too."

"All right, I get all that. But why would the Harrisons risk using a fraudulent health card for the procedure? I mean, why not simply come over here and pay a doctor to do it?"

"They can't. Doctors here don't work for cash, like they do in the United States. If you're an American and you want to use our health care services, you either have to somehow have an OHIP card or you need your own private health insurer to pay for it. Which I assume the Harrisons rejected so there wouldn't be a paper trail with their private insurer. Easier to slip over here and pretend you qualify for our public health care than to risk having it done in the US and having the information leak out. And besides, I don't think many people around here would guess who the Harrisons were or recognize their faces. Speaking of which, who did? You never did tell me where you got this beautiful tip."

"And I'm not going to." She'd protect Ellie, and by extension Marissa, at all costs. For one thing, Ellie would never speak to her again if her name got dragged into this, and for another, Marissa could lose her job or be severely reprimanded for breaching patient confidentiality. Claire began gnawing on the earpiece of her reading glasses, something she did when she had to think through something serious. "There's another potential aspect to all of this." It was one that tore at her heart. "Roe vs. Wade is heating up in the States again. If that ruling gets overturned and women lose their right to an abortion, they might start streaming over the border looking to have the procedure done here." It would be a human rights crisis, but it would also tax the Canadian health care system. It might already be a brewing crisis if others, like the Harrison girl, were finding ways to have an abortion in Canada.

"Good point. I want to keep going with this, Claire. Do I have your permission?"

The story was already growing legs, and quickly. Allowing Jackson to continue to investigate was the right thing to do, even though her heart told her she was on dangerous ground with Ellie. Ellie was clear that she'd spoken to Claire in confidence. She wanted to protect her cousin and protect the girl who'd had an abortion. Claire got that, but if fraud had been committed, the newspaper had a duty to expose it. She closed her eyes briefly. She didn't like these ethical quandaries, especially involving someone she very much cared about, but dammit, this was important. She was doing her job, and doing it properly. Which meant she'd deal with Ellie later, *if* Jackson's legwork amounted to anything more.

"How long before your freedom of information request gets processed?"

"Should only be another week, maybe less."

Claire didn't need to spell out to her most senior reporter that the anonymous information gathered so far—Ellie's tip via Marissa, plus Jacks's ex-boyfriend in the hospital finance department—wasn't enough to base a story on. Anonymous sources compromised the credibility of any story. But if the actual documents supported the fact that the Harrisons lied about residency and had used a government-issued card for an abortion, then she'd have little choice but to approve a story. *Is it wrong*, she thought a little desperately, *that I sort of hope this thing doesn't get that far?*

"All right, look. Keep going with this, but keep it quiet, and do not let any of this see the light of day without consulting me at every step, okay?"

"Don't worry. I wouldn't dream of going rogue on you. Now, when are we going out for another drink?"

* * *

Ellie's stomach twisted in knots as Emily and Elaine ushered her and Erin in. They'd declined dinner, saying they weren't hungry but that they wanted to talk. The mood was somber, and while her gut told her a good outcome was remote, giving their mothers one last chance was a necessary step.

Emily set to making a pot of tea while Elaine tried to initiate small talk.

"I guess you know why we're here," Ellie finally said once tea was served on the back patio.

"What's on your minds?" Elaine said, her tone light but unable to hide a trace of anxiety.

"We need to clear the air," Ellie continued, while Erin, usually the take-charge one, sat in silence. Perhaps because she'd never disappointed their mothers in her life and probably didn't relish the idea of starting now. That was the thing about Erin; she'd grown up without much adversity.

"Sorry, what about?" Emily replied.

Damn. They weren't going to make this easy. She cleared her throat and thought of Claire. Claire who was strong, poised, direct, self-assured. She'd love to channel her right now. "We came here because…because you guys are pissed off at us and we think it's terribly unfair and—"

Elaine's jaw dropped. "Pissed off? Is that what you think?"

"Yes. At me for entering the vet tech program at the college. Well, and not settling into a career yet. Actually, not settling into a career in medicine, to be exact. So I guess this isn't exactly new territory."

Emily pursed her lips and shook her head. "Honey, that's not—"

"No," Ellie said. "Let me finish. Maybe pissed off isn't the right word. Disappointed is probably more accurate. Contemptuous and maybe even disgusted too. And not only with my career choices, but now with Erin because she's pregnant. And maybe because she's bisexual too." Why not throw another log on the fire?

Erin's leg, which was touching Ellie's under the table, twitched in response.

"And," Ellie continued, hardening her voice, "we want you both to know that your lack of support is not acceptable to us any longer."

There was a long moment of silence before Emily finally broke it. "I don't understand what you're saying, Ellie. And Erin, have you lost your voice? Do you agree with your sister?"

Erin cast a nervous glance at Ellie before straightening up and placing her hands on the table. "Yes, I agree with her. We came here to tell you that we may not do things in our lives that meet your approval, but we're adults. We have been for a long time now. And we appreciate everything you both have done for us, but we can't, we can't…"

"We *won't*," Ellie interrupted, "allow ourselves to be subjected to your criticism and disapproval anymore. It's not helpful." That was the understatement of the year. "In fact it's hurtful. Really hurtful. Look, you've raised us with all the tools we need to make our own lives, our own decisions. It's long past time that you let us do that."

"But, but..." Both women spluttered in unison before falling silent. It was so rare for them to be at a loss for words, to be challenged like this, that Ellie and Erin passed each other a glance of surprise.

Slowly and enunciating each word, Elaine said, "What exactly are you two saying?" Leave it to her to distill things down to the bottom line.

Erin found her voice again, thank god. "Look, I'm having a baby some time after Christmas, all right? And I—"

"Speaking of the baby," Emily interrupted, "what are you planning to do about your medical career? And where will you live? What will you do to support you and this child? I mean, what's the *plan*? Do you think everything is going to magically fall into place for you or something? Or that we'll look after it all? Fix everything for you?"

Erin absorbed the verbal blow with a slack jaw and eyes that clouded over. "Of course I don't expect you guys to fix my life or to look after me and the baby! I'm not twelve years old, Mom. I'll figure it out. And I'm not throwing away my career. I'm going to resume my residency in twelve months."

"And who's going to look after the baby when you resume your career?" The words shot from Elaine's mouth with the velocity of bullets. "Do you not realize the long hours involved in a residency? The crappy pay? Plus the work that it takes to look after a baby? How are you going to manage all of this?"

Erin slammed her eyes shut, and Ellie had a new understanding of what it was like to sit and watch their parents verbally skewer one of their daughters. It happened to be Erin at the butt end of it for once, and while Ellie had dreamed for many years of seeing her perfect sister on the receiving end of their mothers' fury, the reality of it wasn't so fun after all. It sucked.

"She will manage," Ellie ground out. "And I'll manage in my new program at the college. What we need from you both is to let us make our own way, but also to support our decisions, to trust that we will sort out our own lives all on our own. Jesus, it's *our* lives! Don't you get that?"

"Of course we get that," Elaine said. "We want to see you girls make the right decisions, that's all. To have the best lives you can possibly have. We've always wanted the best for you both. Always."

"Then let us decide what the best is," Ellie said.

Erin stood in a rush, and Ellie followed her lead. Neither had touched their cups of tea, still steaming in the late August evening air, which was beginning to have a nip in it.

Her voice awash in tears, Erin said to her mothers, "I can't do this anymore. I can't be in your lives if you won't accept me and my baby. I'm going to be a *mom*." She choked on the last word. "And I'm done being around anyone who doesn't respect me, who doesn't respect my choices. And I most certainly won't be around anyone who doesn't love my baby."

She tore out of the house, leaving Ellie to throw a final, despairing look over her shoulder at their mothers. The two women were crushed—slouched in their chairs, their expressions twisted into shock and sorrow. Ellie almost felt sorry for them, mostly because it'd obviously never occurred to them that their daughters might possess spines. And that their daughters might, in one fell swoop, collapse their perfect little world.

"You know where to find us," Ellie said to them.

CHAPTER TWENTY

Ain't No Woman Like The One I Got

"Have you heard anything from them since?" Claire asked Ellie, who'd spent the last ten minutes recapping the ultimatum she and Erin had dropped on their mothers.

Ellie shook her head. There were smudges under her eyes, suggesting she hadn't slept much in the few nights since the big family showdown. Claire found herself wanting to kiss away those dark smudges, to do other things to Ellie that would brighten her eyes, make her laugh, moan, light up, forget her troubles. Tonight they were at one of the wineries along the northern Lake Erie shore, eating braised lamb chops and roasted potatoes, a candle flickering in the middle of their table, bringing out the gold in Ellie's brown eyes.

"I'm sure they'll contact you once they've absorbed everything, had time to think about it. They'll come to their senses, Ellie. How could they not?" If they were reasonable women who loved their daughters, they'd come to the right conclusion, do the right thing. If they didn't, they didn't deserve Ellie and Erin in their lives.

"I don't know. They've never really needed anyone. Their careers and their marriage take up all the space in their lives. It's been like that all along." Ellie's eyes had a faraway look to them. "Sometimes I've wondered why they chose to have Erin and me at all, you know? It was like they were following some sort of script for how to have the perfect lives."

"Making the decision to have children can't be easy, and it's never easy for two women to have children together, so I'm sure they went to a lot of trouble to make it happen. They won't risk losing their daughters and their grandchild. No one with a maternal bone in their body is going to let that happen."

Claire's home life had been the polar opposite to Ellie's. Her father had never been much of a father, even when he was still living with Claire and her mother. He worked all the time; they never took family vacations, rarely did things together. He didn't seem to care that he had a kid. Maybe he was a better father the second time around, with his new family, but Claire didn't really want to think about that. To her, he was a stranger and always would be. Ellie, on the other hand, at least had had two parents who were involved in their kids' lives. Even if that involvement came with a lot of strings.

Ellie sipped her wine in silence. She looked maxed out. "Can we change the subject? I don't want to talk about them anymore. They'll either come around or they won't. It's beyond my control."

"You're right, it is. Sweetie, are you sure you're up to being out tonight?" *Sweetie?* She glanced at Ellie to see if she'd noticed the term of endearment. Yup, she most definitely had, judging by the sloppy grin on her face and the new light in her eyes. The cool thing was that it didn't feel nearly as weird to Claire as she feared.

Ellie leaned closer over the table, her grin firmly in place. "I'm more than up for spending an evening with you, are you kidding me? Looking forward to tonight is the only thing getting me through this week."

Claire blushed hotly because she'd been feeling exactly the same way. She was unsure how this going slow stuff was supposed to proceed, especially when she found herself thinking of Ellie at inopportune moments, like during the morning story meetings at work or while mocking up a layout for the next day's paper. Ellie was the warm breeze that snuck up on you and ruffled your hair, kissed the back of your neck. The kind of breeze where you wanted to close your eyes and lean into its embrace.

"Shall we go for a walk along the lake path?" Dessert was a no-go. There was nothing like a young, hot girlfriend as motivation to watch what she ate.

"Love to," Ellie said, tossing her napkin on the table while Claire gave her debit card to the server. Ellie had earlier insisted on covering the tip, and Claire let her. It was no big deal to Claire to pay for their dates. She was working full time, after all, made a good salary, and her house, which had been her mom's, was fully paid for. But she never wanted Ellie to feel that she was being taken care of, that she was being squired around and treated like a trophy or something. If she could only afford to contribute ten or twenty dollars toward dinner, Claire was more than happy with that. Ellie's company was worth a hundred times that.

Holding hands, they strolled along the paved path that lined the shore of the lake for a couple of thousand yards or so. The night was silent but for the soft lapping of the waves, and always when Claire was near a beach like this, she wished for a home or cottage along the shore, where she could fall asleep and wake up to the gentle rolling swells of the lake emptying itself onto the shore. She breathed in the scent of grass, of salt-less water, and enjoyed the companionable silence between them. It was a refreshing change from what she'd experienced with the women she'd dated in the past, who seemed to feel the need to fill every second of silence, to take up all the air in the room, ultimately smothering any interest from Claire. Ellie let her breathe, let her be. And then the cell phone in her pocket buzzed. *Dammit.* It buzzed again, and again she resisted checking it, until Ellie told her to go ahead.

"No, it's okay," Claire insisted. "Nobody but Jacks or somebody from the paper would be bothering me at eight o'clock on a Friday night. Jacks knows I'm out with you, and I'm off duty at the paper. If there's a problem, the night editor can handle it." She wasn't usually so casual about blowing off a call from work. If she were doing anything else tonight, she'd be all over her phone, but it was Friday night and she was with her girlfriend, and finally, miraculously, she had a life.

"What if it's important?"

"Nothing can be more important than being out with you. I don't ever want to be one of those people who's constantly on their phone when they're with their..." She was about to say loved one, but that might be presumptuous. "...their person." Yes, that was it. Ellie was her person, and the absolute last thing she wanted to have to think about tonight was work. Except it reminded her that she really needed to tell Ellie that Jacks was working on what could end up being a story about the congresswoman's daughter. Ellie would be pissed, even though it might never become a story. Still, she deserved to be told it was a possibility. First things first, though. She plucked her phone from her pocket, refused to look at the screen, and promptly turned it off. No more interruptions tonight.

"I appreciate that, Claire. Thank you."

Ellie's eyes, as they swept over Claire and lingered, were as dark as the water, and Claire shivered in pleasure. She licked her lips, so strong was her need to taste Ellie's skin. She wanted Ellie's arms around her, wanted to relax into her embrace, shelter there. How long had she craved a lover's touch like that? Never, it occurred to her. "Would you, um, care to go back to my place for a nightcap?"

Ellie lifted Claire's hand and twirled beneath it, which made Claire laugh. "I thought you'd never ask."

Claire was unusually fidgety on the drive back to her place, fussing with the radio, indecisive about whether the convertible top should be up or down, and Ellie wondered if she was nervous about the prospect of sex. Which was really confusing, because they'd already had sex. Wonderful, glorious, can't-get-enough-of-each-other, sex. When she couldn't take it anymore, she reached over and stilled Claire's fingers on the radio dial.

"What's wrong, Claire?"

"Nothing. Why?"

"You're acting like you're nervous." She waggled her eyebrows and shot her a teasing look, even though the only light inside the car came from the glow of the dashboard. "Are you scared of me?"

"Should I be?"

Ellie dropped her hand to rest it on Claire's thigh. A thigh that was warm and trembled a little beneath her touch. No, Claire wasn't nervous about sex. Claire wanted her as much as she wanted Claire. She'd hardly been able to take her eyes off Claire all evening. Well, her cleavage, in particular. The swell of her breasts beneath the silky fabric of her shirt and the smooth, slightly freckled skin of her chest left exposed. She leaned closer so she could breathe in Claire's scent—sunshine and mint and something citrusy. "You should only be scared of me if this car can't go any faster."

Claire squeezed the fingers resting on her thigh. "It can go plenty fast, trust me. Look, I need to talk to you some more about that Michigan congresswoman and her daughter. When you told me—"

"No, wait. I told you that in confidence, Claire. You know that's where it has to end."

"The thing is…Jackson's been looking into it."

"What?" Ellie felt her jaw clench, her stomach too. "Please tell me you didn't break our confidence."

"I did, but it was outside of work and I was venting." Claire managed to look contrite, but not enough for Ellie to forgive her. "I didn't ask him to look into it, but he sort of…ran with it. He does not know the source, I promise you. And we never run stories like this without a second and a third source, plus legal advice, so it's a long way from—"

"Wait, a story? You mean he's going to do a *story* on this?" *Jesus Christ*! Marissa was going to kill her, and she'd have every right to. She hadn't meant for Claire to go all reporter on her about this. It was going to be a disaster. "You're his boss, Claire. Can't you shut it down?"

"At this point, no. There's nothing really to shut down because it's still in the exploratory stage. Not to mention that I'd be a shitty editor if I told him to stop. No, not shitty. Negligent. I'd be negligent and incompetent if I made him stop. And it's still very early stages. There's a lot of corroboration, a lot of steps needed before it would ever see the light of day."

"Claire, you can't do this." Ellie removed her hand from Claire's thigh, clenched it into a fist. The only thing she could see, could think about, was that Claire went behind her back. "You don't have a right to invade that young girl's privacy. Or to betray me. Marissa told me in confidence, and then I told you in confidence. It's not right to take it further."

"I know, sweetie, and nobody but me knows where the information came from. I agree with you that the daughter having an abortion isn't news. I mean, it's extremely interesting, given her mother's public views on abortion and other things, but that alone isn't enough to run with, particularly because this newspaper has no responsibility to an American politician's constituency."

"I hear a *but* in there." *Oh, this wasn't good.*

Claire pulled the Mustang into her driveway, hit the button on the car's visor to open the garage door, and pulled in. The door slid noisily down behind them. Claire killed the engine but didn't budge from the car. Neither did Ellie.

"The thing is, there might be more to it than the embarrassment factor for Barbara Harrison. There might be fraud involved. Barbara Harrison and her husband may have defrauded our public health care insurance system. They're not Canadian residents and yet they may have used an Ontario health insurance card for their daughter."

Ellie didn't want to hear any more. "That's not my problem. And it's not yours either."

Claire tilted her head back and squeezed her eyes shut, though her voice remained calm, steady. "It's kind of everybody's problem if a crime's been committed. It's also my tax dollars, and yours too."

"No. That young girl will suffer, and it's not her fault her parents are idiots. And Marissa could get into a lot of trouble."

A minute of silence passed, then another, before Claire spoke. "Do you want me to take you home?"

Ellie's throat tightened, and she cleared it roughly. This whole evening was suddenly going to shit, and it was the last thing she wanted. She wanted to be in Claire's arms and to forget about the last five minutes. "Do you want me to go home?"

"No. I want you to stay."

"All right."

Wordlessly they entered the house. Rolo bounded out to greet them, yawning, tail wagging happily.

"Hi, baby," Ellie said to her, her mood lightening. Dogs always made her feel better because she loved how they lived only in the moment. She reached down and petted the dachshund's soft fur. "Who's my good girl, huh?"

"Come on, Rolo, let's go outside for a pee." Claire stood with a leash in her hand, her face unreadable. They were at a standstill, and Ellie waited until Claire returned from the backyard a few moments later before picking up the conversation again.

"Claire, promise me there'll be no story in the paper until we've talked this out some more. And I need to warn Marissa about what might happen." Claire should never have taken the information further, but Ellie knew some of the blame was hers too. Journalists were like cops or doctors, never truly off duty, and she'd been stupid to think Claire wouldn't at least have been tempted to do something with the information. "I can't let the Harrison girl be part of any story. Not her name and not her situation. I mean, the abortion and stuff."

Claire stepped closer, and it was all Ellie could do not to rush into her arms. But she needed assurances first.

"I promise you nothing's going to happen without my permission and my hands-on supervision. And if it does go forward, I'll do everything I can to mitigate the fallout for the girl. I can't promise anything beyond that."

Ellie hadn't realized she was holding her breath until it more or less exploded out of her. "All right. That's a start. And you'll let me know if it's going to see print?"

"I will."

She moved toward Claire until there were only a couple of inches separating them. "You, um, said something about hands-on supervision?" The thought of Claire touching her heated her from the inside, made her a little dizzy. Her need to be touched was a hunger that annihilated everything else, because she couldn't be this close to Claire and not have the two of them touching one another.

"I did," Claire whispered, her mouth almost, but not quite, brushing her ear. "Do you trust me, Ellie? About the other thing?"

"I do." Claire wouldn't lie to her, wouldn't use her. She placed her hands on Claire's shoulders and gently pushed her against the nearest wall. "I need your hands on me."

Claire kissed her, placed her hands on Ellie's head, threaded urgent fingers through her hair. "You want my hands on you?"

Ellie tugged Claire's lips with her own, claimed Claire's bottom lip and sucked it gently, then harder, then softly kissed her swollen lips. "Yes."

"Where?" Claire whispered urgently. "Tell me where."

It was unreasonable, irrational, how much she wanted Ellie. And not only now that they were alone, in private, but all through dinner and throughout their walk and then on the drive home, she'd thought of nothing but the feel of Ellie beneath her hands, beneath her mouth. She'd even fantasized about slipping off to the restaurant's washroom with Ellie and having her way with her. Taking her right there, in the toilet stall, hiking up the bright summer dress she wore and running her hands all over her. The backseat of the Mustang had tempted her too, even though it was a tight space. She'd never been this excited about making love to anyone before. Not even as a college freshman enjoying her first romance. This insatiable hunger for Ellie was insane. And fucking wonderful.

Ellie had slipped her dress off and stood in Claire's bedroom in a lacy pink bra and matching underwear, and the only thought that managed to filter through to Claire was, *How did I get so freaking lucky?*

"Please," Ellie said as Claire fluttered her fingers down Ellie's side, over her hips, down her thighs in a long, silky caress. Ellie's breath was thready, her voice high and tight. Her eyes were closed, and her neck arched back, as though she were waiting for something divine to happen.

Claire knelt before her, wanting, needing to worship Ellie with her mouth. She placed her hands on Ellie's ass, squeezing gently, inhaling the scent of her arousal, letting Ellie's soft moans of anticipation fill her, energize her. As much as she wanted to hurry things, to give Ellie the immediate release she craved, she wanted to enjoy every second, wanted to remember every little thing about Ellie's body—how it felt, how it looked, how it smelled, how it moved, how it tasted. Especially when she did things to her, like skittering two fingers over the silky underwear, lingering over her heat, and Ellie, with a pleading moan, took Claire's hand and ground it against her.

"Impatient, are we?" Claire said, blowing a breath against Ellie's heat. "I can cool things down if you'd like."

"Don't you dare!"

Oh, how tempting it was to tease and torture. If only she wasn't worried Ellie would pay her back with the same later. That, plus the fact that she wanted to taste Ellie almost more than she wanted to breathe. She moved her mouth closer, placed her tongue against the smooth material of her panties, flicked it slowly and ever so lightly against the damp cloth. It was intoxicating, the moist heat emanating from Ellie, knowing how much she was turning Ellie on, understanding how much Ellie wanted her. *Oh, dear god,* Claire thought, *I could do this for hours and never get tired.*

"Claire." Ellie's breath came in short bursts. "Please. You don't know what you're doing to me."

Oh yes, she knew exactly what. Using one finger, she nudged aside Ellie's underwear, exposing only a tiny part of her sex. Her tongue took the place of her finger, licking and moving closer to the center, almost but not quite reaching its target.

"Oh Jesus, Claire," Ellie whimpered. Her hand was at the back of Claire's head, guiding her closer in need of more friction. But Claire resisted, determined to take her at her own pace.

She licked slowly, edging closer, her hand moving the panties further down to make room for her tongue's exploration. Ellie quivered, her moans growing louder and more insistent with every stroke of Claire's tongue. When Claire found the hard pearl of her clit and took it into her mouth, Ellie let out a cry that nearly made Claire come. Ellie didn't hold anything back in bed—a wild abandon that was new to Claire. It wasn't that Claire's previous sex partners were reserved in bed, it was Claire. She'd never felt free enough, trusting enough, to fully let go. Or perhaps it was because her heart had never been so invested in the act. With Ellie, she wanted to feel everything, right to the depths of her soul. And what she wanted to feel for herself, she wanted to give too.

She wondered if Ellie was so into sex with her because she too was falling in love. Oh, it was true, wasn't it? They were falling in love. Maybe already *had* fallen in love. The realization stole Claire's breath, left her tingling, but not frightened. If this was love, she could do this. Wanted to do this. If that's what this glorious feeling in her chest was. But her thoughts fell away as Ellie rocked against her, faster and faster. Claire's tongue stroked Ellie's clit in time to her demanding hips. She knew Ellie was close, but she wanted—needed—to be inside Ellie when she came. She slipped in a finger, then another, and was met by the kind of warmth and wetness that made her never want to leave.

When Ellie came, her shuddering was so violent and so sudden that it took Claire by surprise. "I've got you," Claire mumbled, holding onto Ellie to steady her. She guided her to the bed, let her down gently, even as Ellie continued to tremble from her orgasm's final spasms. Claire crawled onto the bed beside her and held her, dropping tender kisses on her neck, on her collarbone.

"Oh, Claire," Ellie said. Her voice hitched with emotion. "I…"

Her fingers were in Claire's hair, tousling it, and Claire wished she'd finish whatever she was about to say. But Ellie's mouth had clamped shut, her eyes swimming with unshed tears. If she said she loved Claire, then what? Declaring love was uncharted terrain. It would drive their relationship to a whole new level, one with so many more layers, so many more risks. The idea should have frightened Claire, but surprisingly, it didn't. It exhilarated her.

Ellie had begun moving on top of her, and Claire's arousal flared again. She wanted, needed, Ellie to do all the same things she'd done to her. Methodically, Ellie removed Claire's clothing, and only for a brief second did Claire worry about her body. Ellie seemed completely unconcerned about the few extra pounds Claire carried, and steadily, Claire was beginning to believe Ellie when she called her sexy and gorgeous.

Ellie made love to her tenderly, but not slowly. Every touch, every stroke of Ellie's tongue, was fervent, full of deliberate meaning, and it took Claire only a couple of minutes before she was bucking against Ellie's mouth, her orgasm tearing through her and then leaving her shuddering and weak. Her need was sated but it wasn't gone. It would never be gone, not with Ellie. Ellie moved beside her, pulling Claire against her chest, and stroked her cheek with the kind of tenderness that made her want to weep. She knew it, couldn't deny it; she was in love with Ellie Kirkland.

Ellie awoke not long after the sun was up and tiptoed out of the bedroom, grabbing Claire's robe on the back of the door. Though she didn't have to be at the café until late morning to start her shift, she was used to getting up early, so the fact that it was Saturday morning meant little. She'd given serious thought to snuggling with Claire and softly awakening her with kisses so they could make love again, but Claire was tired, had said something about it being a long work week, so she'd let her sleep.

She whispered to Rolo to follow her out of the bedroom so she could take her into the backyard for a pee. If these overnight dates became regular, and she hoped they did, she'd have to see if she could start bringing Piper with her. It wasn't fair to Marissa and Erin to have to look after her. And she missed Piper.

After letting Rolo out for a pee, Ellie put the coffee on, then went to the front door, because she knew Claire had the newspaper delivered each day, and reading it was something she could do quietly while Claire slept. She picked it up off the porch, pulling it out of its plastic wrapper as she went back inside and closed the door. And there, splashed across the top of the front page in bold black type, was the headline: "Cross-border health fraud?" And below that was the subhead: "Congresswoman's daughter has abortion in Windsor."

Her heart stampeding in her chest, Ellie read the story while still standing on shaking legs. It had Jackson's byline, and it contained everything she'd told Claire about Barbara Harrison's daughter and more. It didn't name the girl, but it didn't have to. Anyone could Google the congresswoman and find her daughter's name and photos of her. The story said the abortion had been done using a fraudulent health card. *Jesus Christ*! Why hadn't Claire told her it would be in the newspaper? She had promised she would tell her first, promised the story wouldn't see the light of day without lots of corroboration and evidence. She'd lied.

Ellie needed to think about what to do. There was an unnamed source from the hospital's finance department, a spokesperson from the Ministry of Health, and a comment from the Harrison girl's grandmother, who lived on the city's west side, saying she didn't understand what was happening, that she hadn't seen her granddaughter in almost a year. There were copies of government documents that listed the Harrison girl as residing with her grandmother since last fall, in direct contrast to the grandmother's comments. There was nothing in the story remotely connecting information to anyone on the nursing staff, but there would undoubtedly be an investigation at the hospital to source the leaks, which could be bad news for Marissa. *Shit shit shit*! She needed to get home, needed to warn Marissa. As for Claire...*Oh, god.*

She halted outside Claire's bedroom door, the newspaper clutched tightly in her hand. A sob caught in her throat. She didn't want to see Claire right now, but her clothes were in the bedroom. She opened the door, unsure whether to wake Claire or to collect her clothes and sneak out.

Claire made the decision for her, waking with a start and sitting up in bed, reflexively pulling a sheet across her chest. "Good morning! I...sorry, I didn't hear you get up."

A fresh wave of anger hardened Ellie's jaw and she tossed the newspaper onto the bed. "So the promise you made, about giving me a heads-up before moving ahead with the story, was that bullshit? Was this the plan all along? String me along? Get as much information out of me as you could?"

Claire's eyes landed on the newspaper, and with her free hand she picked it up. Her mouth dropped as she scanned the headline. "Ellie, I promise you, I had no idea this story was running. I don't understand what happened. I did not approve this." Her voice was high, as if she couldn't quite believe it herself, but that wasn't good enough for Ellie. Nothing could fix this now.

Ellie scrambled to put her clothes on, while Claire wrapped the sheet tightly around herself and leapt out of bed. With propriety came a sure sign their intimacy was in pieces.

"Ellie, wait. We can figure this out together. Let me find out what happened." Claire reached for her cell phone on the nightstand, fumbled with it. Probably the missed calls last night had something to do with this mess, but the details weren't Ellie's problem. What was her problem was the fact Claire had lied to her. And that Claire had ultimately used a private conversation as fodder for a news story.

Ellie backed out of the bedroom and headed for the front door, tears beginning to fall.

"Ellie, please. Don't do this."

Claire followed her, the sheet making her look like a ghost, her expression bordering on panic—something Ellie had never seen before on the always-in-control Claire Melbourne.

Ellie stormed out the front door and began walking, her anger quickening her strides. She'd hail a cab or hop on a bus first chance she got, because she could not stay in Claire's presence any longer, where she was sure she'd say hurtful things, things she couldn't take back. Any guilt she felt for walking out on Claire was no match for her anger and her feelings of betrayal. Clearly, Claire's job was far more important to her than her affection, or love, or whatever Ellie had been stupid enough to believe Claire felt for her.

CHAPTER TWENTY-ONE

My Whole World Ended (The Moment You Left Me)

Claire was in no mood to be pacified or reasoned with when she stormed into the newsroom. She knew the two people she needed to see were here—Bob Tanner and Jackson Hurley—because their cars were in the parking lot, along with that of the weekend reporter.

The first thing that caught her attention was the sound of phones ringing. Everywhere. Jackson was at his cubicle, hunched over, typing on his computer with a phone stuck to his ear. She rushed over to him and hovered impatiently, trying to radiate her unhappiness from every pore of her body. Screaming at the top of her lungs was an idea. So was strangling him. Finally, he hung up, his eyes reluctantly drifting to Claire's.

"I know, I know," he said, holding his hands up as though she were about to rob him. "It wasn't my idea to run it today, I swear."

"What the fuck happened?"

"I was working late on the story yesterday. Tanner was hanging around the office. He came over, demanded to see what I was working on. I couldn't very well—"

"And nobody thought to include me?" They were going to take the story to Tanner later, but only when and if she was confident it was ready to go to print. That was the deal, because she knew the minute Tanner got wind of what they had, it'd be full steam ahead, with or without her reservations.

"I tried to call you last night. So did Tanner, but you weren't answering."

Shit. She'd shut her phone off, wanting no interruptions during her date with Ellie.

"I told him we should wait until we had your approval, but he read it, said there was enough to run the story, and that it was perfect for the Saturday edition, because all the other news outlets would have trouble picking it up over the weekend. He emailed it to our lawyer right away and got the green light to print it. There was no stopping him, Claire. Jesus, you should have seen him, it was like Christmas and his birthday all at once. I—"

"Dammit, Jacks. I trusted you." He could have come to her house, done something to let her know what was happening. But she also understood what it was like to be a reporter breaking a big story—the adrenaline rush, the sense of urgency followed by a satisfaction that couldn't be matched in any other way, except perhaps in playing elite sports. It was easy to get carried away, to get stuck on a single track. As for Tanner, all he cared about was getting head office off his back.

Jackson's eyes dropped from hers as she quietly seethed. The two of them, they'd been a team for so long, which was why it hurt that he had shut her out at the last minute. "I'm sorry," he continued. "I didn't want it to run without you on board, but Tanner insisted. You know how he can be. I wouldn't have let him have it if he hadn't practically wrestled it out of my hands."

"There's always a choice, Jackson. Even pulling your byline as a last resort, which I see you didn't do."

He recoiled as if she'd slapped him. "Claire, please don't hate me. This story is huge, you know that." Now he sounded like a desperate kid pleading to be spared certain punishment. "And Tanner was right about the timing of running it over the weekend. It put us way out front. Hell, reporters from all over the US have been calling here, trying to get something, anything from us. The phones won't stop ringing. And honestly? The story was ready, Claire."

Claire collapsed into the empty chair beside Jackson's. There'd been a permanent knot in her stomach since the moment Ellie held up the offending newspaper little more than an hour ago. The look on her face—shock, hurt, and finally sadness—had cut Claire to the bone. Ellie had not answered her texts or calls since. She brought a hand to her face now, covered her eyes, as she tried to think what to do.

"I'm following it up today," Jackson added, oblivious to the depth of Claire's sorrow. "The health ministry is scrambling, so is the hospital. They're in major damage control. The Harrison family won't say anything beyond no comment, but they've hustled together a couple of lawyers. I'm trying to interview family friends, colleagues of Barbara Harrison's. Tanner says…" Jacks looked at her and finally got a clue. "Wait. What's going on? You look like your best friend died, but I'm alive and well, thank you very much."

Ellie would come around, eventually. She *had* to. *Right?* Claire knew she had broken a trust. Knew she hadn't done enough to keep control of the story, that she hadn't done what she told Ellie she would do. But it would be okay. It had to be, because she couldn't imagine losing the woman she loved over a damned story in the newspaper.

Her throat tightened; she cleared it roughly. What she really wanted to do was cry. "I think I fucked up big time. With Ellie."

"Why? What does Ellie have to do with this?"

Claire shook her head, swallowed back the sob clogging her throat. Right now she needed a friend more than she needed a colleague. "She was my source, Jacks. And now everything's…"

Ruined, she wanted to say. She shook her head in futility. She should have known this would happen. Her job was so much easier when she didn't give a shit about anything—or anyone—else.

Jackson's eyebrows rose. "No. Ellie's a smart girl. She knows you love her. This was not your fault. If it's anyone's fault, it's mine." He shook his head, looking, finally, genuinely sorry. "I didn't know she was your source. Fuck."

"I know. It's how I wanted it."

They stared at one another, two old friends and workmates who had gone many rounds both as a team and sometimes even against one another. But love getting in the way of their jobs? Making them rethink their approach to journalism? That was a first.

"Claire, I have to be honest here. As much as I love Ellie and as much as I love you, this story is bigger than her and bigger than whomever she heard it from at the hospital. And it's bigger than this…this…impasse you're having with her. You know I'm right. We were right to do this story."

Claire stood and paced behind her friend, needing to do something with her coiled energy. Being right didn't feel so good when your whole world was falling apart. "It's not just Ellie I wanted to protect. I wanted to protect the kid. Angela Harrison. What about her? What kind of hell must she be going through now?"

"I'm sorry she's being hurt by this. But this is bigger than her too. You've heard the murmurings about her mother being groomed for the governor's seat one day. *Somebody* would have dug this up eventually. Why not us?"

Claire knew all the arguments. It was the newspaper's duty to report exactly these kinds of stories—government fraud, an entitled politician duping the public. It was terrible that an innocent teenager had gotten caught up in it, and it was one of the unfortunate byproducts of the business. It was exactly why journalists weren't supposed to let emotions—their own or someone else's—dictate their actions. She was no rookie in this business, and neither was Jackson. It was ugly sometimes, plain and simple, but Ellie would never see it that way.

"I know. But it didn't need to happen this way." It would be a while before she would stop being ticked at Jackson. Tanner too. "I'm going to talk to Tanner. Rip him a new one."

"Don't." Jacks placed his hand gently on Claire's wrist to stop her. "You're in no mood right now. And he won't listen anyway. He thinks this is the best thing that's happened around this place in a decade. He's on the phone to CNN right now."

Claire sat back down, slumping in defeat. Sometimes she hated her fucking job. "All right. Show me what else you've dug up today."

* * *

"I should be giving *you* the foot massage," Ellie said, her feet resting in her sister's lap. They were on the sofa in Ellie and Marissa's living room. "You're even starting to show now."

"True, but I'll need the foot massage in about three months when I start getting really big. Anyway, never mind about me. How was your first day?"

She ran through what had been a pretty uneventful first day of her new college program—course outlines and expectations for the rest of the semester, plus meeting her classmates and instructors. Tomorrow they'd start on lab procedures and animal anatomy and physiology. She'd have a little more free time than her classmates, being allowed to skip a couple of general education electives because of her prior education. Though it wasn't truly free time, because she was still working at the café part-time and walking Mrs. Gartner's dog, Maggie, occasionally. Poor Rolo. Since she didn't want to see or talk to Claire right now, she'd texted her to beg off helping out with Rolo, using school as an excuse. It wasn't fair to the dog, but she really needed space from anything to do with Claire right now. What Claire had done was wrong, unforgivable. Who throws a seventeen-year-old girl under the bus like that? And then there was breaking Ellie's trust. And breaking Marissa's trust too.

"I thought you'd be more excited about starting your new course," Erin said, her face acquiring that look that was part worry, part judgment. "It's Claire, isn't it?"

Ellie had already told Erin and Marissa about the news story, about the betrayal. Marissa had predictably thrown a fit. She calmed down only when Ellie explained that journalists didn't give up their sources lightly. In fact, it was usually only on a judge's order. Sometimes not even that. She'd heard of reporters and editors going to jail rather than give up a source, though it was highly unlikely this situation would amount to anything so dramatic.

Erin tried to be Switzerland, announcing that she wasn't taking sides. Ellie knew that wouldn't last long. And it didn't.

"I've let you storm around here and sulk for a couple of days now. It's time to woman up, El."

"What the hell is that supposed to mean?"

"It means you're acting like an idiot."

"What? So this is all *my* fault? I'm not the one who plastered that crap all over the front page of the newspaper."

"So you really think Claire lied to you when she said she wasn't going to print that story until they had more information? And that she would tell you before it went to print?"

"If the shoe fits..." She didn't know Claire to be a liar, wouldn't have expected it of her. But Claire was hardcore when it came to her job. She lived and breathed journalism. If it meant a story that would boost her career or win awards or something, well, who knew?

"Come on. She wouldn't do that to you. She cares about you. And I know you care about her. Just last week you told me dating her was the first right decision you've ever made in your life. How can you throw all that away?"

"How can I throw that away? I'll tell you exactly how! I'm done with people who don't treat me with respect, who act like my feelings don't matter, who treat me like I'm a...a child or something."

"Don't bring our mothers into this. That's not fair."

Ellie extracted her feet from her sister's lap and stood up. "Fair? You want to talk about *fair*? How about that seventeen-year-old kid whose life story is on every news channel and every newspaper from here to God knows where now. That kid who made one mistake and now—"

The front door opened and slammed shut. Marissa dropped her knapsack with a thud and stood at the entry to the living room, her face the shade of a freshly starched tablecloth.

"Oh shit," Ellie murmured. "What happened?"

"That Harrison girl? Angela Harrison? I heard at work she tried to kill herself last night."

Ellie's stomach dropped to her shoes. She was afraid exactly something like this would happen, compounding the tragedy.

Erin spoke first. "Is she going to be okay?"

"Yes, thank god. It was an overdose, but she got to a hospital in time. It happened in Michigan. The husband of one of my colleagues works at the hospital she was taken to." Marissa's eyes bored into Ellie's. "Not a *word* of this to your girlfriend."

Ellie fled from the room before her tears spilled over.

* * *

Claire had no idea how far she and Rolo had walked, except her feet were beginning to ache and Rolo was starting to lag behind at the end of her leash. She picked the dog up, stroked her, apologized to her like she was speaking to a child. Funny how dogs so quickly took on the role of a small child, all cute and cuddly and totally dependent. What she hadn't expected was that she'd become such a doting doggie parent, talking baby talk, stopping at the pet store on the way home from work the other day to buy Rolo a toy because she'd missed her. *I'm becoming a dog lady*, she thought morosely, *with nothing else in my life to occupy my attention. Or my heart.*

When she looked up, she saw Ellie was on a collision course with her, walking Mrs. Gartner's dog straight toward them. She looked around for an escape route, but there was none. *Screw it.* Ellie was the one ignoring her texts and phone messages. A week had gone by and nothing from her, except a one-line text saying it was best if she didn't walk Rolo anymore because she was too busy with school. Fury pulsed through Claire. She hadn't known the damned story was going to run when it did, that it was going to be hijacked by her superior, and yet Ellie was acting like she'd intentionally misled her. Ellie was being unreasonable.

Rolo, the little shit, barked to announce their presence to Ellie, straining at her leash. Ellie looked up. Her eyes widened, then narrowed as irritation clearly supplanted her surprise.

"Hi," Claire said first, deciding to take the high road.

Ellie nodded.

"How's school going?"

"Good. Not too hard."

Well, fuck. Was this really how it was going to be? She'd held this woman, kissed every inch of her body, touched her everywhere, tasted her tears, tasted her arousal, bared her soul to her. She adored Ellie, and being this close to her brought an ache to her soul. Love was such a mystery, a mystery she no longer thought she was up to solving. Not if it was going to be this hard.

"Ellie, please don't."

"Don't what? Make things uncomfortable for you? Like you did for me?"

"I didn't *do* anything to you. That story, it wasn't supposed to—"

"Claire, it doesn't matter about me, okay? But that girl...she tried to kill herself, did you know that? Her life, it's destroyed now."

Claire had heard. Newspapers and news outlets in the United States had run the story about the suicide attempt, though Claire had chosen not to. Not that Ellie was about to give her any marks for that, clearly. "I'm sorry. I'm so, so sorry about that." There was so much more she wanted to say, but Ellie was like a brick wall—impermeable, immovable. Her eyes, there was still something in them, something soft, something like affection when she looked at Claire, and it gave her fresh hope. She reached out a hand to touch her. "Ellie, I miss you. I—"

"No, Claire. I can't do this right now. I'm sorry."

And then she was gone, striding away with Maggie trotting happily beside her. She didn't look back, not even a glance, and Claire's heart shattered into about two hundred tiny pieces that were as sharp as broken glass. How the hell was she supposed to fix this?

She took Rolo home, topped up her water dish, sprinted to her Mustang, and fired it up. There was one place she needed to go, one person she wanted to talk to right now, and the urge surprised her. She wasn't one of those people she saw while driving past cemeteries who sat at a loved one's gravesite, pouring out their hearts. But now she was. *I'm exactly like those people*, she thought as she helplessly dropped to her knees in front of her mother's grave marker a few minutes later. She didn't visit often enough, only on her mom's birthday and the anniversary of her death, but the guilt she felt was overtaken by her anguish.

"Mom, I don't know what to do," she whispered, feeling stupid, but not stupid enough to shut up and get back in her car. "You would love Ellie. I wish you'd gotten to meet her. She's fun and she's sweet and she loves that damned Motown music of yours." Tears ran hot down her cheeks. "But she's so much more than that. Deep down, she's a tiger too." Ellie was so much like Claire's mom, it was almost uncanny. She'd never given her mom enough credit for mostly raising her alone, for working hard at a job to support them both, for being strong even when Claire thought she was being weak. She'd made sacrifices so Claire could go to university, so Claire could follow her dreams. And she'd given her daughter the best possible kind of shelter: love. "God, you two are so much alike." She laughed until she cried. "I can't lose her, Mom. I can't."

CHAPTER TWENTY-TWO

Standing in The Shadows of Love

Ellie knew before she saw Jackson Hurley's face that he was going to try to convince her to give Claire another chance.

She had agreed to meet him at the Café Au Chocolat, after she'd closed it to customers. It was 9:15 in the evening and she was tired from her first week of classes, having grown unaccustomed to schoolwork. She liked Jacks, but the shorter the conversation, the better. Number One, her issues with Claire weren't any of his business; and Number Two, her issues with Claire weren't any of his business. Oh yeah, plus she was exhausted.

He greeted her with a kiss on the cheek. He smelled good, but gay guys always did. He'd once told her, in his big brother voice, that if you smelled bad, it was the first thing people noticed; if you smelled good, it was also the first thing people noticed. *Whatever.* She wanted to go home and curl up with Piper on the couch and a glass of wine.

"Can I make you a cup of coffee?" she asked, trying to sound more pleasant than she felt.

"I would love that, but only if you're having some."

She didn't really want coffee, which definitely meant this was going to be more than a five- or ten-minute conversation. But he looked boyish and sheepish and quite a lot hopeful, and she felt her heart give a little squeeze. He'd always been good to her at the newspaper, a loyal friend. "All right." She went to a coffee machine and placed a prefilled packet of coffee grounds in the basket, pressed the button and waited for it to sound like a miniature mechanic was banging away somewhere inside it.

"Do you miss her?"

She hadn't been prepared for such a blunt opening salvo. Of course she missed Claire. Missed her like crazy, because Erin was right: Claire felt like the only right, the only *good*, decision she'd ever made in her life. After walking out on her, she'd felt carved out, as though a vital organ was missing. A constant sting behind her eyes matched the burning sensation in her chest. It sucked, really sucked, because she'd fallen for Claire. But dammit, it was as though Claire had had no intention of giving any weight whatsoever to her concerns about running the story in the newspaper, that she'd only been placating her by listening, by promising to keep her in the loop. The worst part was not knowing what was a lie and what was the truth and whether she could trust Claire to help her sort it out. That was the root of the problem right there. Could she trust Claire anymore?

She busied herself with the two cups of coffee and carried them to the small table in front of the gas fireplace where Jacks had planted himself. The fireplace had been shut off and she wasn't starting it up again, even though it only involved pressing a button on the remote control. No way was she going to make things too cozy and encourage him to stay long.

"Here you go, on the house." She smiled at him but the effort felt like the slow cracking of cement.

"Thanks, Ellie. You don't have to wait on me. Your shift's done, right?"

"Right." She sat down across from him and doctored up her coffee with a bit of cream and sugar.

"Well?" he said, but there was no urgency in his voice, only kindness. "You didn't answer my question."

"Look, I don't really want—"

"She misses you, you know. She looks like shit. She hasn't smiled or laughed since all of…this. I've never seen her so defeated, so down. It's breaking my heart to see the two of you like this."

"I'm sorry she's not happy, but what's done is done. She can't take back what happened and I…Look, I'm really busy with school right now, okay? And with my sister and other stuff and I …" She sighed quietly, brought a hand reflexively to her temple, where a headache was taking root. What she really wanted was to be left alone.

"Sweetie, listen to me. You and Claire are my two favorite people. You belong together. You're great together, and if you would talk to her, you'd—"

"No. Absolutely not." She wanted to hang on to her fury a while longer, because if she talked to Claire, she'd burst into tears and forget all about being mad. She'd almost done exactly that when she'd run into her the other evening while walking Mrs. Gartner's dog. She'd had to force her feet to stay in one place, pretend they were encased in concrete, and remind herself that she was pissed off because, yes, Claire had looked defeated, had yes, she'd looked like she wanted to fall into Ellie's arms. And while part of her understood it was stupid to let a newspaper story come between them, it was about so much more than that. She needed to be able to trust and she needed to be treated with respect by the people she loved. End of story.

Jackson set his jaw and aimed his gaze at her like two well-aimed darts. "Fine. I can take a hint. But there are some things you need to know."

Ellie sipped her too-hot coffee and listened as he explained that Claire had been completely unaware the story was going to run last Saturday (Had it only been six days? It felt like a month). Their boss decided to green light it without Claire's input or consent, while she had wanted to proceed cautiously and hadn't even fully decided if the story would ever run or if it would end up on the cutting room floor. "I have to tell you, I too agreed with Claire about proceeding cautiously. At first. But the more I looked into this, the more I saw that we *had* to run this story and that we couldn't sit on it much longer. People at the hospital, in the community, were going to start talking. It was going to come out anyway, Ellie, I can promise you that. If not now, a week from now or a month from now, but it would have happened. Being mad at Claire is not helpful. Be mad at me if you want someone to be mad at."

Not helpful? Be mad at him? Ellie started to screw up her face to verbally hurl something back at him when he held up his hand and started talking again.

"I'm sorry, and I know you already know this, but journalism is a nasty business sometimes. It means you have to stomp all over people's feelings, publicly expose their mistakes, their weaknesses. And yes, sometimes it really sucks. I don't like hurting people or embarrassing people any more than you do. And neither does Claire. But Ellie, Claire and I and the others—we have a duty, a responsibility. We can't ignore when laws have been broken. We can't ignore it when people dupe our government or when our government looks the other way or grants special favors to certain people. If we did that, we'd be every bit as corrupt as some of the people and organizations we expose."

Ellie crossed her arms over her chest. What Jackson said, she'd learned in journalism school and in her months of working at the newspaper, but philosophy, when applied, was a son of a bitch some times. "That girl. What about her? Why does she have to pay for all this crap by having her life carved up and tossed around in the court of public opinion? How is that fair to her?"

"It's not fair, of course it's not. And I'm sorry she got hurt. But the decision to run the story didn't come lightly. We tried to spare the girl as much as we could, but..." He dropped his gaze to the table. "Other media, as you know, were only too happy to delve into that part of the story. We can't control every facet of it once it's out there."

Ellie clamped her mouth shut. She knew Jackson had some valid points, but she still ached for that seventeen-year-old girl. And she ached for Claire, too, as much as she tried not to.

Jackson reached for her forearm across the table and gave it a squeeze. "Baby girl, you know I love you, and I'm saying this because I love you. But you need to grow up."

Ellie's ire turned molten hot. How dare he talk down to her, like she was some stupid kid. "If growing up means hurting innocent people, then I won't do it."

"No," he said, and she was surprised by the kindness in his eyes. "Growing up means understanding that sometimes you have to hurt people in the name of the greater good. That sometimes the end does justify the means. It sucks in this case, it really does. But it was the right thing to do, and I think someday you'll realize that too."

He stood up, but she didn't raise her eyes.

"Please call Claire. She doesn't deserve this. She loves you."

He placed a five-dollar bill on the table and slipped away, the bell above the door signaling his departure.

She loves you. Ellie let the phrase repeat in her mind, skimming the surface at first before dropping deep, deep down, like a stone to a riverbed.

* * *

By the time Claire summoned enough bravery (a glass of wine helped), she worried that nine o'clock on a Friday evening might be too late for an almost-stranger to pay a visit. It probably was a little on the late side. Any more procrastinating and it definitely would be. But it was too easy to talk herself out of it (she'd already tried that on for size). She was going to do this. Besides, she'd already lost Ellie. The unexpected meeting on the dog walk only confirmed how awkward things were between them, how little chance there was of reconciling. There'd been nothing but silence from Ellie since, making it pretty clear they were done. There was nothing left to lose.

Claire hesitated only a couple of seconds before pressing the doorbell, which sounded some elaborate tune on the other side. Something classical and so very not Motown.

A moment later, the porch light snapped on and Elaine Kirkland opened the door, surprise briefly silencing her. "Oh… Claire? What…what are you doing here? Is Ellie all right?"

Clearly, Ellie hadn't broken it to them that they were no longer dating. Which meant the estrangement between Ellie and Erin and their mothers continued.

"I…she's fine."

"Elaine, who's here?" Emily's voice emerged from somewhere behind her wife.

"It's Claire, darling."

Emily stepped forward, her face falling for a moment before she rearranged it into something neutral. "Oh. Ah, hello. Would you care to come in?"

"Of course. Thank you. I'm sorry it's so late."

Claire stepped into the foyer, grand with a two-story ceiling, marble floor, and an elegant staircase beyond. For growing up in a home that had to be worth about a million dollars, it amazed her how down-to-earth Ellie was, with her beat-up Honda, the rather simple three-bedroom townhouse she shared with her cousin, her willingness to take jobs that didn't pay much. She respected the fact that Ellie wanted to make her own way. Clearly, Emily and Elaine had instilled a strong work ethic in their daughters, an expectation that they'd need to make their own way in life. Perhaps, in spite of their tough love, they weren't so awful after all.

The two women led Claire into the formal living room. She sat in the chair they indicated, an uncomfortable French provincial flanking the massive gas fireplace. She supposed the chair matched the two women's personalities—stiff, formal, and possessing the attitude that went with it.

"If everything is fine with Ellie," Elaine said, taking the lead, "may I ask the purpose of your visit, Claire?"

Direct was the best course, especially with these two. "This estrangement between your daughters is why I'm here."

Mouths drew into tight lines before Emily said, "I don't see how merely dating our daughter makes this your business exactly."

"Actually, you're wrong on the first count. I'm not dating Ellie right now. We…seem to have ended things."

Elaine shook her head lightly. "I guess you came to realize what a…handful she can be."

"Wrong again." Boy, they didn't like that word. Each time Claire used it, the room dropped about five degrees in temperature. "Ellie is a very special woman. She's kind, she's smart, she's compassionate, she's fun, and she's the most down-to-earth person I think I've ever met. I love that she wears her feelings on her sleeve, that she's not afraid to do that. People, animals, they all gravitate to her, have you noticed that?" She had to clear her throat to gain control of her emotions. And she needed to stop rambling about Ellie before she lost it. "Anyway, it wasn't my idea to end things."

"Surely," Emily said, sarcasm heavy in her voice, "you don't suggest that we have the ability to convince Ellie to take you back. As you know, we really don't have much sway with her at all."

"And why is that, exactly?" Ballsy, which came to Claire easily after all her years in journalism. "Could it be because you'd rather tell her what to do than to listen, than to give her the latitude to figure out what she wants and needs? And could it also be because you'd rather judge and criticize than support her unconditionally? That you'd prefer to control her?"

Elaine leapt to her feet. "This line of conversation is uncalled for. You know nothing about us and very little about Ellie."

"No, wait." Emily held up her hand, which trembled slightly. "If you know something about Ellie that would be…helpful right now, I'd—we'd—like to hear it."

"Ellie loves you both to the moon and back. I know this to be true. You're both her heroes. How could you not be? You went to great lengths to conceive your daughters, I can only assume. You both have careers helping others and are very well regarded in your fields. Ellie's not blind. She understands on an intellectual level that you love her and her sister." Both women visibly relaxed; Elaine sat down again and Emily's hand stopped trembling. "I'm not sure she *feels* that love very often. And the tragedy of it is that you're going to lose your daughters, and a grandchild, if you don't figure out how to show them your love. And that your love comes without conditions and strings." After all, was love really love if it was attached to so many other things? Not likely.

Elaine's face had clenched and gone red. So much for thinking the two were open to listening. "Now hold on one damned minute—"

"Wait," Emily interjected. "Maybe we should listen to what she has to say."

Elaine narrowed her eyes at her wife. "You're prepared to take advice from a stranger?" Then to Claire, "Claire, do you happen to moonlight as a family therapist? Because if not, then I strongly suggest you—"

"Look." Claire huffed out a breath of frustration. What had she expected, that they'd accept her criticism with a smile and a thank-you hug? "Can I be perfectly frank with you both?"

The two women hesitated before nodding in unison.

"I know what it's like to be rejected by a parent. And I also know what it's like not to have parents." Claire told them about her father leaving when she was a kid and how she'd had very little to do with him since. Her mother had tried her best, emotionally, physically and financially. "It was me that let her down, not the other way around." Claire's voice shook. "I had so much anger, contempt, disappointment. And I dumped it all on her. I wasted so many years blaming her for not being perfect, for not doing things the way I would have done them. Years I wish I could take back now." Tears blinded her. She'd lost so much: her father, her mother, now Ellie. And mostly because she'd relented to her pride.

A clock ticked from atop the fireplace mantle.

"My mom died ten years ago."

"I'm so sorry," Emily said quietly. Elaine murmured the same.

"She was so different from me," Claire continued, oblivious to whether or not her audience had any desire for her to continue. "Which I hated for a long time. I mistook her for not being exceptional because she worked at a job that didn't require a lot of education and that didn't pay much more than a living wage." It wasn't that Claire wanted to be rich or above anyone, only that she didn't want to suffer through living barely above the poverty rate. "I credited her optimism as foolishness, her sense of fun, of living in the moment, as being ridiculous and silly. All those years I thought she was weak, fickle. But you know what? She worked her ass off to provide for us. She never once came home drunk or left me with strangers and never took a minute, let alone a day, off from being a parent. And she did all of those things while maintaining her love for life, her love for people, and with a strong moral compass that always gave others the benefit of the doubt. I never gave her credit for her gifts. And now it's too late."

Claire let her tears fall freely. She'd never confessed these things to anyone, not even to Ellie. But this wasn't a pity party, nor did she want it to become one.

"I couldn't see all her attributes, didn't want to see them, I guess, because all I could see was how different she was from me. The path she took in her life, the decisions she made…they weren't the roads I would have chosen. And I condemned her for that instead of appreciating who she was." She looked at Emily and Elaine until they held her gaze. "I would give *anything* to have my mom in my life right now. And the reason I'm telling you all this is because I don't want to see Ellie lose her moms. But it's more than that too. I want her to know what it's like to be accepted and loved unconditionally. To be appreciated for all the wonderful gifts she has, even if those gifts are different from yours."

Part of her wanted to loudly condemn these two fools for what they were throwing away with their pride and their judgy standards. But screw it. She was doing this was for Ellie, so that Ellie hopefully didn't have to go through more years of missing out on the kind of love that should have been hers from the day she was born. But she was also doing this for herself, of course she was. Before she'd gotten to know and appreciate Ellie, *she* had been Elaine and Emily, holding people to rigid standards, standards of her own choosing, and then dismissing them, disrespecting them, if they couldn't meet those standards. She'd pitied people she so contemptuously thought of as living their lives on the sunny side of the street, willfully ignorant of what really went on in the world. But thanks to Ellie, she'd begun to appreciate the small joys, to be more present in the moment, to be brave and take new chances, especially where the heart was concerned. The real world sucked a lot of the time and wasn't always worth fighting. Sometimes, it paid to turn the other cheek. God, there were so many life lessons she wanted to keep on learning from Ellie.

"Not that we need to defend ourselves or explain ourselves to you," Elaine finally said, her voice losing much of its edge. "But we've given our daughters everything they've ever asked for and then some. We've given them a good beginning. No, a great beginning."

"And if we've been hard on them," Emily added, "it's only because we've wanted the best for them."

"I understand that," Claire said. "And I know that comes from love. But the best thing you can do for Ellie? The best gift you can give her? Is to let her be herself. And then love her for herself. That's all she wants from the two of you. Her sister too, I suspect."

There was a long, awkward silence, and Claire had no idea if her advice had hit home or not. She stood, showed herself to the door. Ellie was no longer in her life, but if something, anything at all positive could come from that loss, maybe she could quit crying herself to sleep every night.

"Thank you for indulging me," she said to the two women behind her.

Her words were met with silence.

CHAPTER TWENTY-THREE

I'm Gonna Make You Love Me

Ellie gave the omelet one last flip in the frying pan. After waiting a minute, she cut it in half, then settled the two halves onto plates. She presented Erin with her half and joined her at the small kitchen table, picked up her nearly empty coffee mug—the one that said, "Behind every successful dream is a thousand nightmares." *Huh*, she thought, *I've got the nightmare part of that equation down pat.*

"You don't have to cook for me, you know." Erin quickly stuffed a bite into her mouth, moaning at the results. "Oh man, you make the best omelets. Asparagus and Swiss cheese. Yum!"

"It's about the only thing I can cook. How do you think I've survived the years since I left home? And besides, you're eating for two. I want to make sure you eat." She gulped the rest of her coffee and shoveled a bite of the omelet into her mouth. Not bad. Not bad at all. Except she had no intention of savoring it because she had a mission, and the sooner she got going, the better.

"Jeez, you're going to choke if you keep eating so fast," Erin quipped. She chewed slowly, intentionally. It was so Erin. "Where's the fire?"

Claire. Claire was the fire. All night, Ellie had tossed and turned, thinking about the things Jackson had said to her. It had hurt, the part where he'd told her to grow up, that the news story had been the right thing to do, that Claire didn't deserve to be frozen out of her life, that she'd done nothing wrong. His little speech had been a splash of cold water. Ellie could no longer deny that she was acting like a spoiled brat. She'd taken up that seventeen-year-old girl's cause with a single-minded, stubborn fervor with no regard for Claire's side of things, no consideration for what Claire, and Jacks, might have struggled with. She'd been naïve, obnoxious, with her righteous principles. Hadn't even truly wanted to let Claire explain herself. And now she was angry with herself because her behavior had been straight out of her mothers' books, and being like them was the last thing in the world she wanted.

Stupid stupid stupid. Would Claire even want to see her? Listen to anything she had to say? Sobered by her worries, she stuffed the last piece of omelet into her mouth and pushed her chair back. "Sorry, I need to run."

"Important errand?"

"You could say that." She mentally calculated how fast she could get to Claire's and prayed her stupid car wouldn't die on her. "I'm going to go and see Claire."

"Thank god!" Erin's grin nearly swallowed her face. She followed Ellie to the foyer. "And it's about freaking time!"

The doorbell rang as Ellie struggled to put her jacket on. Erin beat her to the door and opened it, which was a good thing since Ellie's arm was caught inside the sleeve of her jacket. *Shit.* It was her mothers, standing there looking like they were afraid to cross the threshold. Looking, for the first time Ellie could ever remember, scared.

While she tried to rip her arm free of her jacket, Erin stood as mute as a statue. *Great.*

Elaine finally took charge, which was so typical. When Ellie and Erin were kids, it was always Elaine who decided on the family vacation destination. Elaine who decided on a restaurant when the rest of them didn't much care where they ate. "Good morning, girls. May we come in? There's something important we'd like to discuss."

"Sure, yes." Ellie flapped around some more, finally giving up and tossing her jacket to the floor.

The four of them trooped single file into the living room. Thankfully Marissa was working; the fewer witnesses, the better. Even Piper, who came out to assess the situation, scurried away, her tail drooping like the damaged mast of a sailboat.

Ellie remembered her manners, though apparently her sister hadn't. "Um...Mom, Mama. Can I get you anything?"

"We're fine," Emily answered, taking a seat next to her wife.

Elaine pursed her lips, worked her jaw, like she was trying to spit something out. "We're here to...apologize. To try to work things out between us all."

Jeez, that must have hurt, Ellie thought. She could hardly remember a time when Elaine had ever uttered an apology. She stole a quick glance at Erin, who'd gone a little gray.

"We're so sorry," Emily added. "We've come to realize that we've made a big mistake by being so hard on you both, that we perhaps...no, wait." She glanced quickly at her wife. "We understand now that we could have—*should* have—treated you both better. And we don't want to lose you. We very much want you both, and the baby, in our lives." Her voice cracked, a good sign they were being genuine.

"We've only ever wanted the best for you," Elaine added, her glance sweeping across both her daughters. "And sometimes, perhaps, we haven't always taken into consideration what you wanted or what truly was best for you both. We...should have listened more and talked less."

The slightest breeze could have knocked Ellie over. Was this for real?

"We'd like to start over," Emily said. "And with your permission and participation, we'd like for the four of us to see a family therapist to help see us through this...this new way of relating to one another." She patted her wife's knee. "We'd like to be a real family. And that means shedding a lot of old patterns, finding new ways to communicate. And ways to accept one another. It will be a lot of work, but we're willing to do whatever it takes."

Ellie cleared her throat and pointedly looked at her sister.

"Um, okay," Erin said, finally finding her voice. And then she began to cry, big ugly tears rolling down her cheeks. "I'm so relieved, you have no idea." She launched herself at her mothers, who laughed and took her in their arms before chiding her to be careful of the baby. The three of them looked expectantly at Ellie, like they wanted her to join in on this little orgy of forgiveness.

"I do have a question."

"All right," Emily said cautiously.

"What made you have a change in heart?" It was true, she did have a skeptical side. If only Claire could see her now!

"We had a visitor stop by last night," Elaine said carefully. "Claire dropped in for quite a candid chat. She said some things that really hit home for us."

Ellie had to pick her mouth up off the floor. "Excuse me? *My* Claire?"

"Yes," Emily said. "Your Claire. Except we're extremely disappointed to learn that she's not *your* Claire anymore."

"I...um..."

Elaine offered Ellie an uncharacteristic wink. "If I may presume to tell you what to do, for the very last time, I might add, I'd get that woman back. She's a keeper. Don't you all agree?"

The others nodded before Erin ratted out her sister. "Actually, Ellie was about to go over there when you guys showed up."

"Aha," Emily said, laughing. "So you do have good sense after all. I knew we raised you right."

Ellie leapt from her chair. "Will you all excuse me?"

"Gladly," Elaine said. "Get your butt over to Claire's and beg her to give you another chance."

"Excuse me? Beg? You're suggesting a Kirkland woman should beg?" That was new. And weird.

Emily gave her wife's cheek a quick kiss. "Trust me, Kirkland women are not above begging."

"Oh, god," Erin said, rolling her eyes. "I don't think I want to hear this. Don't leave me alone with them, El."

Laughter. Among the four of them. Ellie had to pinch herself. "You guys are so freaking hilarious. Now, wish me luck."

"You got a plan?" Erin called out as Ellie picked her jacket up off the floor.

Hmm. A plan beyond begging? Crying her heart out? "No, but I'm thinking."

Saturdays used to be Claire's favorite day of the week. A day to kick back, do a bit of gardening, cook something nice that she could stretch into two or three meals, take the Mustang out for a drive. Over a glass of wine she'd reflect on the week at work and what had been accomplished, before turning her mind to the stories that needed to be reported on next week. While dating Ellie, Saturdays went from relaxing to exciting because they usually meant a date and a sleepover. Now all she wanted to do was go back to bed and throw the covers over her head. Maybe Rolo would decide walks were too much effort and join her on the bed, the blinds closed to keep the room dark. Failing that, maybe she'd cruise the television channels to find some old movie. Not a romantic movie, mind you. It'd have to be something where lots of people died and things exploded.

"What do you say, Rolo? *True Lies* or *Die Hard?*"

The dog whimpered, placed her paws over her eyes, the gesture so cute that Claire got down on her hands and knees and kissed Rolo's head. *When did I become such a baby around dogs?* It was embarrassing, except it wasn't because nobody was around to see it. Maybe she should adopt about a dozen dogs and sit around in her pajamas all day watching doggie movies like *Lassie* or *Lady and the Tramp*. At least it would beat having her heart ripped out by a woman. Which was exactly what she had known would happen with Ellie. And yet she'd been unable to resist her charms, her warmth, her beauty, her sense of fun and adventure, her kindnesses, not to mention her talents in bed. She'd lost herself with Ellie, lost herself *in* Ellie. And all she wanted to do was go back to the early days of getting to know one another, when things were easy, simple, but never boring. Like riding around together in the Mustang, the roof down, the wind swallowing their words. Lying on their backs on the grass at the fort while the dogs played nearby. Eating a nice meal over a small table with a flickering candle, laughing, talking quietly about things to come. Ellie made her want to dream again, something she'd forgotten how to do. Ellie made her feel desired, desirable. And now she was gone.

Claire couldn't even get excited about the fact that the congresswoman had resigned her seat yesterday, her political career in tatters, plus she and her husband were facing criminal charges. It was a hollow victory, though, because the cost, for Claire at least, had been awfully steep.

Rolo bounded up onto the recliner chair next to the window; it was her favorite place for chilling out while she looked out the window. Probably a dog being walked by had captured her attention. She had bionic hearing, Claire swore.

Wait. Was that somebody singing? It was a lovely voice, whoever it was. The song sounded kind of like…a Motown song? Somebody was outside singing a Motown song?

Rolo's tail started wagging a mile a minute. Claire stepped up behind her and peeked through the blind to see what the commotion was all about. "What the hell?"

It was Ellie, standing in the middle of her front yard, singing a cappella. No, belting it out, a cappella. "And I'm, I'm gonna make you love me, oh yes I will…"

Claire's mouth went dry and she forgot how to breathe. Ellie was singing the lyrics to "I'm Gonna Make You Love Me," her hand on her heart, not caring about the stares from people in passing cars and from neighbors peeking over their fences and through their windows. Not that she had anything to worry about, her voice was that of an angel's. Still…being serenaded wasn't exactly an everyday sight.

By the time Claire raced to her front door and opened it, Ellie was on the porch, finishing the final chorus (Claire knew the words of the song by heart, thanks to her mom). At the song's conclusion, they stood facing one another in silence. Silence that wasn't awkward, but heavy with meaning. It was Ellie who spoke first. Good thing too, because Claire was still trying to figure out how to breathe.

"Claire, will you forgive me? I've been a complete ass. I don't want us to be apart any more. I hate not having you in my life. I hate feeling like I've lost you. Like I've lost us. Losing you ultimately feels like I've lost *me*."

Claire stepped closer, stopping only inches from Ellie's face, and gently clamped a hand over her mouth. "Ellie Kirkland, you're not allowed to say another word until I tell you that I love you. I love you with everything I have and everything I am, including my flawed bits. Especially my flawed bits. This past week has been the worst week of my life and I don't ever want to lose you like that again, because I know I couldn't take it." Too much loss, that's what Claire had had in her life, and it needed to stop. Now. "I'm the one who needs forgiveness." Her voice shook as she softly removed her hand from Ellie's mouth. "Please forgive me. Please love me."

Ellie fell into her arms, kissing her face, her mouth, her neck, her temple, finally resting her forehead against Claire's. "Loving you is the easiest thing in the world, my love."

Claire kissed her deeply, loving the way Ellie's hands moved up her back, down again and around to her stomach, where her fingers fumbled with the hem of her button-down shirt.

"Ha, I think we've already given my neighbors enough to talk about for the weekend. Let's not give them enough to talk about for the next month."

"Fine. But you better get me inside, because I can't be responsible for my actions. I'm a woman in love, you know."

Claire tugged her inside and shut the door. Rolo wanted in on the lovefest, but Claire kept tugging Ellie toward the bedroom, telling Rolo she'd have to wait her turn, which, if all went well, wouldn't be for hours.

Instead of ravaging one another, they lay on the bed facing each other. Which was a miracle, but there were things Claire needed to say first.

"Sweetie, I never meant to make you feel disrespected, or lied to, or that I didn't value your feelings. I hurt you, and I'm sorry for that. I didn't mean for things to happen the way they did."

"No, wait. I'm the one who walked away without understanding what really happened with that news story. Without really considering all the angles. I got caught up emotionally. I let myself get locked into one way of thinking about it. And I let myself doubt you, which I shouldn't have. I get now that the news story wasn't easy for you, that you were struggling with it. And I understand why the story had to run, I swear I do. It still doesn't make me happy, but what really makes me unhappy? Is not having you in my life. *That* I cannot live with."

Claire kissed the tip of Ellie's nose, then searched those dark eyes that she loved so much. Loved from the minute she first saw them, if she were honest with herself. "I love how your instinct is to protect people, to take up for the underdog. You always think about how someone feels, and I'm sorry for all the times at the paper that I tried to disabuse you of that. Because you know what? I'm getting awfully tired of living in a world where we've stopped considering other people's feelings, where we cannot put ourselves in someone else's shoes. Empathy seems to have gone the way of the dodo bird, and I think—"

"Dodo bird?" Ellie wrinkled her nose playfully. "What is a dodo bird anyway?"

"Something outdated. Like my little phrases, apparently."

Ellie kissed Claire on the mouth, smiling as she did so. "I love your little phrases. Do you have one for making love?"

Claire made a shocked face. "Oh! You mean like making whoopee?"

Ellie rolled onto her back and giggled. "Oh my god, that is, like, I don't know what. Nineteen fifties?"

"All right, how about mattress dancing?"

"Really?" Ellie stuck out her tongue and made a face again. "That's kind of stupid, actually."

Claire rolled gently on top of her. "Agreed. How about getting it on? Getting laid? Having sexual intercourse? Ooh, wait, how about some afternoon delight?"

"Yes! I love that! There's a song from the seventies called that, did you know that, Claire?"

It was Claire's turn to make a face. "I might have heard it once or twice on that oldies station. But it is kind of perfect, since it's…" She checked the bedside clock. "Noon now."

"A nooner! Isn't that another one?"

"It is. Now are we going to spend the rest of day talking about sex? Or are we—"

Ellie threw her arms around Claire's neck and pulled her down, kissing her hard. Her tongue parted Claire's lips, and Claire, so hungry for her, let Ellie explore her mouth before she pressed back, using her own tongue to part Ellie's lips. God, she tasted good. But Claire was impatient to touch all of Ellie. She insinuated her hands between their bodies to gain access to Ellie's blouse, a long-sleeved collarless thing with way too many damned buttons.

"Oh, wait," Claire said. Before things went any further, she needed to confess her visit to the Kirkland household last night. Ellie might not be impressed. In fact, she might even get pissed off. But no more secrets between them, no matter the consequences. "I have something to confess."

"You already told me you love me." Ellie reached up and stroked Claire's cheek, and the simple touch of her fingers heated her from the inside.

"I do love you. And I couldn't be more in love if I tried. But there's something you need to know."

A frowned formed on Ellie's forehead. "Okay."

"I went to see your moms last night. I know it wasn't my place to, but I really think that what they're doing is wro—"

"Wait, honey." Ellie pressed a finger to Claire's lips. "I already know all about it."

"You do?"

"They came by this morning. To apologize to Erin and me. They want us back in their lives."

"Wow, really? That's amazing!"

"It is. And it's because of you. At least, that's what they told us. Which means…oh, crap."

"What?"

"I think they might love you more than they love me."

Claire began to laugh, and it was the best feeling in the world, because an hour ago, she thought she'd never laugh with Ellie again. "That, my dear, is impossible. I think they never truly stopped loving you, they just needed a little reminder that—"

"Claire?" Ellie pressed her finger to Claire's lips again.

"Yes?"

"Are you going to make love to me or what?"

"You mean make whoopee?"

Ellie used her strong legs to topple Claire over, and then to straddle her. "I prefer boinking, if you must know."

"Boinking? Ugh! That sounds like a video game."

"Oh, never mind. Buttering the biscuit works. So does creaming the Twinkie."

"Um, wow. You got me there, I've never heard of those."

"And then there's plain ol' making love." Ellie's hands made short work of the buttons on Claire's shirt, and then her own. Ellie snapped off her bra and tossed it to the floor, and oh, god, the way her breasts hung over her while she straddled Claire, it was fucking heaven. Claire could simply lie here and enjoy this view for the rest of her life. If it wasn't for eating. And taking care of their dogs. Oh, and making a living.

"That soooo works for me."

"Does it, now?" Ellie had removed Claire's bra and now she was sucking on her breast. Her tongue and lips were masterful at it, the way she sucked, then circled her nipple with her tongue, then sucked again, throwing in a gentle nip for good measure.

Her tongue flicked across the sensitive skin, and Jesus, she was going to come right now if she wasn't careful.

"Honey," Claire finally managed between moans, "you're killing me here."

"Ooh, then you're going to die one very happy woman."

"You're right, what was I thinking? Go ahead and kill me now. I can't think of a better way to go."

"Not until I have my way with you about one million more times." Ellie stopped and lifted her eyes to Claire's, then stretched out beside her. "Claire, I love you so much. I don't want this to ever end. I'm home with you. I mean, my heart is home with you. All of me is home with you. This is exactly where I want to be."

"Good. Because maybe we can talk later about this, these four walls, being your home too. And all the time, not just Saturdays."

Ellie grinned. "Really? You're asking me to move in with you?"

"Well, if it's all right with Piper. And Rolo."

"I have a funny feeling they'll say yes."

"I do too. And what about you?"

"Oh, Claire." Ellie's eyes misted over and her bottom lip began trembling ever so slightly. "What did I ever do right in my life to deserve someone like you?"

Claire gently pulled Ellie into the crook of her arm and held her tightly. "Motown. That was what did it, the fact that you love Motown music. Who knew that was the way to my heart? Certainly not me." Claire could only think that her mother had something to do with it. "And that song you were singing in my front yard. Did you know that one was my mom's favorite?"

"No. I didn't know. But it's always been my favorite."

Of course it was. Claire smiled, said a silent prayer of thanks to her mother. Thanks for bringing Ellie into her life and thanks for making them both come to their senses. "Your voice is amazing. But there's one problem."

"Oh, no. What? Should I have chosen a different song?"

"Nope. The problem with it is that you don't need to make me love you. Because I already do. And have since the day I found Piper by the side of the road and brought her back to you."

"Okay, wait. You were hugely unimpressed to see me that day when you found out I was Piper's owner."

"Only because I'd fired you. And I felt like shit about it."

"You did?"

"Of course I did. And then when I saw you at your house, looking so worried and then so relieved about Piper, I wanted to take you into my arms."

Ellie propped herself up on an elbow. "Do you feel that way about everyone you fire?"

"No. Well, um, actually you're the only person I've ever fired."

Ellie's eyes widened. "Seriously? Jeez, I must have been really bad if I'm the only one you've ever fired."

"Naw. Everyone else is in the union and it's really hard to fire people in the union. You were easy."

"Easy, huh?" Ellie climbed back on top of Claire and pinned her arms to the mattress. "I think it's time I showed *you* who's boss."

"Oh, yes please!"

"Now who's easy, hmm?"

Claire squirmed, needing Ellie to touch her. "Um, that would be me."

"Well, in that case…" Ellie reached down and pulled Claire's panties far enough down her legs so that Claire could kick them off. "Ooh, that's much better," she whispered into Claire's ear, sending a ripple of pleasurable shivers down Claire's spine. How she craved this woman's touch, which had somehow become as essential as air or food. How had she lived forty-two—almost forty-three—years without it? How had she not known, or at least suspected, this kind of love existed and could actually happen to her? That it wasn't something meant only for others?

When Ellie touched her, Claire jumped from the sheer intensity of it. She was so turned on that every bundle of nerves in her body, especially down there, was ready to snap. She arched into Ellie's touch, cried out as Ellie entered her. Something happened to her whenever Ellie was inside her. It was like she lost her physical sense of herself as a single unit and became an extension of Ellie. Or vice versa. They were one in this moment. It made her heart grow so big she thought it might explode. She squeezed her eyes shut, so that the first touch of Ellie's tongue came as a surprise, instantly pushing her to the edge.

She murmured Ellie's name over and over. Oh, the things her lover could do with her mouth! *It should be a crime.* Hunger, ageless and timeless, surged through her, and it occurred to her that not in a million years would her body ever be sated by Ellie, so great was her need for her.

She came with Ellie's tongue stroking her and two fingers inside her, her orgasm coming in powerful waves that pounded and crested until they crashed her against the shores of her own desire. "I love you, sweetheart. I love you so much. Come here so I can hold you."

Ellie crawled up to her, kissing her on the mouth before settling softly against her. "Oh, Claire, I missed that. I missed you so much. I love you, baby." A tear worked its way down Ellie's cheek, and Claire tenderly wiped it away with her finger.

"Then let's not ever take a break again."

"Deal." Ellie looked into Claire's eyes, searching and then apparently finding what she was looking for. She smiled. "Somehow I think you really mean that."

"With every breath I take."

"Claire?"

"Yes, darling?"

"You're the one thing in my life that's felt exactly right. Perfect. Like it, *we*, were always meant to be. With you by my side, everything else is possible."

"I feel the same. And I don't care how long it takes you to find the job or the career you want. Take all your life. Whatever makes you happy."

"*You* make me happy. But this vet tech course? It feels good. It feels like my heart has found the right calling. I'm kind of loving it."

"That's wonderful. I'm so happy for you."

Ellie giggled. "You know what else would make me *really* happy right now?"

"Hmm, might it have something to do with me making you come?"

"Oh, not only are you pretty much perfect, but you're also psychic!"

"Well, only if reading your mind involves a lot of kinetic activity." She moved her hand down between Ellie's legs. God, she was so wet that all Claire could think about was getting her mouth down there and tasting her, even through her underwear because she didn't want to take the time right now to remove them.

"Oh, I love the sound of that. And the feel of it. Oh, Claire."

Claire's tongue swiped over the damp cotton panties, and Ellie nearly levitated off the bed. She teased some more until Ellie's hands pushed their way down. Claire raised her head and said, "Ah, somebody's in a hurry, hmm?"

"Jesus, Claire, you're killing me. Would you rip that damned underwear off? I don't even care if you ruin them. Just...ohhh!"

As much as Claire would love to keep inflicting this sweet torture on Ellie, it was time to show a little mercy. She pulled Ellie's underwear down her smooth legs, then stroked with her tongue, hard and fast, then light and slow. She held tight onto Ellie as Ellie bucked and sought more friction with her hips.

Some serious swear words erupted from Ellie's lips, but Claire wouldn't be hurried. Her tongue stroked faster and her fingers danced over Ellie's wetness. She could do this all afternoon to Ellie and never grow tired of it...well, her neck might have something to say about it, but her mouth was loving it and her ears were loving the sounds coming from Ellie—moans, gasps, the occasional reference to god peppered with the word fuck. She was driving Ellie crazy, and it made Claire feel powerful. And about twenty years younger.

"I can't...Claire, I'm almost—"

"Not yet, my love."

Ellie so slick, so sweet tasting. Claire could get high on this. She licked and sucked, and right as Ellie's body went rigid, Claire entered her. When Ellie's explosive orgasm came a second later, Claire loved the way Ellie clenched around her fingers, rode them, screamed out her name. How she loved this woman.

Minutes later, their arms wrapped around each other, Claire kissed Ellie's damp temple. "How soon can you move in, sweetie? Because I don't want to spend another night without you here."

Ellie grinned at her. Damn, those dark chocolate eyes of hers were the most perfect thing Claire had ever seen. "Is tomorrow too soon?"

"Tomorrow's perfect. Although tonight would be even better."

"I love you, Claire."

"I love you, Ellie."

EPILOGUE

Take Me In Your Arms (Rock Me A Little While)

The table in front of the fireplace was perfect after a day filled with downhill skiing. Eleven runs they'd managed. Ellie's legs were gone by the tenth; Claire's legs, she'd less than gently complained, were done by the seventh run, but she'd gamely persisted. And now they sipped from glasses of full-bodied shiraz and ate the most tender sirloin Ellie had ever had the pleasure of eating while an actual wood-burning fireplace blazed not more than eight feet away.

"I'm so exhausted," Claire said, but with a smile that lifted right into her eyes. "I can barely raise my fork."

"Crap. I shouldn't have insisted on those last couple of runs if it means you're too tired for, you know, what did we decide on?" She leaned closer and whispered, "making whoopee?"

"I prefer," Claire said with a straight face, "creaming the Twinkie."

Ellie's wine went straight up her nose as she howled with laughter. "Oh, sweetheart." She dabbed her nose with her napkin and snorted. Damn, that wine stung. "I'll cream your Twinkie anytime you want."

Claire raised her eyebrows. "In that case, what do you say to Twinkies for dessert?"

"Ooh, I'm up for that! But we'd better finish our meal first to keep our strength up."

"Good point. You know, it's been so nice to get away with you, even if it's only for a few days. I could sure get used to this, though."

They'd slipped away to Cadillac, Michigan, for three nights at a ski lodge—Claire's Christmas present to Ellie—and tomorrow they'd make the four-hour drive home because Ellie's holiday school break was almost over. Classes resumed Monday and so did Claire's job.

"I wish we could do this once a month. Get away, I mean."

"Me too. But when the baby comes, I think we'll be busy helping out for a little while."

Ellie beamed. "I can't wait for my little namesake to be born. About three more weeks and she'll be here."

"Wait, I thought Erin decided to call her Eliana, not Ellen?"

"She is, but we'll shorten it to Ellie."

"Ah, very clever of you."

"I'm not just a pretty face, you know."

Claire's eyes roamed over Ellie's body. "Oh, you have many pretty things about you. As well as a brilliant mind."

"Whew. For a minute there, I thought you were only with me for my body."

Claire picked up her glass of wine and sipped. "Lucky me that you're the full package. But I'd like to reacquaint myself with…a few things about your body as soon as we can get upstairs to our room again."

A low thrum started between Ellie's legs. Claire did that to her with a simple, charged phrase. Or a look from those sparkling eyes that resembled the frozen Lake Michigan right outside the window—except they were as warm as tropical pools. She loved the way Claire couldn't get enough of her. "I like the sound of that."

"I'm a little worried about all these names that start with the letter E," Claire said. "In fact, I'm feeling outrageously outnumbered in this family."

"True, but at least your name ends with an E."

"There is that, I suppose." Claire took a final bite of steak, rounding it out with the last piece of roasted potato on her plate. "So, if we ever have a baby, does that mean we need not look at anything other than the letter E in the baby name books?"

Ellie swallowed in time before she choked. "What? You want a baby?" Where was this coming from? Or was she joking? She studied Claire's face…the set of her jaw, the earnestness in her eyes. Nope, not joking.

Claire reached across the table for Ellie's hand, waiting until Ellie took it and squeezed it back. "I'd love to have a family with you one day. You're everything to me. And you're enough. But having a child with you would feel like we had not only the stars but the moon too, you know? Hell, we'd own the whole damned galaxy."

"Oh, Claire." Tears pressed at the backs of Ellie's eyes. "You're serious, aren't you?"

"I am."

"Ah, wait, I know what you're up to."

"You do?"

"You know I'm going to fall head over heels in love with my niece and want one of my own. You're a brilliant woman, you know that? Absolutely fucking brilliant." Ellie removed her hand from Claire's so she could raise her glass and offer a toast.

Claire grinned, returning the toast with a salute of her wineglass. "I am rather brilliant, if I do say so myself. But I'm kind of serious."

Ellie let Claire's words sink in, take root. A family. With Claire. God, Claire would make a fantastic mom. So solid, so genuine, so utterly reliable and responsible. Loving too. She'd be a rock. Warmth spread throughout Ellie, a pleasant prickling at the base of her spine. "I…" Her voice came out sounding like sandpaper. "I still have a year and a half of school left. And then I'd like to work for a bit. Establish myself."

"We have time. There's no rush." Claire's voice was as soft and gentle as the falling snow outside the window. "In fact, I'm happy to not have to share you with anyone else until we decide the time is right. *If* the time is right."

Ellie did nothing to stop the tear that slithered down her cheek. "Claire, have I told you today how much I love you?"

"About six times already."

"Good. Here comes the seventh. I love you to the moon and back. No, to the sun and back because that's a hell of a lot farther than the moon."

Claire smiled with eyes that had also begun to swim with tears. "I love you too. So much. You have no idea."

The waiter appeared and removed their empty plates, asking about dessert. Both women struggled to stifle laughter when Claire replied that they had other dessert plans later.

"So," Claire said on the elevator ride up to their room. "I was thinking. Ezra if it's a boy, Edith if it's a girl."

"What are you...? Oh my god. You're incorrigible, do you know that?"

"I do. Deal with it."

"Oh, I plan to."

"Bring it on."

"Gladly." Ellie let them into their room and locked the door behind them. They eyed one another in pretend challenge until Ellie pointed to the bed. "Bed. Now. Clothes off. Now."

Claire did as she was told and lay down naked on the bed. "Twinkies anyone?"

Ellie grinned and walked toward the bed, her heart full, her body on fire. She would never grow tired of this. "I'm starving for dessert. How did you know?"

Motown Playlist

Nowhere To Run To....................Martha Reeves and the Vandellas
Every Little Bit Hurts..Brenda Holloway
The Way You Do The Things You Do....................The Temptations
Come See About Me..The Supremes
Too Busy Thinking About My Baby..............................Marvin Gaye
My Mistake (Was To Love You)..........Diana Ross and Marvin Gaye
Something About You..The Four Tops
Heaven Must Have Sent You..The Elgins
Love Is Like An Itching In My Heart.......................The Supremes
It Takes Two....................................Marvin Gaye and Kim Weston
What Does It Take (To Win Your Love)......................Junior Walker
I Heard It Through The Grapevine............................Marvin Gaye
Baby I'm For Real..The Originals
Just To See Her.. Smokey Robinson
Ooh Baby Baby.......................Smokey Robinson and the Miracles
The Hunter Gets Captured By The Game.............The Marvelettes
How Sweet It Is..Marvin Gaye
If I Could Build My Whole World Around You............Marvin Gaye
and Tammi Terrell
My World Is Empty Without You..............................The Supremes
Ain't No Woman Like The One I Got......................The Four Tops
My Whole World Ended (The Moment You Left Me)...David Ruffin
Standing in The Shadows of Love............................The Four Tops
I'm Gonna Make You Love Me..Diana Ross
and the Temptations
Take Me In Your Arms (Rock Me A Little While)........Kim Weston
Bonus Track: *You Keep Me Hanging On*................The Supremes

Bella Books, Inc.

Women. Books. Even Better Together.

P.O. Box 10543
Tallahassee, FL 32302

Phone: 800-729-4992
www.bellabooks.com